ELIMINATION

What Reviewers Say About Jackie D's Work

The Rise of the Resistance

"I was really impressed by Jackie D's story and felt it had a truth and reality to it. She brought to life an America where things had gone badly wrong, but she gave me hope that all was not lost. The world she has imagined was compelling and the characters were so well developed."—*Kitty Kat's Book Review Blog*

"Jackie D explores how racist, homophobic, xenophobic leaders manage to seize, manipulate, and maintain power."—*Celestial Books*

Infiltration—Lambda Literary Award Finalist

"Quick question, where has this author been my entire life? …If you are looking for a romantic book that has mystery and thriller qualities then this is your book."—*Fantastic Book Reviews*

"This book is an action-packed romance, filled with cool characters and a few totally uncool bad guys. The book is well written, the story is engaging, and Jackie D did a great job of reeling the reader in and holding your attention to the very end."—*Romantic Reader Blog*

Lands End

"This is a great summer holiday read—likeable characters, great chemistry between the leads, interesting and unusual premise, well written dialogue, an excellent romance without any unnecessary angst. I really connected with both leads, and enjoyed the secondary characters. The attraction between Amy and Lena was palpable and the romantic storyline was paced really well."—Melina Bickard, Librarian, Waterloo Library (London)

Lucy's Chance

"Add a bit of conflict, add a bit of angst, a deranged killer, and you have a really good read. What this book is is a great escape. You have a few hours to decompress from real-life's craziness, and enjoy a quality story with interesting characters. Well, minus the psychopath murderer, but you know what I mean."—*Romantic Reader Blog*

Pursuit

"This book is a dynamic fast-moving adventure that keeps you on the edge of your seat the whole time...enough romance for you to swoon and enough action to keep you fully engaged. Great read, you don't want to miss this one."—*Romantic Reader Blog*

Visit us at www.boldstrokesbooks.com

By the Author

After Dark Series

Infiltration

Pursuit

Elimination

Lands End

Lucy's Chance

The Rise of the Resistance: Phoenix One

Spellbound (co-authored with Jean Copeland)

ELIMINATION

by
by
Jackie D

2020

ELIMINATION

ISBN 13: 978-1-63555-570-7

This Trade Paperback Original Is Published By
Bold Strokes Books, Inc.
P.O. Box 249
Valley Falls, NY 12185

First Edition: February 2020

CREDITS

EDITORS: VICTORIA VILLASENOR AND CINDY CRESAP
PRODUCTION DESIGN: SUSAN RAMUNDO
COVER DESIGN BY MELODY POND

Acknowledgments

Thank you to Victoria Villasenor, you're a fantastic editor, and I couldn't do this without you. Thank you, Bold Strokes Books, for sharing my stories with the world. To my friends and family for taking this exciting, frustrating, and invigorating journey with me over and over again. Finally, thank you, Alexis, none of this would be possible without your support, understanding, and toddler wrangling.

Dedication

Alexis, of all the choices I've made,
you'll always be the best.

CHAPTER ONE

Tyler Monroe pushed the door open and stepped inside. She heard a voice she recognized and waited for her eyes to adjust to assess the situation.

"I'm going to kill you. I'm going to tear you apart limb from limb. Your body will be so unrecognizable, your parents won't be able to identify you." Caden squinted in the darkness, her fingers trained on the trigger in her right hand.

"What are you doing?" Tyler flipped on the lights and sat down next to Caden on the couch.

Caden adjusted her headset and leaned forward. "Whatever you have to tell me is going to have to wait. We almost have this level cleared."

Tyler grabbed the beer on the table and took a sip. "We? Who's we?"

Caden shook her head and motioned toward the television. "My team, obviously. Now, be quiet, you're distracting me."

Tyler leaned back on the couch and crossed her legs. "I don't think you'll want to wait to hear this."

Caden scooted away from her on the couch as if the few inches would help her concentration. "Five minutes, Monroe."

Tyler focused on the screen. There was a group of five animated soldiers moving behind buildings, shooting from around corners, and lobbing grenades. "This seems excessively violent."

The door opened, and Jennifer and Brooke walked in, laughing. Brooke kissed the top of Tyler's head and wrapped her arms around Tyler's shoulders from behind the couch. "What are you two doing?"

Caden leaned over farther and adjusted her headset. "Can't a girl get five minutes of peace around here?"

Jennifer sat on the arm of the couch. "You're in my apartment."

Caden dropped the controller and fell back, sighing. "We lost. Are you three happy? Now I have to explain to my team why I couldn't get to the rendezvous point in time." She crossed her arms. "They're going to be pissed."

Jennifer slid onto the couch next to her. "You play with four teenage boys. They'll be fine."

Caden glared at Jennifer. "We're ranked number three."

Tyler sucked in a breath. "Wow! I'm sorry to hear that." She patted her back. "Don't worry, with enough practice I'm sure you'll eventually be number two."

"In the world. We're number three in the entire world." Caden motioned to the controller as if this would prove her point.

"Which is good, but there are still two teams out there better than you. I don't like those odds." Tyler looked at Brooke for agreement. "I mean, we wouldn't play with you."

Caden grabbed her beer out of Tyler's hand and rolled her eyes. "When did you become such a comedian, Monroe?"

Tyler shrugged. "I never had enough material before I met you."

Jennifer rubbed Caden's shoulders, and her face relaxed. "We got called into work." She pointed to Caden's phone on the kitchen table. "If you aren't going to keep the ringer on, you should at least keep it near you, so you can hear it buzz."

"We all got called in?" Caden leaned into Jennifer. "It's supposed to be our last weekend off before we leave for Dubai."

Tyler marveled at the recent transformation in Caden. She had only been seeing Jennifer for a few weeks, and she was already counting down the days to her weekends. Caden, before Jennifer, would've been perfectly happy to work every day, twenty hours a day. She was different now, more settled.

"Why do you smell?" Caden asked Tyler. She scrunched up her nose and moved farther away from her.

But Caden was still Caden. Tyler sniffed her armpit and fought the urge to smack her when she realized she'd fallen for the joke.

"Brooke and Jen went to the movies, so I went for a jog. I was down the street from Jen's apartment when I got the call, so I figured I'd swing by and see if you were here."

Brooke kissed Tyler on the cheek and let her mouth linger for a moment. "I like the way you smell."

"You two are gross," Jen said. "Let's go. We have to be there in thirty minutes. Tyler, I assume you have clothes at work to change into?"

"You know I do," Tyler said.

Tyler followed Brooke down to her car. Brooke shook her finger at her. "Don't you dare. Throw a towel down on the seat. I don't want it all sticky."

Tyler pulled a towel from her gym bag and laid it on the seat. "I thought you liked the way I smelled?"

Brooke laughed. "I don't want your sweat sticking to my leather seats for the next two weeks."

Tyler opened the glove box and pulled out a pair of sunglasses. "Do you know anything yet about why we're being called in?"

Brooke laced her fingers through Tyler's. "I don't know any more than you." She kissed Tyler's hand. "But it makes me nervous whenever we get called in. That usually means you'll be sent out on assignment soon."

She squeezed Brooke's hand. "I always come back to you."

This was all Tyler could say. They'd had this conversation in one form or another more than a dozen times. She couldn't make Brooke comfortable with it, no matter what she said. She also knew Brooke understood she'd never walk away from an assignment. Her job was as much a part of her as the blood that pumped through her veins. It was who she was, and Brooke loved that person. Tyler just hoped it was a promise she'd always be able to keep.

CHAPTER TWO

Emma Quinn paced back and forth inside the analysis room. She ran her thumb and pointer finger over the rosary she kept in her pocket. It'd been a gift from her grandmother, a family heirloom. Somewhere along the way, it had transformed into a good luck charm and she'd developed a nervous habit of rolling the tiny beads inside her pocket.

She looked around at the monitors that sat on the long table and along the wall. They looked precisely like the ones in her workspace, except for the logo that danced across the screen. The emblem of the CIA rotated across each of these, a tangible reminder that she was stepping outside her usual daily activity.

When Captain Hart had tapped her for this assignment, she'd been over the moon. She'd spent the last five years analyzing data, putting together messages, and following breadcrumbs. Now, she might get the chance to see all her hard work come to fruition. That part was exciting. The portion of the assignment that had her pacing was the part where she'd have to work with a group of people. Apart from her third assignment, her work had been solitary. There was no team she dealt with daily, no one she had to bounce her ideas off. She only answered to her supervisor. And she liked it that way.

She'd read the profiles on the four women she'd be working with. Two were computer analysts from the CIA, and the other two were Rambo types from Homeland Security. Individually, they were impressive, but as a team, they were outstanding. Together, they'd managed to infiltrate a terrorist organization and take down one of the foremost leaders. They'd uncovered a plot to assassinate the president and vice president, as well as proving the Speaker of the House, Carl O'Brien, had been behind the entire operation. They were a well-oiled machine. Now, they'd have an odd sprocket thrown into their mix, and Emma wasn't sure how that would affect their symmetry.

She heard the door beep, signaling an entrance, and she quickly looked around for a chair, not wanting any of them to know she'd been pacing. She sat in the closest one and put her hand on her chin, then changed her mind right as the door swung open.

She recognized each of them immediately from their files. Jennifer Glass and Caden Styles entered first. Caden had apparently said something wrong because Jennifer was instructing her to shut up. Brooke Hart and Tyler Monroe came immediately after, smiling at each other as if there was a joke no one else in the world knew but them.

Emma sat up a little straighter and forced herself not to play with her hair. Tyler noticed her first and walked directly to her. She was an overwhelming presence, stronger than Emma had initially pictured, despite reading all about her. She could see the outline of the muscles in Tyler's shoulders through her shirt, but her blue eyes were soft and kind. Emma was so overwhelmed by the contradiction, she didn't notice right away that Tyler had stuck out her hand to introduce herself.

"I'm Special Agent Tyler Monroe." Tyler smiled. "And you are?"

Emma stared at Tyler's hand for a moment. There were scars all over her knuckles and calluses on her palms. She must have taken too long to respond because Tyler tucked her hand back in her pocket, her expression bemused.

"I'm sorry, I'm Emma Quinn. It's nice to meet you." Emma felt her face run hot and hoped no one else noticed. She wasn't good at meeting new people, and now she'd never be able to get her first impression back.

The door beeped again, and Captain Calvin Hart came bounding through. Captain Hart was the kind of guy who entered every room as if everyone was awaiting his arrival. Which, Emma realized, was quite literally probably every room he entered.

Emma knew Captain Hart was Brooke Hart's father, but what she would've never known from her file was the way Brooke's body shifted when he arrived. Brooke looked uneasy, and she'd placed Tyler between herself and her father. *Interesting.* From everything Emma had read about Brooke, she was a star. She'd received excellent marks through college, during her training with the CIA, and then her work with this team. She seemed to take on each assignment with a level of determination and ferocity that supervisors couldn't wish into existence. But there was definitely some story there.

The captain waved his hand toward the chairs in the room. "Has everyone met the newest addition to the team?"

Emma knew they were shaking their heads, but she couldn't bring herself to look up, still embarrassed by her earlier freeze with Tyler.

He walked over to her to make the introduction. He smelled of Old Spice and new car, a peculiar combination. "This is Emma Quinn. She's a civilian NSA intelligence analyst, and her expertise is in Russia. There will be a sixth member of the team, but I can't reveal their identity until we arrive in Moscow."

Emma was more thrown by the revelation than she wanted to admit. She'd not been advised of a sixth member. She hadn't prepared, she didn't have the briefing information, and she didn't like surprises. She tried to calm her mind, wanting to fit into this group of women that functioned, even thrived, on change. But that was easier said than done. She could feel her blood pressure rise, and she fought the urge to rub the rosary beads in her pocket. She did her best to refocus her energy on the conversation that was taking place around her. She needed this information. She needed as much information as possible.

Caden raised her hand and spoke. "I thought we were going to Dubai. What's in Russia?"

Captain Hart tapped Emma on the shoulder and pointed to the screen. Emma realized he wanted her to pull up the file they'd gone over an hour before. She inserted the thumb drive into the computer and opened the folder. When the picture appeared, he motioned for her to talk.

Emma stood up, felt herself wringing her hands, and then stopped herself by picking up the computer remote. She willed herself to speak with authority and confidence. "Our sources indicate that Carol O'Brien is taking refuge in Russia. Moscow, to be exact. The original assumption that she headed to Dubai was nothing more than clever computer hacking." She pushed the button, clicking through a series of photographs. "She's been there for about three weeks." She sat back down, unsure what else to add.

Captain Hart looked at her for a long second before he spoke and his eyes held a flash of annoyance. "The extradition treaty has been long abandoned between our government and Russia. We want her back to face trial, so we're going to have to go get her." He walked toward the door. "We'll finish the briefing on the plane. We leave tomorrow at zero-four-hundred. Do not be late and do not bring anything to wear that identifies where you work."

Emma took the thumb drive out of the computer and placed it in her bag. She was going to leave when she noticed the four faces staring back at her. She slumped back in her seat, unsure what to say.

Caden leaned forward on the table and laced her fingers together. "I assume since the captain didn't introduce us, you already know who we are."

Emma nodded. "You're Special Agent Caden Styles. You're thirty-two years old, graduated sixth in your class from the University of Florida, where you studied criminal justice. You started out in the FBI but moved over to Homeland Security four years ago. Your father spent twenty-five years in the Coast Guard, and your parents have been married for thirty-five years. You're the oldest of four and the only female."

At first, Emma thought Caden was angry; her expression was blank, and she merely blinked at her. Then, a smile started to creep across her face. "So, you've seen all our files?" Caden asked.

Emma nodded and pointed at Tyler. "Special Agent Tyler Monroe. Thirty-years-old, both parents are deceased. You spent your teenage years living with your aunt in North Carolina. Your uncle was killed during the World Trade Center attacks on nine-eleven. You started your career in the Marines, and you did four tours in Iraq before being injured. Then, you taught for six months at the CIA training facility, Camp Peary, where you met Hart, Glass, and Styles. After that, you came to work for Homeland Security."

Emma didn't know if she should continue, but her nerves didn't allow her to stop. "Analyst Brooke Hart, twenty-six years old. You've excelled at everything you've ever done. You played several varsity sports in high school and then went on to play in college. The CIA recruited you and you went straight to the Farm after college. You were a Navy kid and raised on several continents, and you speak four languages. You also are the only female of four children." Brooke stopped making eye contact, and Emma decided not to mention her parents. She looked over at Jennifer Glass, who had started tapping her fingers on the table. Jennifer seemed uneasy about the personal disclosures, and Emma didn't want to continue, and no one pushed her.

Caden chuckled. "That's a pretty neat trick. You seem to have our files memorized, but we don't know anything about you." Caden leaned back in her seat, clearly waiting for Emma to answer a question she didn't ask.

Emma looked at the four expectant faces staring at her. They were right; she'd had the advantage of knowing who she'd be working with before today. She knew they could look her up. Hell, they could investigate anyone in the world with their resources. But they wanted to hear from her, a step in the direction of cohesive teamwork.

Emma nodded and tried not to bite her lower lip. "Okay, well, I have an older sister and a younger brother. I grew up in Texas, right outside of Dallas. I graduated high school at sixteen and Texas A&M at nineteen. The NSA approached me right after graduation, and I've been with them since then."

Jennifer cocked her head to the side when she spoke. "How old are you?"

Emma pushed her glasses up the bridge of her nose. This was a question she was asked often, and the answer was rarely well received. "I'm twenty-five."

Brooke smiled at her. "That's very impressive." Her eyes were genuine, which relaxed Emma.

Emma was accustomed to people shrugging off her capabilities because of her age, but she didn't see that in Brooke's reaction. She assumed it was probably because Brooke often faced the same reception as she did regarding her age versus her capabilities. But

Brooke apparently had something she didn't—self-assurance. Maybe some of that would rub off on Emma. She hoped so, anyway.

Tyler stood and put her hand out again. This time, Emma took it. "It's nice to meet you, Emma. We're looking forward to working with you."

Emma continued to shake her hand. "Thank you. I'm very excited about this opportunity."

Tyler smiled, and Emma realized it was probably because she was still pumping her hand up and down.

"Do you want to go get dinner with us? We could all get to know each other better."

Emma felt her breath catch in her throat. She looked around at the faces staring back at her. She shouldn't go out to dinner; she needed to get ready to leave. She'd never been off-site for a mission, and she wasn't even sure what to bring. But that's not what came out of her mouth.

"Okay." The surprise of her own answer forced her body to release Tyler's hand.

Emma picked up her bag from the floor and put it on her back. "So, I'll follow you to the restaurant? Or you could just tell me where we're going." She pulled the straps of her backpack forward. "Are we going now or did you all want to go later? Is it too early to eat? What time is it?" She blew out a breath. "I ramble sometimes. Like when I'm nervous. Or when I'm not sure what to say." *Just stop talking, Emma.*

The blank stare on Tyler's face transformed into a wide, amused smile. "We're going to Rocco's. Do you know where that is?"

Emma nodded her head once. "The pizza place. Yes, I know where it is. I'll meet you there."

Tyler shoved her hands in her pockets and moved toward the door, and the other three followed her. "See you in a few."

Emma waved, and Tyler cocked her head and smiled again before the door closed behind them. Once there was only the quiet hum of computers in the room, Emma covered her eyes and shook her head. *What is wrong with you? Get it together, or they're going to think you're an idiot, and you'll never be let out of your little box again.*

Chapter Three

Tyler was practically salivating when they pulled up to Rocco's. It was home to some of the best brick oven pizza she'd ever tasted, and she was already mentally ordering when she got out of the car. They were about to embark on the final leg of their long sought-after objective to put Carol O'Brien and her organization down for good, but that could wait until tomorrow. Tonight, she was going to enjoy Brooke, her friends, good food, and try to get to know the newest member of the team.

She heard Caden before she saw her, explaining to Jennifer her initial thoughts about Emma. "I'm just saying she's a bit odd."

Jennifer was holding Caden's hand, but her face showed her annoyance. "You need to give her a chance. She's clearly brilliant, and not everyone has your charm."

Caden stopped, turned, and put her hand against her heart. "You think I'm charming?"

Jennifer rolled her eyes and walked past her. "I've changed my mind."

They were able to get their favorite round table in the corner of the restaurant without any issue. Tyler and Caden took their usual spots, backs to the wall, with a clear view of the front door and the windows.

"Are we splitting a pizza or are we each ordering?" Caden asked, and she looked over the menu.

Brooke put her hand on Tyler's, but she spoke to Caden. "Let's wait for Emma."

Caden frowned, but she tossed her menu onto the table. "I was just planning ahead."

The server brought water over, and Jennifer told him there would be one more. Then she turned her attention to Caden. "What is your deal? You don't know her well enough to not like her."

Caden sipped her water. "I didn't say I didn't like her. I'm just not sure she's going to fit in with us. Like I said, she's a bit odd."

"There's nothing wrong with being odd. I'm odd, and you like me," Jennifer said.

Caden leaned over and kissed Jennifer's cheek. "Yeah, but it took a while for you to grow on me."

Jennifer pushed Caden away, but she was smiling. "Not everyone is wired like you and Tyler. Give her a chance."

Tyler sipped her water. "Don't drag me into this. I'm always more comfortable when I'm familiar with the people I'm working with. Why else would I have started hanging out with Caden?"

Caden hit her in the arm. "I'm the—" She looked over at Brooke and shrugged. "Second best thing to ever happen to you."

Tyler was about to make a smart-ass comment back when Emma came through the door. She took a moment to study her in the few seconds she had before Emma found them and came over to the table. Tyler didn't agree with Caden in this instance. She didn't think Emma was odd as much as she was a little socially awkward. She had graduated early from both high school and college, meaning she was constantly around people who were slightly older and probably intimidated by her. Tyler didn't think many sixteen- to twenty-two-year-old people would've gone out of their way to befriend her, much less bother to get to know her. This would've made her socially isolated and probably lonely. She assumed Emma would've become accustomed to these interactions and never bothered to try something different when she graduated. Emma just needed someone to give her the opportunity to be herself.

Emma had her hands pulled underneath her sleeves and her arms crossed. She pushed her glasses up on her nose and tucked her short sandy hair behind her ear, even though it hadn't fallen in her face. All these little tells indicated to Tyler that she was right. Emma wasn't odd; she was nervous and probably overwhelmed.

Brooke patted the chair next to her, and Emma took a seat. "Hi, Emma. Did you have trouble parking?"

Emma shook her head and grabbed the menu. "No, I rode my bike. So, no issues."

This seemed to pique Caden's interest. "Oh yeah? What kind of bike do you have? I have a Ducati Scrambler, and I love it." She leaned forward on the table, waiting for Emma's response.

Emma scrunched her nose. "I ride a Schwinn, but I don't remember the model. You can look at it after dinner if you'd like. It's very comfortable."

Caden leaned back in her seat and put her arm along the back of Jennifer's chair. "That's okay." She was trying to suppress a laugh. "I'll take your word for it."

Brooke shot Caden an annoyed look and then opened her menu. "Everything looks so good." She turned to Emma. "Did you want to share something with us, or did you have something in mind?"

Emma's shoulders relaxed slightly. "I could go for a veggie pizza if anyone is interested."

Brooke closed the menu and smiled at her. "That sounds perfect."

Tyler didn't want a veggie pizza. In her book that didn't even count as pizza. But she could make this small sacrifice to show Emma they wanted to be friends. The server came, and Brooke ordered a veggie pizza, and Caden ordered a meat lover. Tyler's stomach rumbled at the mention of Caden's order but said nothing. Caden gave her a sideways glance, topped off with an annoying smirk.

Dinner continued without any significant missteps. Emma seemed thoughtful and kind, a stark contrast to the people Tyler usually worked with. The chatter was light and simple. They were in an unspoken agreement that after today, their time would be filled with the harsh realities of their jobs.

Tyler took her time, enjoying the people she was with. Meeting Brooke had helped her develop this skill. She now saw the beauty in the comfortable and secure instead of always looking for the next new thing. She took Brooke's hand under the table and felt the butterflies bubble in her stomach when Brooke squeezed her hand while laughing at something ridiculous Caden had said. Tyler wished she could stop time at this moment so she could enjoy it a little longer.

❖

"Packing is a science," Tyler said, laying out all the items she'd be taking into neat and precise stacks.

Brooke came up behind her and ran her hands up her back and onto her shoulders. "You treat everything you do like a science."

Tyler smiled and grabbed her hand, pulling her around in front of her. "Not everything." She kissed her lightly at first and then with more determination. Tyler wanted to convey the depth of her feelings with her body, not just her words.

Brooke put her hands on Tyler's face and smiled. "I don't know what I did to deserve you."

Tyler kissed her forehead and pulled her into a hug. "I feel the same way."

Brooke stepped out of Tyler's embrace and went back to packing her own bag. "How do you feel about working with my father?"

Tyler rolled each of her shirts and placed them along the bottom of her bag. "Captain Hart is one of the most decorated military officers we have working in our country right now. I consider it an honor." She rolled her pants next and placed them on top of her shirts. "But the real question is, how do you feel about it?"

Brooke looked through her toiletry bag and zipped it up. "I don't know. He makes me nervous."

Tyler sat on the bed, turning her full attention to Brooke. "Tell me more about that."

Brooke glanced up at her and smirked. "You sound like a therapist."

Tyler knew Brooke was deflecting, but it wasn't going to deter her. Brooke rarely showed a chink in her armor, and if she was now, they needed to talk. "Do you want to talk about it?"

"No." Brooke threw a shirt in her bag with a bit more force than what was necessary. "I mean...after everything that has happened between my parents and us, now I'm just supposed to be around him like everything is normal?" She continued to throw items of clothing in her bag. "They think you're a phase of some kind, and the very idea of that is insane. They act like you're the first woman I've ever told them about. It's just infuriating that they don't listen to me. They treat me like a child who doesn't know what she wants. My dad says that he's going to have an open mind, but you have no idea the power my mother has over him." She sat on the bed.

Tyler pulled Brooke to her, allowing her head to rest against Tyler's stomach. "Do you want my advice?"

Brooke kissed the top of Tyler's hand and then intertwined their fingers. "Always."

"Treat your dad exactly how you'd treat any commanding officer on this mission. He'll see what you're capable of, that you're no longer a child, and just how good you are at your job. Your mom, well, we can deal with that when we get home," Tyler said.

"It's hard for me to even look at either of them. Denying you is like denying a part of myself. I'm not comfortable with any of it." Brooke's voice was quiet and uncertain. It was a sharp contrast from her normal confident tone.

"We'll get through this. I promise we will."

Brooke kissed her hand again. "I know. I've never had any doubt."

Tyler didn't know what else to say. She'd been young when her parents died and her aunt Claire had been exactly who Tyler needed her to be when she came out, and she'd accepted it immediately. She didn't know if she'd given Brooke good advice or if it fell into the realm of asinine. But Tyler knew, regardless of how Brooke's parents felt, she'd never give up on Brooke. Tyler would never leave her, would never walk away, and would never turn her back on her. Brooke was all that mattered.

CHAPTER FOUR

The early morning sun that slipped through the makeshift curtains helped to enhance the hangover Dylan Prey felt throbbing in the front of her head. She looked down at the arm draped across her body and followed it up to the stranger's face. Dylan tried to remember the woman's name. *Misha? Yana?* It didn't really matter. Dylan would never see her again, not if she could help it, anyway.

Dylan carefully removed the woman's arm and slipped out of bed, a small creak from the frame when she moved the only announcement of her actions. The woman made a slight noise and rolled over, giving Dylan the perfect opportunity to leave unnoticed. She found her pants, shirt, and shoes lying in different locations around the small room. She made sure she had her phone and keys and slipped out the front door.

Once outside, she pulled her phone from her pocket. There was a notification from her handler, which she cursed herself for missing. It came in the form of a package delivery update, and she only had an hour to get there. She looked around, knowing full well her car was here somewhere. Even in her most intoxicated states, needing her car would've made it through the haze. She remembered asking one of her guys to drive them back to the woman's apartment last night. Which, of course, he did without hesitation. She walked to the back of the apartment building and felt a sense of relief when she laid her eyes on her Lada Granta.

In all honesty, she hated the car. It looked like a Toyota Echo and a Mitsubishi Lancer had an ugly baby. But they were popular here, and it helped her blend in to the culture. Dylan got to the car and opened the trunk. She pulled out a fresh pair of jeans and a shirt. She looked in the mirror she kept in her bag, unimpressed with what she saw staring back at her. There were mascara circles under her eyes, and her face was blotchy from the heavy drinking the night before. She grabbed a bottle of water from the trunk and splashed it on her face, and then ran some through her hair. She did her best to smooth her hair back, attempting to give herself a fresh look. She knew her handler would see right through the attempt, but this was all she could do for now.

Dylan got in her car and plugged her phone into the charger. She now had forty-five minutes to make it from the Lyublino District, to the FedEx location in Moscow, where her package was waiting. It was only about seventeen kilometers, but in the morning traffic, she'd use every bit of her allotted time.

Dylan was nine minutes late when she pulled into the parking lot of the FedEx store. The traffic that morning had been particularly unforgivable, but making Merrick wait was even worse. She found his car parked on the other side of a dumpster and got into the front seat.

"You're late." He growled at her from the driver's seat. He pulled a cigarette from his pack and lit it with the one already burning between his fingers. "It's dangerous to just sit out here like this. Especially in the daytime."

"I know," she said. She did her best not to cough from the smoke that was swimming all around her. "I didn't see your message until this morning. I had to go out last night."

He scratched at the stubble on his chin. "Were you with Alekperov?"

She rubbed at her eyes, the hangover worsening from the smoke. "Yeah. I think we're getting close. It's taken three years, but he trusts me. We're going to be able to pick him up and flip him soon."

Merrick reached into his breast pocket and pulled out a piece of paper. "We need you to help on this assignment, too."

She took the paper but didn't open it. "I'm too close to be pulled off now."

"Relax," he said. "We aren't pulling you off anything. This new assignment plays right into your current one."

She opened the paper and memorized the address, date, and time. She handed the paper back to Merrick, and he lit it on fire and then tossed it into a tin box. He'd finish getting rid of it later.

She put her hand on the handle of the door, wanting to get out of the car and into the fresh air. "Anything else?"

"This new assignment is important. The team is permitted to have full access to any information you have on Alekperov and his associates. Don't be a dick about it." He nodded to the door, indicating she could leave.

"When am I ever a dick?" Dylan asked.

He laughed and started the car. "Every single day that I've known you. That's what makes you good at your job. You don't have any emotions, so they never get in the way. Good luck, and stay safe."

She got out of his car and walked into the store. Part of the ruse was that she'd actually pick up a package. That way, if Roman Alekperov, the *pakhan*, the boss of the Russian mafia she'd been trying to get close to for the last several years, hacked her phone and saw her messages, she would've been where he thought she should be. She didn't use any encrypted technology when she was around him. He needed to be able to hack her phone if he pleased. He needed to believe she was exactly who she said.

She tossed the small package she'd retrieved from the FedEx store onto her front seat. She didn't know exactly what was in it. She placed random items into her Amazon cart, and when the CIA needed her, they'd pay for one of the items and send it her way. It usually happened once every two to three months, rare enough to not raise suspicion, but frequently enough for Merrick to keep tabs on her when she couldn't get to their satellite office.

She drove toward her apartment, wondering what new mission would be bringing her agency to Moscow. It had to be big enough to pull her in, potentially risking a position she'd cultivated for the last three years. She knew all this, but it didn't help to squelch the irritation she felt for being put in this position in the first place. She was so close, and she wasn't going to jeopardize her progress for some idiot who didn't want to put in the work. Sure, she'd do what was asked of her, but she wasn't going to bend over backward for anyone.

Her phone rang, and she looked down at the screen. It was Nikolai. Nikolai was the *derzhatel obschaka*, or bookkeeper, that she reported to in the Bratva. She'd started out at a lower level, being a *shestyorka,* a kind of errand girl, and moved her way up to a brigadier, only last year. The structure of the Russian mafia was similar to all other gangs around the world, the names were just different. Dylan didn't have to answer to many people, but Nikolai was definitely someone she needed to pick up her phone for, without question. Dylan's transition from herself into Sasha wasn't a difficult one. She could barely tell the difference between her two personalities anymore.

"Hello, Nikolai," she said in Russian. "What do you need?"

"Sasha, where are you?" His connection was spotty at best, and she pushed the phone harder against her ear to hear.

"I just picked up a package from FedEx," she said. There was no reason to lie about her whereabouts. He could easily find out where she was.

"I need you to go over to the candy store. There's a shoplifter." He ended the call with no further information.

The Bratva didn't fear the police force in Moscow. They had no reason to; these were their streets and their rules. But they still spoke in coded language in case other agencies were listening. Agencies like the CIA. He was informing her that one of the warehouses where they kept and dispersed their drugs was in danger. The candy store told her which one she was needed at.

She drove for fifteen minutes to the textile factory and parked her car with the mass of others in the lot. Anyone passing by would assume the vehicles belonged to employees of the factory, spending their days making traditional Russian cloth. This wasn't entirely inaccurate, because there was an entire workforce that did just that every day. What took place in the bowels of the warehouse was an altogether different business. Asian opiates were cultivated here, as well as cocaine and cannabis. They were cut, measured, packaged, and then shipped out all over Western and Central Europe, and occasionally to the United States.

She opened her trunk and removed the false floor. She grabbed extra ammo for the small pistol attached to her ankle and slid it into the black vest she'd wear inside. She placed another handgun in the back of her pants and slid her favorite knife into its holster around her belt. She didn't think any of these weapons would be necessary, but she couldn't risk going in without them.

She pulled her leather jacket on and zipped it up, wanting to hide her vest. She moved quickly toward the warehouse, hands in her pockets and her head down. She didn't want her face on the decidedly low-tech security cameras the textile factory used. The employees knew Roman Alekperov owned the building and that it was used as a cover for a drug operation, but the fewer people who could identify her, the better. She opted for the back entrance, wanting to see what happened without anyone being able to give warning that she was coming.

She used her key fob to enter at the bottom of the staircase and pushed open the heavy metal door. Her arrival on site was met with a sea of surprised faces. It wasn't often that someone in her position would stop by the operation, and that fact would be the key to discovering the thief. There were about a dozen low-level *shestyorkas* inside, working on cutting up and weighing the drugs, while three *boyeviks*, the middle management, monitored their work. Each boyevik had the same expression and body language, ready to pounce for any minor infraction.

She walked over to the boyevik closest to the only window in the space, keeping her eyes trained on the shestyorkas hovering over their work. She spoke to him in Russian. "How long since the last shift change?"

The tall, broad man uncrossed his arms and looked down at her. "Forty-five minutes. Is everything okay?"

She noticed one of the men in the corner of the room. His hands were trembling with what she assumed were nerves. He was pretending to stare intently at the beaker in his hand, but his eyes were actually on her. She walked over to him, forgetting the boyevik she'd been speaking with.

"How long have you worked here?" she asked him, stepping closer to him than necessary.

He tried to look unfazed, but she could see the sweat at his hairline starting to form. "Three months."

She pulled the gun from the back of her waistband and set in on the table. "And how long have you been stealing from us?"

The man's eyes bulged, and he put his hands out in front of him, pleading. "I'm not stealing. I'd never steal from the pakhan." His voice shook with trepidation. He was lying.

She saw the three boyeviks take a step in their direction and she put her hand up, indicating she had it under control. "You don't have a lot of options here. You can either tell me the truth and I kill you. Or, you lie, and I let them kill you." She waved her hand at the three hulking men, practically salivating in her peripheral, waiting for her signal.

He knew, just as she did, that dying at the hands of the boyevik was a fate far worse than death. Their souls fed off the carnage and pain of others. Their efforts wouldn't be quick or minor. The boyevik would take their time, enacting a lifetime of hellfire and suffering into the experience.

His eyes flicked back and forth between her and the men. The answer was clear, but she understood that agreeing to your own death could take a moment. "I'll go with you."

She nodded once and slipped the gun back into her waistband. She grabbed him by the arm and pushed him toward the door. None of the boyevik said anything to her as she shoved the man outside; they wouldn't dare. There was no room to question her or ask where she was taking him. They knew they weren't privy to that kind of knowledge and they didn't need to be part of it. One of the reasons the Bratva was so successful was because everyone knew their place and adhered to the structure. Anything less would result in your death, and a hundred people were waiting to take your place. Everyone was expendable or exchangeable.

They got to her car, and she opened the trunk. "Get in."

He got on his knees, tears rolling down his cheeks. "Please don't kill me."

"You should've thought about that before you stole from the pakhan. You've left me no choice." She motioned to the trunk and put a hand behind her back, where her gun was holstered.

He reluctantly got into the trunk of the vehicle, and she zip-tied his hands and feet. She placed a piece of duct tape over his mouth and shut the trunk. She got back into her front seat and took a swig out of her water bottle. This wasn't how she wanted to start her day. She pulled a box of tampons from underneath the passenger seat and retrieved a small black device that looked like a pen. She pushed the button and started toward the other side of town. It was going to be a long day.

Emma sat in the leather seat of the plane and secured her seat belt. She pulled on it once for good measure, wanting to make sure it was placed correctly. She pulled her laptop out of her messenger bag and plugged it into the bulkhead outlet. She'd intentionally arrived earlier than the rest of the team. Getting comfortable with her surroundings without people watching her was one of the ways she put herself at ease. She powered on her computer and pulled the thermos from her bag, pouring some of the contents into her travel mug. She was about to take her first sip when she heard voices.

"All I'm saying is that it's real damn early," Caden said to someone behind her. She tossed her backpack onto an empty seat and dropped onto the bench a few feet from Emma.

"The flight is almost ten hours. I'm sure you can take a nap. I hope you aren't this whiney the whole time," Tyler said. She was right on Caden's heels but stopped to put her smaller bag in a compartment near the bench where Caden sat.

Jennifer entered next, seemingly in a conversation with Brooke. She stopped and picked up Caden's backpack and put it in a secure compartment before sitting next to her. "Are you still complaining about being tired? I told you to go to bed."

A slow smile started on Caden's lips and she winked at Jennifer. "If I remember correctly, that's not exactly what you said."

Jennifer smacked her arm. "Knock it off, Styles. Or that will be the last time you see me in bed for a while."

Emma hoped her face didn't show the surprise she felt. She knew Tyler and Brooke were a couple, she could tell by their interactions, but she hadn't realized Jennifer and Caden were as well. The knowledge made her slightly uneasy. She hoped these four women would be able to maintain their focus. Otherwise, they'd all be in a lot of trouble.

She hadn't realized she was staring at Jennifer and Caden until she felt a hand on her arm.

"Are you okay?" Brooke asked.

"Yes, I just didn't realize that all of you were in relationships... with each other." Emma could've lied, but that wasn't how she was built.

Brooke glanced across the table at Tyler, who was scrolling on a tablet, before looking back at her. "There aren't any rules saying that people in the CIA can't date people in Homeland." Brooke sounded a little defensive, but not angry.

Emma remembered how her words were sometimes received as blunt, and that hadn't been her intention. "Oh, no. That's not what I meant. I was just surprised, and I'm rarely surprised."

Tyler looked up from her tablet. "Yeah, we were surprised that Styles convinced Glass to date her too." She laughed while ducking a blow from Caden over the top of the bench.

Jennifer put her arm on the back of the bench and looked at Emma. "What about you? Are you seeing anyone?"

Emma almost choked on her coffee as she tried to stifle a laugh. "Me? No. People aren't interested in me."

Jennifer cocked an eyebrow. "I find that hard to believe. You're brilliant, successful, and beautiful. I'd think plenty of people would be very interested in you."

Emma fought the urge to cover her face, embarrassed by the attention. "I'm also socially awkward, nervous, and a bit neurotic."

"You *are* a bit weird," Caden chimed in from her spot on the bench.

Jennifer smacked her without looking back. "Don't listen to her. She rarely knows what she's talking about."

Emma smiled, watching Caden impersonate Jennifer behind her back. She really enjoyed this team. She hadn't been sure of what to expect, but their cohesiveness was apparent, and their camaraderie palpable. It was enjoyable just to be in their presence.

Emma was about to tell them about her one romantic experience in college when Captain Hart entered. He looked at all of them and then turned to the cockpit, disappearing behind a barrier.

Brooke let out a sigh next to her. "Fun's over, time to get to work."

Even though Brooke was sitting across the table from Tyler, her body language was clear as she leaned toward her. She wondered if Brooke realized how drawn to her partner she was, seeming to need even a minuscule adjustment in their proximity when she felt distressed. Brooke might not have realized it, but Tyler did. Tyler watched Brooke's face and winked at her. Emma wondered what it would be like to have someone feel like that about her. What it would be like to have someone so in tune with your emotions that they threw you small lifelines without having to be prompted or asked? What it would feel like to have someone care about you so intensely?

Her thoughts were cut short when Captain Hart sat next to Tyler, asking Caden and Jennifer to move closer. He put his bag on the table and started pulling out items as the plane began rolling forward. He handed each of them a passport with a different name and airline tickets to match. "We're flying into Norway, from there, you'll take different commercial flights into Moscow. Monroe, you stay with Hart and Glass. Styles, you're with Quinn. I'll fly in on this plane for a scheduled meeting. Once you arrive, pick up your rental cars, and we'll meet at this safe house." He handed them a map with a location circled in red.

Caden looked at the map and then back at the captain. "What's the time frame for the mission, Captain?"

"Whatever it takes, Styles. We need to get Carol O'Brien out of there and back to the States, but we're pulling in someone who's been undercover for years to help with the extraction. We need to do everything we can to help keep their identity intact, and that may mean it takes us longer than we'd like," he said as he slid folders in front of each of them.

Emma opened her folder. Inside were dozens of pictures and organizational charts. She felt her breath catch in her chest. "Is this what I think it is?"

Captain Hart nodded his head. "Our temporary team member is Dylan Prey. She's been deep undercover for the CIA for the last three years, working her way up the ranks inside the Russian mafia. She has the connections to help us locate, allocate, extract, or if need be, eliminate Carol O'Brien. O'Brien is currently under the protection of the Russian mob." He pointed to the folders. "Inside your folders is everything we have on the mob, or as it's known there, the Bratva. Their safe houses, their organizational chart, their hideouts; everything. I need you to memorize everything in these folders. I need you up to speed when we land. You need to be able to recognize who these people are so we don't put Prey in danger."

Emma put her hand over her mouth, astonished by the sheer amount of information on the pages. She'd worked for years putting bits and pieces of this information together for the NSA, but she'd never seen it in its complete form.

"What's a pakhan?" Caden asked from beside her.

"He's the boss," Emma said, still scouring the information on the pages. She looked up at Caden when there wasn't a response.

Caden blinked back at her. "Want to help us out here? It'd probably be easier to digest all this info with a little assistance."

Emma nodded. "Sure." She spread the papers out across the table and pulled her laptop over. She pulled a stylus from her bag and started writing on the tablet. A push of a button sent the image to the large screen in front of the table so everyone could see what she was drawing.

"Russian mafia, Bratva, or Red Mafia, the organization goes by many names. Their criminal résumé includes almost every illegal activity in existence. This organization has its fingers in just about every country worth any money in the world. I know it might seem like they're one large group, but they aren't. The Russian mafia is an umbrella term for a network of autonomous criminal groups, a kind of consortium of mafia groups." She pulled up another set of images onto the screen. "The one thing all these groups do share, besides their Soviet roots, is a commitment to being involved in any activity that will turn a profit. They're terribly resourceful and have zero limits. We're talking money laundering, drug and human trafficking, weapons smuggling, extortion, sex work, kidnapping, smuggling, and murder." She blew out a breath. "They're difficult to take down because there are so many sects. Removing a few of the higher-ups wouldn't cripple them, and they'd be replaced within the hour. This aspect sets them apart from the crime families we've dealt with in the States."

Brooke pointed to one of the photos of Dylan Prey, where she was speaking to a muscular man with a cigarette dangling from his mouth. "So, Prey is in the thick of all this?"

Captain Hart nodded. "There are Bratva clans all over Russia, but the particular one she's been working with is the largest in Moscow. They're responsible for nearly forty percent of all of the drugs that leave Asia."

"Do we know where they're hiding O'Brien?" Tyler asked.

Captain Hart shook his head. "No, but if anyone can find out, it's Prey."

Emma studied the picture of Dylan Prey. She was thin but muscular, her arms were covered in tattoos, her dark brown hair was cut above her ears, and she had the greenest eyes Emma had ever seen. Her lips were full, and the angles on her face were stark. She thought that even if someone did mistake her for a man, she wouldn't be any less attractive. She had the urge to run her finger over the photo but stopped herself when she was pulled from her reverie by Tyler's voice.

"Emma?" Tyler said her name as if she'd already done so several times.

"Yes, sorry." She turned all her attention to Tyler.

"Can you pull up the maps of Moscow? I think we should study the streets and their names. We need to familiarize ourselves with the area before we get there. Also, we'll need landmarks and how different districts are divided. Whatever you have," Tyler said as she pointed to the screen.

Emma did as she was asked, grateful to have someone as pragmatic as Tyler on her team. Emma tended to get lost in the minutia of tasks, often losing sight of the big picture. Yes, it made her good at her job, but it was also one of the reasons she struggled in other areas of her life. She hoped, and not for the first time, that she could learn something by being around these women.

Chapter Five

Dylan parked her car at the designated location under the Renaissance Moscow Hotel. She walked over to the keypad in the corner of the parking garage and entered her authorization code, waiting for the door to beep. Once inside, she walked through the underground tunnel that led to the CIA station operating under the Baker & Hughes building. If anyone in the Bratva were to check her location, it would come up as her being at the fitness center next door. But this only gave her about two hours to conduct any type of business she needed to handle, and the number of times she could visit needed to be limited. She couldn't raise suspicion, and she'd still need to make an appearance at the gym itself, to be seen on the cameras.

Merrick didn't bother getting up from his seat when she came through the door. "I just saw you, so imagine my surprise when you hit your transmitter. This better be good."

She leaned against his desk and took one of the jellybeans from the dish on the corner, popping it in her mouth. "I've got a thief in the car, spent the last few months cutting up drugs. You could probably flip him. He's going to need relocation."

He pulled the dish toward him and took four red candies out, shaking them in his hand. "What do we want with a low-level thief? Does he have any other info? Has he seen any murders? Does he know where the pakhan lives?"

She pushed herself off the desk and started toward the data center in the back corner of their office. "That's your job to find out. I can't do everything. He's in the trunk of my car."

She knew the last part would piss Merrick off. He hated being told what his job entailed. That was partially why she said it. It wasn't often that she could ruffle his feathers, and she loved doing it.

She slid her phone over to a young man hunched over his keyboard, examining several monitors. "Hey, Tony, can you scan my phone for me? I want to make sure it's not being tracked."

He glanced down at the phone but didn't make eye contact with her. "That's your CIA phone. It's not being tracked. I'd know."

Dylan did her best to hide her smile. She liked Tony's no-nonsense approach to dialogue, even though some found him off-putting and brash. "It'd make me feel better, please."

He plugged her phone into his computer. "Emma Quinn will be here in seventeen hours."

She looked at him and waited for him to continue. He didn't, so she was forced to ask a follow-up question. "Who's Emma Quinn?"

His fingers streaked over the keyboard, clicking at a speed that didn't seem human. A moment later, a picture appeared on the screen, along with a full bio. The woman staring back at her from Tony's monitor was beautiful. She had sandy blond hair, pulled back into a bun, striking blue eyes, and a small birthmark below her left eye.

Tony nodded toward the screen, his fingers never leaving the keyboard. "That's Emma Quinn. I've never met her, but we have exchanged messages via our encrypted messaging system for work purposes. She's brilliant."

"Are you being replaced?" Dylan asked, scanning Emma's bio.

Tony looked confused. "No, of course I'm not being replaced. She's coming here to work with you. Well, her and four other people, your type of people."

"My type of people?" she asked and smiled.

"You know, they carry guns and like chasing people in dark alleys. Well, two of them do, anyway. The other two are computer analysts, like me, but not as good as me."

So, this was the team she was supposed to be helping. She hadn't gotten much information out of Merrick, as was his style, but maybe she could from Tony.

"Can you pull up their info?" she asked.

He thought about it for a minute and shrugged. "Special Agent Tyler Monroe, Special Agent Caden Styles, Analyst Brooke Hart, and Analyst Jennifer Glass." He sat back in his chair. "You can read the rest."

She leaned forward on the table, scanning the information next to their pictures. She'd be lying if she said she wasn't impressed. Still, she didn't understand why they needed her help.

"Do you know what the assignment is?"

He unplugged her phone from the computer and handed it back to her. "Yes."

She took the phone from him and put it in her back pocket. "Are you going to tell me?"

Tony shook his head. "I can't. You know that. You'll be informed of your assignment when—"

"When the agency deems fit. Yeah, I know the drill," she said.

He nodded once and turned back to his monitor. "Be safe out there."

"Thanks, Tony. See you soon."

Merrick glared at her when she walked past his desk. "We took care of your car issue."

"I knew you would."

She went back through the tunnel and into the gym. She'd need to get on the treadmill in the far corner, directly in front of one of the security cameras. Running wasn't her favorite workout, but it was the most efficient.

Dylan hopped on the treadmill and did her best to clear her head. As the speed increased, she recalled the information she'd read about the women. Her mind kept flashing to the image of Emma Quinn. Yeah, she was probably brilliant like Tony had said. But what Dylan couldn't shake from her mind were those blue eyes. They weren't cold, the way most people looked in their company files. Emma's eyes seemed kind, almost welcoming.

Dylan increased the speed on the treadmill and shook her head. She needed to switch her train of thought because she was close now. She knew with a little more time she'd be able to flip Nikolai, and that would deal a devastating blow to the Bratva. That needed to be all that mattered. She'd worked too hard to be distracted by a beautiful blonde, regardless of her piercing blue eyes.

❖

"Can I speak with you for a minute?" Captain Hart asked, looking a bit nervous.

Tyler closed her laptop and looked around, but they were the only people awake. She pushed herself out of her chair and followed him to the back of the plane.

He ran his hand over his chin and leaned against the bulkhead. "Is Brooke still upset with me?"

Tyler instinctively turned in Brooke's direction. She could only see her feet, propped up on the edge of the couch. "I'm not sure this is a conversation you should be having with me, sir."

He nodded. "I'm not trying to put you in an uncomfortable situation. I want to do right by my daughter, but I can't control my wife's reactions."

Tyler studied his face and saw his sincerity. "She's hurt. It's going to take time, and you're going to have to accept her for who she is. That means letting go of who you thought she was, or whoever you wanted her to be, and making room for the real her." Tyler shoved her hands in her pockets. "She's worth it, you know." She nodded in Brooke's direction. "She's amazing, and if you two can't get past your feelings, you're going to be missing out on one of the best people any of us have ever known."

Captain Hart leaned toward her. "She's lucky to have you, Tyler. I mean that."

Tyler chuckled. "I'm the lucky one, sir. Once you see that, you'll be ready to get to know her."

Tyler walked back over to the couch and opened her laptop. Brooke leaned into her and rubbed her eyes.

"Everything okay?" Brooke asked with a yawn.

Tyler smiled at her. "Yeah. Go back to sleep."

Brooke pulled the thin airplane blanket closer to her chest, and a moment later, her breathing became rhythmic and deep.

Tyler pulled out the small box she'd been carrying around for the last two weeks and opened it, wanting to look at it again. The ring wasn't anything fancy. The band was made of white gold, with a solitary one-carat diamond.

"It's beautiful," Jennifer whispered from behind her.

Tyler turned to look at her, a little embarrassed that someone had been watching her. "It was my mother's."

"She'll love it."

Tyler leaned a little closer, not wanting to wake Brooke. "Are you sure? It's not too simple?"

Jennifer smiled. "Have you seen the way she looks at you? She'd wear a gum wrapper if it meant marrying you."

Tyler closed the box and put it back in her pocket. "Thanks, Jen."

"When are you going to ask?"

Tyler shrugged. "When we aren't in extraordinary danger, I guess."

Jennifer rolled her eyes. "Oh, God, don't wait for that. If you do, it will never happen."

"Ask me what?" Brooke asked from under Tyler's arm.

"Nothing, go back to sleep. I'll wake you up in an hour so we can keep prepping." Tyler kissed the top of her head because no one was watching, and because she couldn't help herself.

CHAPTER SIX

Carol O'Brien looked out the window from her penthouse apartment. She could just make out the colorful tops of the Kremlin. She took a deep breath, uncrossed her arms, and plastered a smile on her face. Dealing with Roman Alekperov, the Russian oligarch, was always an exercise in patience.

She turned and faced her visitor. "I thought when you agreed to hide me, you'd put me in a subtler location, Roman."

He scratched at his salt-and-pepper beard. "I own building. There's no problem."

Carol sat on the couch next to him and watched his eyes travel over her body. She allowed him a minute to take her in. "Roman, I gave you twenty million dollars. I should at the very least have security here, don't you think?"

Roman laughed and shook his head. "Boyeviks all over building. Getting to you is impossible. Americans, always so untrusting. Relax, enjoy your new home. Let Nikolai know if you need something." He stood to leave. "You should look forward to gala. It will be fun. Lots of food, dancing, and vodka. You have good time."

"Hmmm," she said as she walked him to the door. "See you then."

Carol opened the encrypted laptop Roman had given her and started scanning the pages of the American news sites. As far as she could tell, the search for her was alive and well, but still focused in Dubai. She read dozens of think pieces on why she'd done what she had. Speculation regarding her fear of people of color, of the LGBTQ community, her hatred for the "other." People needed to believe she was a monster; it helped them sleep better. They needed to believe hatred was easy to spot. They needed to be able to point to a specific characteristic and tell themselves that was the reason, that if they didn't share that particular belief, they were safe. But like most things, the truth was far more complicated.

Carol had done things the right way her entire life. She did as she was told and waited her turn. Waiting gradually progressed from months to years to decades. It wasn't until she took her place toward the top that she realized that was as far as they'd let her go. The men above her would keep her tethered to her spot, a beacon of false promises and lies they told children. *You can do whatever you set your mind to.* Bullshit. She'd made her share of questionable deals, traded votes for fundraising dollars, let people go without clean water to achieve more considerable backing from oil and coal. She'd said nothing as the men shook hands and made deals behind closed doors. She ignored the extramarital affairs of the so-called "family value advocates." Hell, she'd even helped reelect a congressman who'd killed a sex worker during a night of particularly brutal sexual play. She'd thought she was putting a string of wins in her column, a column that would place her in line for the presidency. But when her time came, she was pushed aside for some no-name out of the Midwest and a bumbling idiot from the East Coast.

It was at this point that she found her people, her followers who would go to the ends of the earth for her. All she had to do was validate their belief systems. It started innocently enough, a few rallies, some backroom meetings, sitting through their church sermons. She found an energy bubbling under everyday life in America. Energy fueled with hatred, mistrust, and the belief that people were cutting in line in front of them. It was then that she realized hate was a better motivator than love would ever be. Anger forced people beyond limits that society deemed unconscionable. They knew the proverbial line; they simply didn't care where it was. They wanted back what they'd felt was taken from them. They wanted people to see them instead of just looking past them. They were tired of hearing about the elites. Tired of being told they weren't worthy. They were tired of the college degrees and high-paying jobs that were kept just out of their grasp. They wanted to matter.

So, she became their voice. She gave them structure, funding, and leaders to help them organize. She found people to develop websites where they could find each other and share their thoughts and feelings, without the input of the rest of society. She gave them the home and safety they'd been searching for all along. When she thought they were strong enough, she mobilized them. She gave them a purpose, a sense of being. She saved them. Her own beliefs didn't match, but that didn't matter in the least.

Luckily, her country spent over a dozen years focused on threats from outside their border. Security agencies weren't paying any attention or sinking any funding into tracking their movement. They were easy to write off—extremists, loons, racists, homophobes. No one believed they deserved any real attention. The media and the government turned a blind eye when they started stacking police forces, school boards, and even local government commissions with people loyal to their cause. She changed the way they viewed themselves and the way the rest of the world saw them. The days of the white hood and burning crosses were long gone. These were community members, business owners, and people's friends. It was incredible what a nice shirt and slacks could do for one's image.

The wave started slowly. People sitting at dinner parties giving anecdotes about how their cousin had lost a job to an immigrant who was already receiving Social Security benefits. Having people write blog posts about how their children were being taught homosexual sex in schools and instructed how to pray to Allah. It didn't matter if it was true. It was actually better that it wasn't. They felt like they were privy to a world everyone else was too stupid to see. She made them believe that they were the insiders, and the rest of the lot was too blind to see what was happening right under their noses. It ignited fear and unease in communities. People would wave to their Mexican neighbors and then behind the cloak of the voting booth, put people into power who would send the very same neighbors back to their country of origin. Fear was an excellent motivator, and no one stoked the red-hot flame of fear better than her.

Of course, she'd made a few mistakes along the way, too. Michael Thompson and Nathanial Lark were two of those mistakes. Michael was so hell-bent on destroying a single Marine, Tyler Monroe, he almost tanked the whole operation. Then there was Lark. He could have been something special. But Lark was busy playing games when he should've stayed on task. Both of their failures had all but led Tyler Monroe and Caden Styles to her doorstep. Had she handled their duties herself, she'd be sitting in the Oval Office, instead of stewing in a country with no extradition treaty. She should've known better. She knew better than to send a man to do a woman's job.

Roman could reassure her until he was blue in the face. She knew the truth; she could feel it in her bones. Monroe and Styles were coming for her because it was personal now. But this time, she was ready. There would be no maiming, no toying, no kidnapping, no threats. This needed to be handled once and for all. Carol knew what their end game entailed: arrest or elimination.

Carol was no fool. She understood that simply killing Monroe and Styles wouldn't prevent her home country from continuing to pursue her. But if she could get rid of them, she'd be able to buy herself enough time to disappear. It would take months to get a new team up to speed, and she'd use that time wisely. She wouldn't have to spend the rest of her life looking over her shoulder. She could disappear and finally lead the life she deserved. All she needed was the right person for the job. She needed someone who could do what the others failed to do. Get rid of them. She was sure Roman or Nikolai could help her with her plan. Now, it was just a waiting game. It wouldn't take them long before they realized she wasn't in Dubai, and when that time came, she'd be ready.

CHAPTER SEVEN

Dylan left her car at her apartment and took the bus, then the Metro, and the bus again to make it to the address in Ostrov she'd memorized from Merrick. She did a double take when she arrived, unsure if she was in the right place. There was nothing but open grassy fields as far as she could see. She decided to walk a bit up the path, and she knew she was headed in the right direction when she came to an old rusted gate. It wasn't the gate that signified she was at a CIA house of operations, it was the lock attached to it. The gate was so old and rusted it could be easily knocked down by a Prius, but the lock was new and slightly advanced. She turned the lock over in her hand, and a red light showed from underneath. She lifted it to her face, knowing that it was a camera, and the people on the other side would need to see her. A few moments later, the lock came unlatched, and she pulled the gate open.

When she finally made it to the old farmhouse, she waited, knowing someone would be out to get her soon. It only took a few minutes before a woman she recognized from the pictures came out from behind the house.

"Agent Prey, I'm Special Agent Tyler Monroe. Thanks for coming all the way out here," she said, sticking her hand out.

Dylan uncrossed her arms and took the offered hand. "I didn't really have a choice."

Tyler gave her a smile and motioned to the house. "Well, thanks anyway. Let's talk inside."

They walked around to the back of the house, and Tyler pulled up an iron door from the ground. They descended the stairs into a well-equipped room. There were monitors on every wall, computers humming, and several words scribbled onto a whiteboard in the corner. At the table in the center of the room sat the other women Dylan had seen in the bios from Tony.

Dylan nodded at them. "I know who you are, so no need to introduce yourselves. I just need to know why I'm here. I don't like risking my cover, and I don't like team projects. So, what's the deal?"

"Well, I like her." Caden smacked the table.

Brooke didn't seem as enthusiastic as Caden about her approach. She glared at Dylan. "Look, we know that you've been undercover out here for quite a while, so you may not be up to speed with everything happening in the United States, so let me fill you in. The leader of the National Socialist Movement, a white nationalist organization, attempted to assassinate both the president and the vice president. That's after her team of goons broke into the Farm and compromised several CIA assets. Oh, and she tried to have each of us killed on more than one occasion. She's hiding somewhere here in Russia, and we intend to bring her back to face trial."

Dylan ran her hand through her hair and took a seat at the table. She had seen snippets on the news about what was happening back in the States. She knew about the organization Brooke had mentioned, but she didn't know they'd narrowed it down to one person being at the helm. "Do you know who she is? People have a pretty easy time disappearing here."

Emma hit two buttons on the computer, and a picture appeared on the screen in front of Dylan. "Yes, Carol O'Brien."

Dylan rubbed her chin and cursed to herself. "The Speaker of the House, Carol O'Brien? Jesus Christ." She felt her blood run cold, unsure if it was her surprise that so much had happened back home without her knowledge or that she knew she really had no choice but to help them.

"Is that a problem?" Jennifer asked.

Dylan leaned back in her chair. "A person with that kind of political notoriety just doesn't slip between the cracks. The mob, the

Russian government, or both, are involved in hiding her. To get any of you near her is going to require me to use up all my favors, all the trust I've built, and will most likely cause me to give up my cover. I've been working on this assignment for years, and I'm so close to getting to the top. If I can get one of the top players to flip, it would mean intel that we've never had access to before. It would mean being able to save the lives of hundreds, if not thousands of people stuck in human trafficking, drug disbursement, and other despicable activities. It would make a real difference in the world." She switched positions, putting her arms on the table, and intertwining her fingers. "I assume if there were another way, you wouldn't be here?"

Tyler looked at her for a long moment while the rest of the women watched Tyler, clearly waiting for her to take the lead. "I understand your trepidation. You've poured your heart, soul, and safety into this assignment. I get it, truly. But believe me when I tell you, if we had another way to get her, we would. I just don't see a path to her without you. We need your help."

Dylan was surprised by the candor in Tyler's statement. This line of work was filled with overly inflated egos, people who believed the fate of the free world lay solely in their hands alone. But that's not what she saw in Tyler's eyes when she spoke. She saw honestly, loyalty, with a dash of recklessness for good measure.

"Okay," Dylan said.

"Okay? Like you'll help us, or okay like pound salt?" Caden asked from the other side of the table.

Dylan couldn't help but smile. She instantly liked Caden. "Okay, I'll help you. With one catch—we do things my way. I know these people, this area, and what the real-life risk is if we get caught. These guys…" She blew out a breath. "They're animals. They won't think twice about cutting you open and sending your heart to your loved ones back home if they find out who you are and what we're doing."

Dylan saw both Brooke and Jennifer bristle at her words. Caden's and Tyler's responses came in unison. "Deal."

Emma, who had said nothing until this moment, had seemed to anticipate her response. Her voice surprised Dylan; she'd expected it to be quiet and maybe a bit timid, but that's not the sound she heard.

Emma's voice was raspy. Dylan found the contrast both fascinating and a little sexy.

"I'm going to need access to your files. I don't mean the files the CIA keeps either, I mean *your* files." Emma tapped her pen against her keyboard and pushed her glasses up the bridge of her nose.

Dylan put her feet up on the desk and crossed her legs. "I don't keep anything from my superiors. You and I both know that would be against regulations. I'd lose my job."

Emma cocked her head to the side, seeming to appraise her. "Bullshit."

Dylan crossed her arms and tried to read Emma's expression. There was no challenge in her statement. "Which part, exactly, is bullshit?" Dylan tried not to smile at Emma, who seemed so resolute in her appraisal of the situation.

Emma shrugged. "All of it. You absolutely keep files that your superiors don't know about because that's what good CIA Agents do. Also, you're not worried about getting fired. The arrogance is written all over your face. Lastly, the sly smile you keep flashing in my direction may work on other women, but it won't work on me. I know your type."

The boldness surprised Dylan, and from the look on Emma's face, surprised her as well. Dylan couldn't help but smile. "What type is that, exactly?"

Emma's face flushed, either from embarrassment or surprise, Dylan couldn't tell which. "I, um…"

Whatever she was going to say was cut off by Caden. "So, what's the plan, Prey? What do you need from us?"

Dylan had to force herself to pull her eyes off Emma to answer. "Nothing." She tapped the table and stood. "Let me see what I can find out before we formulate any kind of plan."

Tyler stood, mimicking Caden. "When can we expect to hear back from you?"

Dylan studied Tyler. There was no accusation, no hint of annoyance, the question was precisely what it seemed. "Give me two days."

Tyler nodded, although Dylan could see the rest of her team wasn't as understanding. She chose to ignore them and walked past the other three women sitting around the table. However, when Emma looked up at her, she made sure to wink. She enjoyed the way Emma looked away, her face turning pink. Dylan smiled to herself, enjoying the premise of throwing the computer hotshot off her game.

When she had finally gotten out of earshot, she pulled her phone out and located the familiar contact. He answered on the fourth ring. "Sasha, where are you?"

Dylan hurried along the path, hoping to catch the next bus. "Nikolai, I was visiting a friend. I need to speak to you."

He was quiet for a moment, and Dylan was sure he was going to put her off, but he let out a long sigh. "Fine. Meet me at Chemodan." He hung up the phone.

Dylan made it to the bus just in time. She was going to need every moment of this trip to formulate a plan on how to approach Nikolai without raising suspicion while still getting the information she needed. Nikolai, by nature, was untrusting and paranoid. She'd have to choose her words carefully. She leaned her head against the window, hoping she'd made the right choice in helping. If not, she'd pay with her life.

Emma stared at her keyboard, still unsure what had come over her. It wasn't like her to be outgoing in any way, but you'd never know that by the way she had just interacted with Dylan. Emma had consumed every bit of information she could find on Dylan before she'd arrived, but it hadn't prepared her for the presence Dylan commanded. Dylan gave off an aura of strength, independence, and a little bit of mischief. On top of that, she was painfully attractive, and her pictures hadn't done her any justice.

Emma rolled her neck, thinking about the way her body had reacted under Dylan's appraisal. Her mouth had grown dry, and her hands had become clammy. The visceral reaction wasn't one Emma had been prepared for and her head was still swimming a bit.

"Emma?" Brooke must have said her name several times because her face was etched with concern. "You okay?"

Emma blinked at her and sat up a little straighter. "Yes, sorry. Did you need something?"

"I was going to go make lunch for everyone up in the main house. Did you want to come?" Brooke asked.

"Yes, I could use some fresh air, too." Emma pushed away from her computer station and followed Brooke out of the room.

Once inside the house, Brooke started pulling ingredients for sandwiches out of the fridge and placing them on the counter. "What do you think of Prey?" Brooke asked while she laid bread out on a large tray.

Emma unscrewed the tops of the mayonnaise and mustard. "I think she's good at her job. Her list of accolades and awards is unlike anything I've ever seen for a CIA agent at her age."

Brooke placed turkey on several of the pieces of bread and roast beef on the others. "All true, but what does your gut tell you?"

Emma stopped putting condiments on the bread and looked at Brooke. "I don't know what you mean. All the data supports my original analysis."

Brooke smiled at her. "How very formal of you." She bumped Emma with her shoulder. "I know you're new to these team assignments, but I'm not. Tyler is going to be following her into whatever comes next and I'm just wondering if you find her trustworthy. Sometimes my opinions are skewed because of my feelings for Tyler."

That made sense. "You want to know if I think Prey will be reckless."

Brooke nodded. "Yes, that's exactly what I'm asking."

Emma placed several pieces of lettuce on the sandwiches. "Aren't they all a little reckless? I mean, I've read Tyler's and Caden's files; they'd run directly into a burning building if there were even a glimmer of a reason for them to do so."

Brooke's jaw clenched. "You aren't wrong."

Emma wasn't good at this whole friendship thing and got the feeling she might have added to Brooke's discontent, which wasn't something she wanted. "Their files also indicate that they're the best at what they do, the very best."

Brooke gave her a rather sad smile. "You aren't wrong about that, either."

Emma chewed on her bottom lip, unsure how to phrase her next question. She decided just to go for it. "Is it worth it? I mean, is the concern, the not knowing, the late nights, the near-death encounters— is Tyler worth it?"

Brooke turned around and leaned against the counter. She used the back of her hand to wipe an errant hair out of her eye and looked thoughtfully at Emma. "Yes." She smiled and looked up at the ceiling. "Tyler isn't just the very best at her job. She's the very best person I've ever known and an even better partner. She's strong, confident, and unwavering in everything she does, but she's also thoughtful, kind, gentle, and loyal. She makes me want to be better, to do better. She brings out the very best in me." She turned back around and took a deep breath, chuckling to herself. "Wow. Sorry about that. It seems I got a little emotional there for a minute."

Emma watched Brooke blush, and she couldn't help but smile. "You're fortunate. I've never felt like that about anyone or anything. I wonder if most people do?"

Brooke cut up the sandwiches and went to work on cutting up apples. "God, I hope so." She glanced over at Emma. "Have you ever been in love?"

Emma shook her head vehemently. "Me?" She laughed. "No." She bit down on one of the apple slices Brooke had laid out. "You'd be underwhelmed by my dating résumé. I've only kissed three people and had sex with one." Emma took another bite of the apple. "Sex was awkward and terrible. I honestly don't understand why people are so obsessed with it."

Brooke raised an eyebrow. "At the risk of sounding like an obnoxious guy, you were probably with the wrong man."

Emma shook her head. "Not a man. I've known that I like women since I was seven. It was science, really. I've never had any interest in men. I find them to be overly aggressive and unappealing." She turned away, remembering that she tended to overshare her internal dialog.

Brooke laughed and picked up the tray. "I couldn't agree with you more. Let's get these out to everyone before Caden starts to really annoy Jennifer."

Emma fell in step next to Brooke. "They're a peculiar pairing."

Brooke nodded. "They're good for each other though. They balance one another."

Emma thought for a moment. Maybe she had been doing the calculations wrong in her head. Perhaps she had been focused on finding someone like her instead of someone different from herself. *The Law of Polarity. Why didn't I think of that?* Her thoughts went to Dylan and the way her body had reacted to her. Her stomach flipped just thinking of the way her green eyes had traced over her face and the desire she'd had to touch her. She shook her head. That type of intensity might be a bit too much. It seemed dangerous to allow such strong emotions to someone's physical appearance to grab such a foothold in your psyche. No, she'd need to start with something much more straightforward, more comfortable to manage. She had a feeling Dylan Prey would be anything but easy to manage.

CHAPTER EIGHT

Dylan paced in the waiting area of the restaurant. She wouldn't be allowed admittance into Nikolai's private area until he deemed fit. She examined the old pictures that hung against the wallpaper. She picked up a few pamphlets that sat next to the door and flipped through them absently. Nikolai loved making her wait, and she had no choice but to do as he pleased.

"You can go back," the short, plump woman said to her in Russian.

Nikolai was at his regular table, laughing boisterously with another gentleman, whom she didn't recognize. "Sasha, you made it."

She plastered on her very best smile. "Yes, I need to speak with you."

He motioned to the empty seat at his table and slid over a glass of kvass. Dylan hated the cider; it was made from fermented rye bread, and the tartness made her lips pucker. She took the drink anyway and sipped on it.

"What is so important that you wanted to interrupt my meal?" Nikolai lit a cigar and inhaled deeply. Smoking had been banned in restaurants for two years, but that didn't matter to him.

"You're keeping me out of the loop Nikolai, and I want in." She leaned forward on the table, hoping to drive home her point.

He stared at her for a moment, squinting. "I don't know what you're talking about."

She reached across the man sitting next to her and pulled the bottle of vodka over. She finished the rest of the kvass, and then proceeded to pour the clear liquor into the empty glass. "You think my guys don't talk to me, Nikolai? You think I don't know about the person we're hiding?" She took a large gulp of the vodka. "I've been a good brigadier for you, but I want more."

He blew the cigar smoke into her face. "I owe you nothing, Sasha."

She knew her face didn't show the fear that bubbled in her belly. She was far too good at her job for that, but it was there all the same. Nikolai could end her with a single phone call; there was a list of people willing and eager to take her place. She was expendable; she had no disillusions about that. Still, she needed more information.

"Let me take over the security detail, so I can prove to the pakhan that I'm ready for more." She took another large gulp of vodka, partially to seem unfazed and partly to calm her nerves.

He studied her. She saw rage in his eyes but also a hint of admiration. Her ears were buzzing, and she tried not to falter under his scrutiny. Finally, he pulled a notepad from his jacket pocket, jotted a few words down, and slid it across the table to her.

She put the paper in her pocket without looking at it and was relieved to see her hands weren't shaking. "Thank you, Nikolai."

"If you fuck this up, it will cost you your life, Sasha. Don't thank me yet." He blew a massive plume of smoke up toward the ceiling.

She nodded and pushed herself up from the table. "See you soon."

She got back to her car and pulled the piece of paper from her wallet. Just as she assumed, it was an address. She typed the location into her GPS and set off in the direction it dictated. She made it to Chapaevsky Lane and blew out a long whistle. *Who knew being a white supremacist paid so well?*

She walked through the expansive doors made of wood and glass and up to the man sitting behind a desk. "I'm here to see Anna Golubev." She knew the name Nikolai had written on the paper was fake, but it would lead her to Carol O'Brien.

The man looked down at a piece of paper he had in front of him and nodded. "Floor twenty-three, number forty-two."

Dylan wasn't sure exactly what to expect, but it definitely wasn't the five-foot-nothing woman who opened the door. *She looked much taller on TV.* Carol O'Brien looked at her with a small amount of anger and trepidation.

"Well, don't just stand there, come in." Carol retreated into her apartment.

Dylan walked in and took in the room. It was gaudy, covered in gold, mirrors, expensive drapes, and rugs. It made her a little dizzy. She put her hands behind her back, waiting for Carol to say something, not wanting to seem too eager.

"Do you speak English?" Carol said from behind the kitchen island, where she held a glass of red wine to her lips.

"Yes, ma'am." Dylan made sure to emphasize a Russian accent. "I'm Sasha Katov. I'll be taking over your security."

Carol sipped her wine and a slow smile split across her face. "When Nikolai told me I was getting new security, I have to be honest, you weren't what I was expecting."

Dylan turned to her and gave her a curt nod. "I'm very capable."

Carol raised one eyebrow. "I'm sure you are." She came around the island now, wine glass still in hand. She stood in front of Dylan and looked her over again, this time allowing her eyes to linger on her body a little longer. "You'll be with me night and day?"

Dylan broke eye contact and looked at the wall in front of her. "No. I'll be available to you, but I will be in your presence only when necessary."

Carol sipped her wine again. "Who decides when is necessary?"

Dylan stepped around her and made a show of examining the apartment. "Whenever you leave the property, I'll need to know."

Carol let out a long sigh. "I'm afraid I won't be going out much. Too many eyes in the area."

Dylan nodded toward the phone in Carol's hand. "Let me give you my cell phone number."

Carol unlocked the screen and handed it to her. Dylan smiled and entered a series of numbers, opening the phone to cloning. She smiled and gave it back. She opened her phone, cloning Carol's. *This was much easier than I'd expected.*

"Call me, so I have your number," Dylan said.

Carol gave her a mischievous grim but did as she was asked.

"I'm going to send a few guys up to set up some cameras in your apartment." Dylan made a circle with her hand, indicating the space they were in.

"Is that really necessary?"

Dylan nodded. "Yes, I need to make sure you're safe at all times."

Carol studied her for a moment, looking into her eyes. "I'd like to go shopping, but since I know that isn't possible, could you help me bring a few trusted shop owners here so I can get some new clothes?"

"I'll see what I can do. How does Thursday work for you?" Dylan asked, pleased that Carol was so trusting.

"That will be fine. If I need anything between now and then, I'll give you a call." Carol walked her back toward the front of her apartment.

Dylan opened the door and turned to look at her. "I'll be back tomorrow to check in on you. My guys will come up to set up the surveillance equipment, but don't let anyone in who doesn't have the proper identification."

This seemed to amuse Carol. "You all have mob identification cards?"

"No, but ask to see their chest. They'll have a pair of eyes tattooed there if they're with us." Dylan leaned against the doorframe, waiting for Carol to respond.

Carol took a step closer, staring at Dylan's chest. "What about you, Sasha? Do you have eyes tattooed on your chest?"

Dylan pushed herself out of the door. "See you tomorrow."

Once Dylan made it to her car, she let out a long breath. Carol hadn't been what she was expecting, and everything had happened with great ease. For someone running for her life, she didn't seem to grasp how much danger she was in. She placed a quick phone call to one of her guys and asked him to go and install the camera system at Carol's apartment. She wasn't met with any resistance, as people in this world were good at taking and following orders.

She couldn't risk going back to the CIA safe house the same day she'd just been there, so she opted for the next best thing. She picked up her CIA phone and dialed Tony. She might not be able to go there, but she could bring the new team to her. She tried to tamp down the smile she felt form when she thought of Emma and being able to see her again. Distraction was dangerous, but just a bit of visual pleasure couldn't hurt, right?

CHAPTER NINE

Emma was focused on Tyler and Caden. Their arms were crossed, and there was a look of concern on their faces.

"I don't think it's a good idea to let her go out unprotected," Caden said.

Tyler gritted her teeth and looked between Caden and Emma. "No one knows who she is, though, whereas if the wrong eyes spotted us, we could blow the whole thing. Prey knows what she's doing. We need to trust her."

Tony raised his hand to speak, looking a little sheepish. "If I may, she'll be with me."

Caden raised her eyebrows. "Is that supposed to make me feel better?"

Tony reached into his pocket and retrieved a small canister. "I have pepper spray."

Caden looked over at Tyler and put her hands on her hips. "Is he fucking with me? He has to be fucking with me."

Tyler put her hand on her shoulder and then directed her attention at Tony. "Prey told you to come get Emma and bring her to the apartment, right?"

Tony put the canister back into his pocket and nodded. "Yes, then I'll bring her back here. She has some information, but she can't come back and forth to the safe house. It's too risky. We are to go over there and find out what she needs to tell us." He motioned between Emma and himself. "We both speak Russian, so we're a little less conspicuous than, well, you two."

Caden narrowed her eyes, and Tony took a step back. "If anything happens to Emma, we're coming for you."

Emma pulled her fingers off the rosary in her pocket and put her hands up, wanting to deescalate the situation. "Everyone relax, we'll be fine. If something goes wrong, I promise to hit my panic button. It won't be a big deal." She looked over at Jennifer and Brooke, who were sitting behind computer monitors. "They'll be tracking me the whole time. Everything will be fine, and we need an update."

Tyler nodded. "Agreed. I'd like to go with you, but I think this is the best option for this particular set of circumstances." She handed Emma a bottle of wine and Tony a tray of food. "If anyone sees you walking up, it will look like you're going for dinner."

Emma took the bottle, cradling it in her arms. "We'll be back soon."

Caden formed a peace sign with her fingers, pointed to her eyes, and then turned them on Tony, indicating that she'd be watching him. He audibly gulped next to her.

Once inside the car, Tony seemed even more nervous. He tapped his leg several times and pulled at the collar of his shirt. "So, how's the NSA?"

Emma watched the changing landscape out the window. "It's good. This is my first team assignment, so I'm a little nervous."

Tony continued to drum his fingers. "Yes, I know. So far, so good, though. I've seen some of your work, it's awe inspiring."

She turned and looked at him. "Thank you. Yours is pretty good too."

"I know," Tony said, matter-of-fact.

Emma didn't think it was possible, but perhaps she found someone as socially awkward as her. The thought was reassuring, and she relaxed a little bit, letting her guard down.

"How long have you been here in Russia?" she asked.

Tony put on his blinker and cautiously checked his surroundings. "Three years."

"So, you've been here as long as Dylan?"

Tony shook his head. "No, she's been here a week longer than me."

Emma stifled a laugh; Tony was very literal. "Do you like working with her?"

Tony changed lanes, again, checking all his mirrors. "She's smart. Not smart like you and me, but very smart. She can read people, knows how to interact with everyone. She brings me gifts sometimes, things that I like, because she pays attention. She brought me an R2-D2 lunch box from nineteen seventy-seven that she found at a rummage sale. I don't think she has any idea that it's worth twenty-five hundred dollars, but she thought of me."

Emma smiled, thinking of the stoic Dylan carrying around an R2-D2 lunch box. "That was very kind of her."

Tony nodded as he pulled into an open parking spot. "Would you prefer to carry the wine or would you be more comfortable if I did it?"

Emma cocked her head at him, thinking that maybe he was even more awkward than she'd initially assumed. "It doesn't matter, Tony. Whatever you prefer."

He took the wine from her hands and opened the door. "I prefer to carry the wine."

Emma followed Tony the short distance to the apartment and waited as he knocked three very specific thrums on the door. She could hear music playing behind the wall and was surprised to hear it was Johann Sebastian Bach.

Dylan opened the door a moment later, wiping her hands on a dish towel. She grabbed Tony and greeted him in Russian. "Cousin, welcome!"

Emma felt her neck flush as Dylan turned her eyes on her. "It's nice to finally meet you, Nada, please come in."

Emma handed her the tray, hoping the transfer of items would prevent Dylan from wrapping her in an embrace as well. Although she immediately regretted it, because she suddenly had an overwhelming urge to touch Dylan.

Dylan motioned toward the couch. "Please, have a seat. I'll be back in a second."

Emma looked around, wanting to take in this peek into Dylan's life. The walls had exposed brick, and the floors were hardwood. The kitchen was lined with white subway tiles and wooden countertops.

A chandelier hung in each room, and there were accent walls of light greens and blues flowing throughout the space. It was elegant, tasteful, and not what she'd expected.

Dylan came back in and handed them each a glass. She looked at Emma and cocked her head to the side. "Everything okay?"

Emma nodded and took the glass of wine. "This isn't what I expected." She waved her hand around.

Dylan sat and draped one of her legs over the other. "What did you expect?"

Emma was watching Dylan's slightly bouncing leg, the knee-high leather boots another contrast that had caught her off guard. "I'm not sure." She forced herself to swallow. "Perhaps something not so put together."

Dylan smiled and brought the glass up to her mouth, taking a slow sip. "I'm full of surprises."

Is she flirting with me? No, I must be misreading the situation. She can't possibly be flirting with me.

Tony, who hadn't bothered to lean back onto the couch, put his glass on the table. "What's happening? What do you need us for?"

Dylan pulled her eyes from Emma, but it seemed forced. "Do you want to have dinner first? You need to spend at least two hours here to make a visit with my cousin and his friend believable."

Tony blushed slightly. "I don't have any record of your apartment being under surveillance."

Dylan swished the wine in a slow circle. "I'm not, but people talk. It's better to be safe than sorry, just in case. I haven't gotten this far without playing it smart."

Tony stood abruptly. "I need to use your restroom facilities."

Dylan pointed behind her toward a hallway. "First door on the left."

Emma felt her back stiffen, and she forced herself not to reach into her pocket in search of her rosary beads. She willed herself to find that tiny bit of gregarious behavior she'd had when she first met Dylan. "I didn't mean to offend before when I said I didn't think your place would be put together. I'm sorry about that."

Dylan pushed her hand through her hair and focused on Emma. "You're going to have to work a little harder than that to offend me, Emma." Dylan smiled and sipped from her wine glass.

Emma tried not to focus on the way Dylan's bright green eyes seemed to transform under this light. They reminded her of the way trees first bloomed in the springtime. They were vibrant, full of life, and held a little bit of the unknown. Emma was captivated.

Emma sipped from her glass, hoping Dylan hadn't just noticed her staring. "Still, I do that sometimes...offend people without intending to."

Dylan uncrossed her legs and leaned forward, putting her elbows on her knees. Emma couldn't stop herself from staring at the exposed lines of Dylan's collarbone, dipping out from beneath her black V-neck shirt. She felt her throat go slightly dry and her heart rate picked up without warning.

"What's your favorite movie?" Dylan asked.

Emma was puzzled by the abruptness of the question, but she didn't seem any harm in answering. "*Looper*, without a doubt."

"The one with Bruce Willis and Joseph Gordon-Levitt?"

Emma shrugged. "And Emily Blunt."

Dylan cocked an eyebrow. "Of course, how could I forget the exquisite Emily Blunt?"

Tony came back from the bathroom and sat back down on the couch, but Dylan never broke eye contact with Emma. The sensation was both intoxicating and overwhelming. Dylan was so focused, so intense, so purposeful; being her sole focal point, even for a moment, was enthralling.

"I prefer *Edge of Tomorrow*," Tony said. "As far as Emily Blunt movies go, that's my favorite."

Tony's cinematic preferences broke the trance between her and Dylan. She didn't know if she wanted to smack him or thank him. Dylan got out of her chair and walked into the kitchen. Tony grabbed the remote from the table in front of them and turned on the television. Emma only thought briefly about staying rooted in her spot, but she decided instead to see if Dylan needed any help.

"What are you making?" Emma leaned against the counter and folded her arms. She thought, for whatever reason, the simple stance could protect her from Dylan's magnetism.

"Lemon pepper chicken, salad, and some noodles." She pulled the wine from the counter and poured more in her glass, then poured more into Emma's. "I'd like to say this will be the best dinner of your life, but that would be categorically untrue." She chuckled to herself. "I'm not a very good cook. This is one of the only things I know how to make."

Emma didn't mean to say what she'd been thinking, but it slipped out anyway. "I can't imagine anything you aren't good at."

Dylan took a step closer to her and leaned against the counter. "You've spent some time imagining my skill set, have you?"

Emma watched her lips as Dylan spoke, mesmerized by the way they moved and turned into a sly, seductive smile. "Yes...I mean, no. I mean, it's my job to know what you're good at." *Nice save, Emma.*

Dylan put her hand on the counter, inches from where Emma's hip was resting. "Is there anything you want to know that isn't listed in my file?"

Emma stared at Dylan's hand. It was scarred, like Tyler's. She wanted to turn it over and see if they were calloused in the same places too. She wanted to touch it. Emma was feeling nothing like her usual self, and the feeling was terrifying and liberating. She wanted to know what Dylan's skin felt like under her fingertips. She wanted to see if Dylan reacted to her touch. Emma wanted to see if the electricity she felt would actually transmit between the two of them. A buzzing sound started from behind Dylan before she had a chance to let her thoughts morph into purpose. Dylan moved away, started pulling dishes from the oven, and gathering plates.

Emma took the plates and brought them over to the table, happy to make herself busy with something else. She knew she didn't have a great deal of experience in this area, but she was pretty sure Dylan could feel whatever had just happened between them as well. Her eyes had glimmered with the same awareness Emma had felt in her belly. She wasn't sure if she should be elated or go running back to the safe house. She wasn't accustomed to having such conflicting emotions, nor was she sure how to manage herself in a situation like this because Emma couldn't afford the distraction Dylan had the potential of becoming. She'd worked too hard to be taken seriously. She wouldn't blow it now because a beautiful woman looked at her with a little bit of lust in her eyes. All she could do was hope that her good sense would prevail when it came to Dylan Prey.

❖

Thank goodness for small miracles and the fact that Dylan couldn't cook by sight or smell alone. If that timer hadn't gone off and pulled her from her moment with Emma, she would've surely kissed her. Which, for about one hundred different reasons, was a terrible idea.

Once she'd brought all the food over to the table, she sat down. She noticed that Emma wasn't making eye contact. *That's probably a good thing.* Luckily for both her and Emma, Tony seemed to be oblivious to anything having transpired between the two of them.

"I'd like the update now. We have seventy-one minutes until it's appropriate for us to leave, and I want to allow for question and answer time," Tony said it with so much determination, Dylan almost stopped everything to answer him.

But then she remembered his place, and her own, and started cutting the chicken on her plate into pieces. "I've managed to secure the spot as lead security for Carol O'Brien."

Emma's eyes grew into the size of silver dollars. The blue was shining with excitement and a bit of fear. "Is that a good idea?"

"Do you have a better one for being able to know her comings and goings on a daily basis? For being able to have access to her?" Dylan made sure to keep her voice even and soft. She wasn't trying to be combative, but she was trying to make a point.

"I think this is the most efficient way to complete your objective," Tony said, nodding thoughtfully. "I hope you've taken into account that if this particular mission of extracting Carol O'Brien is successful, the probability that your cover will be blown by the end, or worse, they'll kill you, is highly likely." He scratched his chin and looked up at the ceiling. "In fact, the probability of them killing you outright once Carol is taken back to the States, is about ninety-six percent." He refocused on his plate and started to eat.

"Tony, as always, your analysis is very helpful." Dylan shook her head and kept eating. Hearing the odds out loud made her stomach turn.

Emma pushed the food around on her plate, looking uncomfortable with Tony's calculations. "The team is going to ask what you need from them. What should I tell them?"

"As soon as I'm familiar with her schedule, I'll give them a window to grab her." She forked a piece of chicken. "Hopefully one that won't land me in the bottom of a river." She saw Emma wince at the statement, and she wanted to make the pain on her face go away. "Don't worry, if we're all as good as we think we are, everyone should make it out of this alive."

Tony shook his head. "Very doubtful."

Dylan took a deep breath. "Thanks, Tony. I always knew I had your vote of confidence."

Tony shrugged and continued eating.

"I'm also having security cameras set up in her apartment, and I'll have a location tracker on her as well," Dylan said. She slid her phone to Tony. "I managed to clone her cell phone too…you're welcome." Dylan suppressed a laugh when Tony's face lit up. "There will be audio attached to the surveillance in her apartment. I trust you two can get into it without being caught."

Both Emma and Tony nodded at the same time. Dinner took all of twenty-seven minutes, and Tony announced they had forty-four minutes remaining and that he'd do the dishes. After, he'd get the cloned information out of Dylan's phone and transfer it to his computer.

Dylan reached into her pocket and slid over a thumb drive to Emma. "Here's what you asked for. I trust you'll use it appropriately."

Emma looked at the device and then at Dylan. "I'll plug it into an air-gapped computer. Thank you for trusting me. I know that must not come easy in your line of work."

Dylan leaned closer, captivated by the changing emotions on Emma's face. "Are you always so transparent with your thoughts?"

Emma let out a nervous laugh. "Unfortunately, yes, it's a terrible habit."

Dylan had an overwhelming urge to touch her arm, but she stopped herself. "I think it's rather endearing."

Emma's eyes were so profoundly blue, they might have seemed green in specific lighting. Her blond hair was pulled back into a ponytail, and Dylan absently wondered what it would look like if she let it down. *Beautiful.*

"Dylan?" Emma asked, pulling Dylan from her thoughts.

"Hmm?"

"Will you come back to the States after this?" Emma asked without eye contact.

Dylan took a sip of her wine. "I'll go wherever the CIA wants me. Best-case scenario is that my cover isn't blown and I'm able to finish out my mission here. I'm hoping the team can help me with at least part of that."

Emma traced the top of her glass with her finger. "What has your mission entailed, exactly?"

Dylan gave her a half smile and shook her head. "Tsk-tsk, Ms. Quinn, you know I can't tell you that."

Tony appeared beside her a moment later, startling her. "I'm done with the dishes and the phone. We should leave now."

Dylan knew better than to argue with him, so she stood to say good-bye. "Tell the team I'll be back over as soon as I can. If I need you before then, I'll find a way to let you know."

Emma looked like she was going to hug her, but changed her mind and shoved her hands in her pockets. "Be safe."

"Good night, Dylan. I'll see you soon," Tony said, and then turned to leave before she could answer.

Emma got to the open door and Dylan would've given anything to know what she was thinking. "Thank you for dinner," Emma said in Russian.

"My pleasure." Dylan shut the door behind them.

Dylan took a deep breath after the door was closed. She was trying to shake off a feeling of loneliness she wasn't accustomed to that was working its way through her chest. She walked around her apartment and thought briefly of going out, finding a bar, and falling into a woman she wouldn't be able to pick out of a lineup the next day. She decided against it, figuring she needed a hot bath and a good night's sleep to clear her head. She needed to be on her game if she was going to get out of this in one piece. She poured the remainder of the wine into the glass and headed toward the bathroom and the hot bath she'd just promised herself.

There was no valid reason for Emma to be affecting her the way she was. It wasn't as if Dylan hadn't been in the presence of beautiful women before. Dylan knew what the look in Emma's eyes had meant. Emma wanted her too. Dylan would typically use this to her advantage, but she got a distinct impression that Emma was different. Emma wouldn't take well to being manipulated for any reason, and she wasn't the kind of woman you bedded and walked away from. Dylan knew she was attractive. She knew the way men and women alike looked at her. It had always been an advantage she held, a card she could play. But with Emma, she didn't have the desire to play any of the games she'd mastered. Dylan didn't know why, but she cared about how Emma would feel about it, how it would affect her.

She climbed into her bath and let her back descend through the slippery surface. She picked up her wine glass from the table next to her and took a sip. She wondered if Emma's lips would've tasted like this wine had she taken the chance to find out. Dylan rolled her eyes at her internal musings. *You're ridiculous.*

CHAPTER TEN

Tyler listened intently as Emma and Tony explained the plan Dylan had put in motion. Well, it wasn't a plan yet, but it was definitely the beginning of one. Brooke and Jennifer were busy transferring the cloned phone information onto one of the monitors in the room, as well as opening the video feeds from Carol O'Brien's apartment.

Caden swiveled in her chair. "I have to admit, I had my doubts about Prey, but this is fantastic." She slid her chair over to the video feed and watched. "This is really going to be it. We're finally going to get her."

"What do you think?" Tyler asked Emma.

Emma looked surprised that she was being consulted but leaned forward to give Tyler her full attention. "I think this is good for us and bad for Dylan. If the Russians find out what she's doing, they'll kill her."

Tony put his finger in the air. "There is a ninety-six percent chance she gets found out and eliminated." He put his hand back down and nodded his head once to make his point.

Tyler's hand twitched at the information. "Is it really that high?"

Tony looked confused by the question. He furrowed his brows and stared at her. "Yes."

There was an inherent risk to their jobs, to the choices they made daily, but the probability of this ending in Dylan's death was a lot to plug into the calculations. Tyler got out of her seat, needing to move her body. She paced in the small room, trying to sort out her thoughts.

Brooke walked over to her and put her hands on her shoulders to stop her movement. "What are you thinking?"

Tyler rubbed the back of her neck and looked at Brooke, her heart rate slowing under her calming touch. "We aren't just going to go in guns blazing. I know Dylan says she'll give us an opening, but we need a better approach than that. We need to ensure her safety as well."

Brooke nodded and continued to rub Tyler's arms. "Nothing is set in stone yet. Let's do surveillance for a few days, then we'll regroup with Dylan and come up with something we can all agree with."

Tyler nodded her approval and put her hand over Brooke's. "Yes." Tyler reached into her pocket and pulled out her phone. "I need to call Captain Hart and update him."

The captain was thrilled with the progress Dylan had made and with the direction the mission was heading. He informed Tyler that he had a few meetings the following day and then would arrange for a place they could meet in Moscow. It would be too conspicuous for him to head out toward the sparser countryside where they were staying.

Tyler ended the call and took a seat next to the others. Everyone was glued to the screen, watching Carol O'Brien mill about her apartment. Her behavior seemed so ordinary, so unexceptional. She didn't look like an individual who wanted to incite civil war in her own country. She didn't look like she'd cultivated a plan that would have murdered the leaders of the free world, someone who hoped to make white supremacy a way of life. Tyler felt her jaw tighten as she watched her, wanting nothing more than to reach through the screen and pluck her out, to lock her away in a dark hole from which there was no escape.

Tyler reached into her pocket and felt the box that now seemed like part of her uniform, she'd been carrying it for so long. The thought of placing the ring on Brooke's finger calmed her anger and brought a sense of serenity. She decided to focus on that sensation, instead of one she couldn't control at the moment. Brooke. She was everything.

❖

Carol inspected the cameras the crew had installed. There was one in the northeast corner of her ceiling, one facing her balcony, and one pointed toward the entryway. She thought it was a bit excessive, but she was glad someone was finally taking her safety seriously.

She poured herself four fingers of scotch and walked to her balcony window, taking in Moscow at night. She wanted to get out of the suffocating apartment, but she knew the risk involved for momentary excitement wasn't worth it. She had no idea if Tyler Monroe or Caden Styles were here, but she knew it wouldn't be long. All it would take was one surveillance picture of her wandering the streets, and they'd descend like locusts. She took a large gulp of her scotch and silently cursed the women.

She sat at her coffee table and opened her laptop. White nationalism was taking the country by storm, her disappearance giving fuel to the cause. She wasn't entirely sure what she'd envisioned when she first started out down this path, but she never dreamed it would turn into such a movement. She read op-ed pieces about the way society was shifting, how prejudice was winning out, and what happened to the country.

She chuckled and took another large sip from her glass. *What happened?* The morons who wrote these pieces, they were so out of touch with the real America it was ridiculous. Academic types who thought people were inherently good and wanted peace were falling all over themselves to come up with an answer. Such a naive little world they lived in, where ignorance was indeed bliss. People weren't inherently good; people were inherently selfish. People could be relied upon for one thing, and that was to look out for themselves. Most people didn't care about the poor, the homeless, the people held down by systemic racism. They wanted to know how to keep those things out of their communities, scared it might be contagious, scared of being a victim. She just happened to be brave enough to say it out loud. Media outlets wrote her off as a blip on the radar, an anomaly that could be flushed out—punished and dealt with. She knew better. She had contacts all over the world who shared the belief system she helped bolster. She'd benefit from her connections while she sat back and watched America crumble, only to be reimagined by the very people they feared. Writing off her followers as weak or stupid had always been a mistake her opponents had made. There was security in numbers, and danger with people who thought they had nothing else to lose.

She opened her phone and leaned back on her couch, swirling the scotch around in its glass. She entered the familiar number and started a text message thread.

Where are you? She sipped her scotch, waiting for the reply.

I'll be there soon. Are you safe?

She almost rolled her eyes. He didn't actually care if she was safe; it would be easier for him if she weren't. Still, part of their passionate affair relied on their love/hate dynamic.

Just hurry up and get here. It annoyed her that she was at his whim now, and he was free to roam about while she was trapped in this cage, albeit a very nice cage.

I'll see you at the gala. We're nearly there.

The gala. Even if Monroe and Styles weren't here by then, they'd hear she was there and show up shortly after. She'd make certain they'd never be an issue again. Then, she'd finally be able to move on with her life. She finished the remainder of her scotch and set the glass on the table. She waved to the cameras as she walked toward her bedroom, hoping Sasha was watching her.

CHAPTER ELEVEN

Dylan's morning run along the river edge at Gorky Park was her favorite time of day. The city was just starting to wake up, foot traffic was minimal, and the cold air from the river was a perfect natural air conditioning source. She'd just started her fourth mile when a person appeared next to her. Dylan had to do a double take and fight the instant reaction to punch the woman because of her surprise appearance.

"What are you doing here?" Dylan asked as she quickly glanced around, more out of habit than anything else.

"O'Brien has a boyfriend she was texting with last night," Emma said, her breathing labored.

Dylan slowed her pace, wanting to give Emma a chance to explain. "Who?"

Emma shook her head. "We don't know. The number is encrypted, and it hasn't hit on any of the programs we've run it through. Brooke, Jennifer, and Tony are still working on it, but it's very odd."

"Do we know anything?" Dylan started walking.

"Oh, thank God." Emma slowed to match her pace. "I thought I was going to die. I've been out here running for almost two hours looking for you." She put a hand on Dylan's arm and breathed heavily. "We think he's from the States, but it can't be good if he's high up enough to have that kind of encryption."

"What does Monroe think?" Dylan was trying to keep the conversation on track but was very focused on the hand that rested on her arm.

Emma shook her head. "She's not sure what to make of it, but she's worried we all may be sitting ducks now." Emma seemed to realize she was still holding on to her and removed her hand quickly.

Dylan pointed to a bench, and Emma sat down. "I need to go see O'Brien this morning, but I'll try to stop by the safe house this afternoon." Dylan stretched. "Why two hours? Surely Tony could have given you my location."

Emma pulled up her shirt and dried the sweat from her face. "What?"

Dylan watched Emma's stomach muscles move in and out and turned her attention quickly back to the ground. "Why didn't you just have Tony give you my location?"

Emma leaned against the bench, her breathing more in control. "You don't have your phone."

"Yes, I do." Dylan reached into the zipped pocket of her pants. "Shit. No, I don't."

Emma motioned, indicating the expanse of the park. "You left it in your car. Hence, the two hours."

Dylan laughed. "Sorry, I parked, had breakfast, watched the ducks for a while, and then started my run."

Emma stood and pulled on her leg, stretching her quad. "You had breakfast and watched some ducks? Perfect." She rolled her eyes.

"I never leave my phone. I don't know what my problem was this morning," Dylan said.

Emma stretched her other leg. "It's okay, I needed the exercise. Maybe not this much of it, but I'm trying to make the best of it."

Dylan watched Emma's lean body move back and forth as she tried to ease the tension out of her muscles. Emma was in much better shape than Dylan had initially thought. She'd assumed she was built more like Tony, thin and soft from their sedentary jobs. That definitely wasn't the case. Emma clearly took care of herself, and Dylan allowed herself to appreciate Emma's efforts.

"What? Is there something on my face?" Emma asked, breaking Dylan's focus.

Dylan started walking back toward her car, embarrassed that she'd been caught staring. She motioned for Emma to follow. "No,

I'm just surprised you could run so long. It's not really in your job description."

Emma quirked an eyebrow at her. "Do you only do what's in your job description?"

Dylan realized how ridiculous that sounded and shook her head. "No, I guess not."

Emma bumped her shoulder. "Running is one of the only things I enjoy outside of work. I don't really have any friends, I don't watch a lot of television, and I have no family in the area. So, if I'm not working, I'm reading or running, and sometimes I do both at the same time." She shrugged.

"I don't have any friends either. This job is hard on all relationships." Dylan was surprised to hear the sadness in her voice. "But it does have its perks," she said, wanting to sound more upbeat than she had.

"Like what?" Emma squinted when she looked at her, the sun in her eyes.

"Lots of beautiful women," Dylan said it to be funny but wished she could take it back when she saw the look on Emma's face.

Emma's expression was one of hurt and annoyance. She put her hand over her eyes to shield the sun and pointed down the road. "I should get going. I just wanted to give you a heads-up before you went in today." She increased her pace toward the direction of her car.

"Emma, wait. We're going the same way." Dylan didn't fully understand Emma's reaction, but she wanted to fix things.

Emma was already several steps in front of her when she yelled back in Russian. "It was nice seeing you."

Dylan watched her disappear into the distance and wondered what had happened. A throwaway comment about women shouldn't have made her run, and it wasn't like they were a couple or anything, although Dylan knew Emma found her attractive. *Well, this is why you don't get involved.* She shoved the confusion aside and pushed on to complete the rest of her run, putting a little more exertion in than was necessary.

"You're overreacting, Quinn. Get it together," Emma said to no one as she drove back toward the safe house.

Dylan's comment about beautiful women had caught her off guard. It wasn't that she thought Dylan was a saint of some kind, in fact, she knew she wasn't. It was that she wasn't prepared for how her body had reacted to the comment. Dylan's casual comments had ignited a burning sensation that started in her chest and worked its way down to her fingers. It wasn't until she reached the car that she was able to identify the anomaly as jealousy. *Fucking perfect.*

Emma was losing her mind. She had no reason to be jealous. She was acting like a child, petulant about something she wanted and someone else had. Dylan didn't belong to her, she had no claim, and she had absolutely no reason to react the way she did. She knew that intellectually, she understood all of this, but it didn't stop her body from having a visceral reaction to the information. *What does "lots" mean?* She sighed, even madder at herself now for understanding what was happening and perpetuating it.

She needed to get her head on straight. This was her first real opportunity in her career to show what she could do, that she was capable of more than sitting in a room alone for sixteen hours a day. She needed to take advantage of the opportunity in front of her and knock it out of the park. There was no room or time to be fantasizing about some CIA spy who probably wouldn't give her a second look had they met anywhere else. Dylan was a distraction and a player, and Emma had to remember that. *Don't blow this, Quinn.*

She arrived back at the safe house feeling as though she'd thoroughly and properly chastised herself to the point of understanding. It didn't matter how good Dylan Prey looked in running pants, or how her eyes crinkled when she laughed. It didn't matter how every time Emma looked at her, she wondered what it would be like to have her hands on her, or how her skin tasted. *Oh my God. Seriously? We just talked about this. Knock it off.* She blew out a deep breath and tried to calm her mind with what she knew scientifically about her reaction to Dylan. *Lust is triggered by estrogen and the desire for sexual gratification and our need to reproduce. Attraction involves the brain pathways for reward and includes the intervention of dopamine and norepinephrine. These will make you giddy, energetic, and euphoric—your reaction to Dylan. It's all a chemical reaction and something you can get a handle on.*

She was lightly pounding her head against the steering wheel when a knock on the window completed the circle of her embarrassment.

"You okay, Quinn?" Jennifer asked, looking concerned.

Emma pushed the door open and got out of the car. "Yeah, I'm great! Why?" She was a little too excited, compensating for the whole hitting her head on the steering wheel thing.

Jennifer cocked an eyebrow at her. "Umm…because that isn't the behavior of someone great." She pointed to the steering wheel.

Emma didn't want to explain any of this, so she thought as fast as she could. "No, just psyching myself up for the day." She lifted one hand in the air. "Go, team!" She shook the hand around. "Yay!" *I wish Caden had found me. She's not nearly as observant.*

Jennifer crossed her arms. "Did everything go okay with Prey?"

Emma got out of the car and pointed toward the house. "Yup, passed all the info along." She started walking faster. "I'm going to go take a shower. Be back in a jiffy."

A jiffy? So what, now you're from the nineteen fifties? Emma didn't bother to look back at Jennifer. She could feel her eyes on her, probably trying to figure out how they got stuck with such a weirdo.

Thirty minutes later, Emma headed back down to their makeshift control center. The cold shower had done her a world of good, and she'd almost convinced herself that she was back to normal, whatever normal was for her. She hoped Jennifer hadn't made too big of a deal about their earlier conversation. Emma wanted nothing more than to put it behind her.

When she came into the room, everyone's attention was on the screens that hung on the main wall. Jennifer and Brooke sat behind their computer stations, ready to type in whatever information might be helpful. Caden was on the ground doing some overly ambitious rendition of push-ups, and Tyler was jumping rope.

Brooke looked over at her and smiled. "Carol just got off the phone with Dylan, and she's on her way up to her apartment."

What better way to get her mind off Dylan than to watch her for the next several hours? Sound logic. She took a seat next to Brooke and pulled out her laptop, ready to do her part.

CHAPTER TWELVE

Carol opened the door and smiled. "Good morning, Sasha."
Dylan dipped her head. "Good morning, ma'am."

Carol grabbed her hand and pulled her inside. "Is this when I ask you to show me your identification?" She winked at her.

Dylan didn't want to egg this on in any way but thought a small amount of playing along could yield results. "Would you like to?"

Carol ran one finger down Dylan's jaw and across her lips. "Not yet, I prefer some mystery."

Dylan was grateful for her response. She had all the necessary tattoos, fake of course, that would allow her to pass for her leadership level inside the mob, but she didn't want to take her shirt off.

"How was your evening?" Dylan asked and walked to the large window on the other side of the room.

"Uneventful. Being stuck inside is starting to do things to my head." Carol sighed dramatically and stood next to her.

Dylan decided to try to pry a bit of information out of her. "You're attending the gala, yes?"

Carol bit her bottom lip and continued to stare out the window. "Yes."

"There will be a few shop owners here today, cleared through us. You can try on some things and decide what you'd like. Before I inform them what to bring, is there a specific look you're going for?"

Carol tapped her finger against her lips. "Formal wear, obviously." She looked out the window a bit longer and shrugged. "But maybe something a little fun, kind of flirty."

Dylan made sure not to smile at the answer, which gave her an opening. "Flirty? Is there anyone in particular you hope to catch the attention of?"

Carol turned and looked at her, a little bit of anger flaring in her eyes. "No. I dress for myself and no one else. Always have, always will."

She turned and headed in the direction of her bedroom. "I need to freshen up. Don't touch anything."

Dylan had clearly hit a soft spot of Carol's, and she didn't want to lose what small bits of progress she'd made. She wanted Carol to trust her, to let her guard down. She'd have to avoid this topic unless Carol brought it up again. Dylan glanced down at Carol's computer and thought briefly about downloading all the information from it, but she wasn't sure how much time she had until Carol returned and she couldn't risk it. She'd wait until Carol was trying on clothes and then make her attempt. They really needed to know who this person was that Carol was dating or, at the very least, sleeping with.

Dylan stepped closer to the large sliding glass door when she heard Carol coming back into the room. "I'm sorry if I overstepped. It wasn't my intention to upset you."

Carol waved dismissively and tossed a file folder onto the table. "I need your security people to be on the lookout for these individuals, specifically."

Dylan picked up the folder. "Have they threatened you?" She flipped open the cover and forced herself not to react when she saw Tyler, Caden, Jennifer, and Brooke. There were random photos of each of them—coming and going from buildings, getting into cars, and drinking coffee.

"They're the reason I'm here." Carol let out a long breath and rolled her eyes. "They want nothing more than to see me dead."

Dylan closed the folder and slid it under her arm. "I will notify my men immediately. How would you like us to handle them if they show up?"

Carol sat on the couch but turned her focus toward the window. "Would you kill them if I asked?"

"Without hesitation," Dylan answered.

Carol turned and smiled at her. Dylan fought the urge to ask more about her plans. She knew Carol was playing a game of some kind and would only reveal information at her own pace. Any coaxing on Dylan's part would tell Carol more about Dylan than vice versa. She knew Carol's type; she'd been surrounded by people like her for most of her career. People like Carol only cared about themselves and would sacrifice whatever, and whoever, necessary to ensure they came out on top. Carol had no allegiance, no sense of loyalty, no desire to protect anyone but herself. It served her well in this world, but the damage it would leave behind would be visible on her soul.

Dylan's phone buzzed and she glanced at the screen. "Ma'am, the shop owners are here to see you now."

Carol smiled and stood. "Excellent." She let her eyes linger over Dylan. "Feel free to stay, so you can let me know what you think. That is, unless you have somewhere else to be."

Dylan could think of about a million places she'd rather be. "My place is here with you until you dismiss me."

Carol's eyes sparkled. "I like that."

Dylan wasn't sure what kind of game Carol was playing, but she knew it was a game all the same. Dylan was familiar with the games people played because she'd participated in more than she could count. There were games of seduction, manipulation, power, revenge, and pure self-interest. Dylan just needed to narrow down Carol's motivation, but she assumed it was a mixture of them all. This made Carol not only unpredictable but even more dangerous than she'd initially thought. Cornered animals would fight their way out, no matter the cost.

She watched the shop owners wheel in cart after cart of elegant clothing. They bristled with excitement as Carol traced her fingers over the pieces and practically fell over themselves to help her try on the garment of her choosing. Carol was devouring the attention. Dylan could tell by the way she let her fingers linger, wanting to increase the excitement. She clearly loved her role as predator, no matter how small the prey.

Dylan glanced up at one of the cameras, wondering if the team on the other end was picking up the same inflections she'd been. But of course, they were, they knew Carol O'Brien better than anyone. They'd spent years chasing her, tracking her, learning what she was capable of. That was why Carol had given her their pictures; she was scared of them. She knew her manipulative words wouldn't work on them. They'd managed to take her down, peg by peg.

Carol turned in front of the full-length mirror, ensuring her dress was hugging her in all the right places. She looked up at Dylan and winked at her, wanting to make sure Dylan took her in completely.

The proverbial light bulb went off, and she gave Carol a brief nod before looking away. *I know who her boyfriend is.*

CHAPTER THIRTEEN

Tyler felt the force of the heavy bag as she heaved her fist into it for at least the thousandth time. The small, dimly lit garage was a poor excuse for a gym, but it was all they had. Sweat continued to burn her eyes, and her muscles felt like molten lava. She should've stopped fifteen minutes ago, but her mind wasn't clear yet. It was still hazy around the edges with the uncomfortable realization that so much of this mission was out of her hands. Tony's words kept echoing in her mind. *Ninety-six percent.*

She heard Brooke before she saw her. "What did that bag ever do to you?"

Tyler slowed the bag with her gloved hand, and her body instinctively gasped for the air she'd been denying it. "How did you find me?"

Brooke pushed herself off the wall and walked over to her. She put her hands on Tyler's face and kissed her softly. "I know you better than you know yourself, sweetheart. This is the first place I looked."

"Am I really becoming that predictable? That doesn't bode well for my career." Tyler unlaced her gloves and took the towel Brooke offered.

Brooke wiped some hair out of Tyler's face. "You want to tell me what's going on?"

Tyler gulped down the water she'd brought with her, enjoying the tiny streams that escaped her mouth and fell onto her chest. "Four percent."

One of the things she loved the most about her and Brooke's relationship was how little she had to explain to her partner. Brooke understood her on a level she'd never experienced before. Brooke knew the expectations she had for herself professionally and personally. Tyler knew she couldn't control every situation or every set of circumstances, but she didn't like playing games or taking chances where other people were concerned.

"I could tell you that Dylan knew the risk she was taking when she agreed to help us," Brooke said. "I could also tell you that four percent is still four percent, and we've beaten tougher odds." She sat on the bench. "I know none of that will make you feel better. So, instead, I'll remind you that we're the best backup Dylan could have in this situation. I'll also remind you that there's no one anyone would rather have on their team than you."

Tyler searched Brooke's eyes and found what she always saw staring back at her, honesty. She took a seat next to Brooke. "You know, it still catches me off guard sometimes."

Brooke put her head on Tyler's shoulder. "What does?"

Tyler kissed the top of Brooke's head. "How much I love you."

Brooke smiled against Tyler's shoulder and then kissed the top. "Good. I hope we never take each other for granted."

Tyler looked over to the pile of folded clothes in the corner of the room. The ring was there in the pocket of her pants. These moments of quiet where the rest of the world seemed to fall away weren't something either of them enjoyed in abundance. Tyler considered going over, getting the ring, and proposing to Brooke right then. But she didn't. She still needed to speak with Brooke's father. Not to ask permission, or seek his approval—no, that was an archaic custom. She wanted him to know her intentions so the news wouldn't put a deeper strain on Brooke's relationship with her parents. She wasn't sure it would matter, but at least she'd know she tried.

"What are you thinking about?" Brooke asked as she ran her hand along Tyler's jaw.

Tyler leaned her head into Brooke's touch. "Just that you're the best thing to ever happen to me."

Brooke kissed Tyler's nose. "Don't ever forget it." She stood up. "Now, go take a shower and come eat something."

Emma walked into the room and turned red. "I didn't mean to interrupt anything."

Tyler tossed the towel over her shoulder. "You didn't. What's up?"

Emma pointed behind her. "We got a message from Langley. I thought you'd want to see it right away."

Tyler nodded and followed them out the door. She steeled herself for whatever kink the higher-ups were about to throw their way. They hadn't been here long enough to have done anything wrong, and communication was supposed to be sparse for fear of foreign interception. This could only mean one thing—her job was about to become significantly more complicated.

Emma rubbed the rosary in her pocket as she watched Tyler read the message they'd just received. She wasn't sure what their next step would be, but she was sure Tyler would have a plan. *There has been a change in strategy. Stand down until you receive the proper authorization. We're awaiting further instructions.*

Caden smacked the table. "What the hell does *stand down* mean? This is bullshit. We're already here, we're already working on a plan, we already have people out there. Do they realize what it could mean if we stand down?"

Emma shared Caden's confusion and anger; she just wasn't as animated in her delivery. "What do you want me to do?" It didn't matter who answered, Emma only wanted to do something.

Tyler continued to stare at the screen, her hand on her chin. "I assume you authenticated the message?"

"Yes, of course," Emma said.

Caden stood up so fast her chair fell over behind her. She stood next to the screen on the wall where the message was on display for the team to see. "You aren't seriously going to listen to this, right? If we alter the plan now, we'll be putting Prey in more danger than she's already in."

Emma's stomach tightened, and her face flushed hot. She could feel the sweat starting at her brow. "It came directly from CIA Director Walker. I have yet to hear anything from Director Ericson at Homeland."

Caden threw her hands in the air. "Since when do we answer to Walker?"

"Since we're on loan to the CIA," Tyler murmured. She turned, looking at Emma. "You need to get a message to Captain Hart. We need to see him as soon as possible."

Emma nodded and sat at her station, happy to have something to keep her occupied. After she sent the message out, she watched her teammates. Caden was still ranting to no one in particular. Brooke and Jennifer were busy typing at their stations, probably checking to see if there had been any computer interference. There wasn't, she'd already checked. But Tyler, she stayed cemented in her spot, still staring at the screen. Her facial expression had yet to change, and Emma wondered what she could be considering.

Emma's computer dinged, and she opened the message. "Captain Hart will be here within the hour."

Tyler nodded toward the screen. "Pull up O'Brien's apartment."

Emma did as she was asked. She was relieved to see Carol was now alone in her temporary home. Dylan had apparently left, and Emma found herself wondering where she'd gone. She told herself it was out of concern for whatever was happening among the ranks far above her own. A tingling in her chest told her that wasn't entirely true. She thought about what Dylan did when she wasn't working. She was curious as to who she was with and what her activities included. She rolled her shoulders, hoping to push the thought away. It didn't matter, not right now.

Tyler took a step closer to the screen, observing O'Brien. "What are you up to?"

"What are you thinking?" Jennifer asked from her computer station.

Tyler turned and looked at her. Her face was calm, but her brows were furrowed. "We've been chasing O'Brien for over a year. At first, we had no idea she had anything to do with the white nationalists. She wasn't even on our radar until Thompson got sloppy. Her position as Speaker of the House helped to shield her place. It's foolish to think she was able to maintain that kind of autonomy without having friends in high places."

"You think someone is still protecting her?" Caden's voice was filled with anger and resentment.

Tyler shrugged. "I'm just saying she's been able to stay a step ahead of the smartest people in our field for quite some time. She must know we'd be coming for her. Is it so hard to believe that she'd call in one last favor?"

Caden growled with fury. "If this is one of our own, I swear I'll burn the whole place down. I will take that place apart, brick by brick."

The alarm sounded, and Emma looked down at the security cameras. Her skin prickled at the sight of Dylan coming through the gate. "Dylan is here."

Emma watched her as the cameras tracked her progress coming up the long drive. She was still in the clothes she'd been wearing at Carol's earlier that day. The navy suit hugged her in all the right places. Emma felt her heart rate increase when she saw the white fabric of her shirt pull across her chest as she walked. *Jesus. We could all be in real danger here, get your head together.* Her mind tried to give her a warning, but her body didn't listen. It was too busy reacting to the question of where Dylan kept her gun in the perfectly tailored suit.

Chapter Fourteen

Dylan didn't realize she'd made the decision to go to the safe house until she was already on the road that took her out to the countryside. She wasn't sure if they'd think her hunch was crazy or not, but she had to tell them. It wasn't just her life that could be in danger if it was true. It had been a long time since Dylan had taken the time to consider the safety or well-being of others. It wasn't that she was callous, it was because it had been quite some time since it was necessary. Her life was one of solitude, just how she liked it. Now, the lives of five other people were in her hands.

Five expectant faces stared at her when she opened the door. "Um, hi." She walked to the center of the room. "I have to tell you all something."

Caden snorted. "Yeah, us too."

Tyler pointed at her. "You first."

Dylan nodded. "O'Brien's boyfriend has to be someone at the very top of the CIA. It could possibly be Homeland, but my money is on the CIA."

Tyler crossed her arms. "Why do you say that?"

Dylan took a deep breath. She was relieved they hadn't laughed her out of the room yet, but there might still be time for that. "First, she isn't quite scared enough. She handed me a file with pictures of Monroe, Styles, Hart, and Glass. She wants me to be on the lookout for all of you, but that was it. She has no fear of anyone else. She knows damn well the entirety of the United States wants to see her brought home to face treason charges, but she's only worried about the four of you. If she weren't getting some type of protection it wouldn't matter who was searching for her, she'd be terrified of being caught. Even if she could get rid of all of you, they'd just send another team. Second, she clearly uses her sexual prowess as a weapon. It's so ingrained in her nature, she probably doesn't even need to think about it. Last, the whole idea of going to this gala is bananas. If the full power of the United States were behind her apprehension, she'd be terrified to show her face anywhere in public, but she's not. It's almost as if she's making this appearance with the intention of it being in public. She's planning something, and for her to feel this secure about it, she has to have reassurances." She exhaled, not meaning to speak as quickly as she had.

Caden was standing with her hands on the table, rocking back and forth. "Dammit. She's right."

Dylan glanced over at Emma, wanting to see her response. Emma was chewing on her thumb, her eyes locked on Dylan. Dylan wanted to tell her that it would be okay. She wanted to say to her that they'd figure all this out, but she didn't want to make promises she couldn't keep. She wanted to ease some of the fear Emma had etched on her face, but she did nothing. It wasn't her place, and she wouldn't even know where to start. Consoling people wasn't one of her strong suits.

Tyler turned her attention to the three computer analysts. "Pull up everything on Dylan's assignment. I want to know who has access and who has final authority on her objectives."

They started typing furiously. The door opened, and Captain Hart walked in. He looked as if he'd just come from a dignitary dinner of sorts, and Dylan's hackles were immediately on alert. She didn't feel as if anyone above their pay grade could be trusted. It didn't matter to her if he was Brooke's father or not.

"What's the problem?" Captain Hart barked as he walked to the center of the room.

Tyler passed along the information as if he were part of their inner circle. Dylan wasn't sure about that, but she trusted Tyler knew what she was doing. To his credit, he listened intently. He didn't make any move to dismiss their suspicions, nor did he try to make them feel insane for their apprehensions.

"This needs to stay in this room," Captain Hart said. "If this goes as high up as you believe it does, it would put everyone in danger if it got out." He rubbed his hands over his face. "You're sure about this?"

Tyler nodded. Her eyes were unwavering. "It's the only thing that makes sense. Whoever sent this message has to either be in on it or the person responsible. There are very few people with the credentials to send us a message like this, but there's no signature. We're uncertain who it came from, other than the fact that it came from headquarters." She looked over at the screen with the message still on it. "Do we stand down?"

Captain Hart turned his focus on Dylan. He stared at her for so long, Dylan had to shift her weight under his scrutiny. "The file O'Brien handed you, Quinn wasn't included?"

"No, it was just the others," Dylan said. "I'm not sure what that means."

He sighed. "I brought Quinn over from the NSA as a favor. I cleared it through Deputy Director Martin, but he clearly hasn't reported it back to his supervisor. Meaning, Martin knows something is up, or he's in on it too, and he's waiting for us to make a mistake."

Tyler shook her head. "I really don't believe Martin has anything to do with this."

Captain Hart shrugged. "I don't trust anyone right now." He rubbed the back of his neck. "Reply that you're standing down and awaiting further instruction. We can't raise any suspicion."

Caden started to protest, and he put his hand up. "That doesn't mean we stop working." He looked at Dylan. "Is there anything more you can find out without raising suspicion?"

Dylan wasn't sure if she should share this information with him, but the others seemed to trust him. She had no choice but to follow suit. She was either on this team or she wasn't. "There's a dinner tonight at Nikolai's."

"Were you planning on going?" He took a step closer to her, and she forced herself to stay rooted to her spot.

"Yes, I always go. It's a good opportunity for intel."

"Do you usually go alone?"

Dylan wasn't sure why she glanced at Emma, but she did. "No. It's easier to get information when the situation is casual, and there's nothing more casual than having a date with you." She wasn't sure why that last part was important, but she felt like she needed to say it.

"Perfect." He pointed at Emma. "You're taking Quinn."

She was going to protest, but Tyler beat her to it. "That's not a good idea. Quinn isn't trained for this kind of situation. She can't protect herself."

Captain Hart cocked his head at Tyler, seeming not to believe the words that were coming out of her mouth. "Do you have a better idea? Quinn has been tracking these people for quite some time. She knows better than any of you what information could be important and what isn't. Plus, she'll be with Prey. She'll be perfectly safe. It's not like one of you can go in her place. That would risk this entire operation." He looked at his watch. "This is as close as we can get to standing down on our current operation while still obtaining intel." He pinched the bridge of his nose. "It's like I'm loaning the NSA to the CIA for Prey's primary mission." He made a move toward the door. "I have to go. If I'm not at this summit, it will raise suspicion. Let me know what you find out." He looked at them one last time. "And be safe."

Dylan turned and looked at Emma. Her face was pale, and her hand was in her pocket. "You'll have to change."

Emma sat in her chair and chewed on her lower lip. "I…I'm not sure I'm ready for this."

Dylan wanted to say something to ease her mind, but she couldn't think of anything that would make her feel better. She was taking Emma into the proverbial belly of the beast. She was still thinking about what it meant to take Emma when she was saved by someone much more capable.

Brooke pulled up a chair next to Emma and put her hand on her arm. "I know you're scared, but it will be okay. Dylan will be there with you the whole time. If you get uneasy, let her know, and I'm sure she'll get you out of there."

Dylan nodded. She wasn't sure about this either, but she didn't want her to know that. It wasn't that she didn't think Emma was capable, Dylan knew she was. It was the thought of Emma being in the vicinity of some of the most diabolical men Dylan had ever met. They'd take one look at Emma's blond hair and blue eyes and fall all over themselves. The thought of Emma being manhandled all night was enough to make her stomach turn. She wouldn't be able to let Emma out of her sight, that she knew for sure.

Dylan cleared her throat. "You'll need to wear something more—" Dylan tried to choose her next words carefully.

Caden interrupted. "Brooke, loan her that leather skirt and jacket you brought." She looked at Dylan. "Is that the look you mean?"

Dylan nodded. "Yeah, something like that."

Brooke and Jennifer took Emma to the main house. Dylan watched Tyler and Caden. Caden was practically vibrating with righteous fury. Tyler sat at the large table in the center of the room. She was looking through a variety of files that had been strewn along the surface. The two were so different, a damn near perfect pairing. She could see how'd they complement each other in the field, and in friendship.

Tyler swiveled in her chair to face Caden. "Captain Hart—"

"He doesn't know O'Brien like we do. He's never had any skin in the game. He has no idea what she's capable of." Caden was yelling to no one in particular.

Tyler crossed her arms and stared at Caden. "That's not true. His daughter has been front and center since the beginning. He's one of the best military minds of this generation. He knows what he's doing."

Caden's sarcastic laugh indicated her feelings, but she voiced them anyway. "Your misplaced hero-worship could get Quinn killed. It could blow this entire mission to shreds. Do you get that?"

Dylan thought Tyler might come out of her seat and meet Caden's anger, but she didn't. Tyler's voice grew even calmer. "The only person responsible for potentially blowing this mission to shreds sits at the head of the CIA. As far as getting Quinn killed, Dylan would never let that happen. You need to get hold of yourself, Styles. I need your clear mind and tactical approach at a hundred percent if we're going to beat the odds. He's keeping us in play, and we're not actually standing down. Focus."

Dylan had known she liked Tyler, but now she respected her. "What do you need from me?"

Tyler seemed relieved to have someone else to speak with. "Just find out what you can about the arrangements O'Brien has made, without putting yourself or Quinn in danger, of course."

Dylan nodded. "Of course." She sat at the table. "I'm not sure I'll be able to bring Quinn back here tonight. She may have to stay with me."

Tyler nodded before standing and moving away slightly. "I trust your judgment."

Dylan started pulling clothes from the bag she'd brought with her. "Mind if I change here?"

Tyler was already speaking to Caden in hushed tones and she hadn't bothered to answer. She watched the two for a moment. She couldn't blame Caden for being angry. This mission was something they'd worked on for quite some time. She was clearly passionate about their objective, an attribute she'd want on her side. She got the sense that Caden was fearless in the face of danger, bordering on reckless if the situation called for it. Tyler, in contrast, was deliberate, calculating, and focused. The two of them were probably unstoppable. Unstoppable, that is, unless the orders came from the very top. Dylan had never wanted a partner, but watching them made her wonder if, one day, she should consider it. If she made it out of this alive, anyway.

Dylan finished changing into her jeans, knee-high boots, and sweater. "I'm going to meet Emma upstairs."

Tyler nodded her approval. "Be safe."

Dylan ascended the stairs, sending a silent promise to Tyler that regardless of what it meant for her, she'd make sure Emma was safe.

Chapter Fifteen

Emma tried to get into the car without embarrassing herself. She'd never worn a skirt this tight and had no idea how to properly sit without revealing too much. She held her breath when her back hit the seat. She looked down, still not believing this was the situation she was in.

"You look nice," Dylan said from beside her.

Emma laughed. "Nice? I have no idea how to wear anything like this."

Dylan started the car. "I'm sorry you're uncomfortable. It's just that I normally show up with women who…well, they dress similarly to what you're wearing."

Emma put her hand over her face. "I wish you could've taken Brooke. I'm sure she'd be much better at this."

Dylan kept her eyes focused on the road. "I'm glad it's you with me."

Emma wasn't sure what to say to that. Brooke was strikingly beautiful, she was quick-minded, and she could hold her own if shoved into a dark corner. No one had ever looked at Emma the way people looked at Brooke, and she had no idea how to hit anything.

"Brooke would've been better backup." Emma stared out the window, not wanting to see Dylan's agreement.

"She's not my type. It would've raised suspicion."

Emma turned to look at Dylan. "I can't imagine Brooke not being anyone's type."

Dylan shrugged. "She's not mine. I like blondes." Dylan gripped the steering wheel a little tighter. "So, someone may ask where we met. We need a rough back story."

"Tell them I've done some hacking for you, that I'm a friend of your cousin. I doubt they'll ask for more specifics, but if they do, at least that's an area I'm comfortable discussing." Emma looked back out the window, confident in her response.

"That won't work," Dylan said and touched her arm. "I don't normally bring women around who would work in that capacity." Dylan's expression was pained, almost apologetic. "The cousin aspect is fine, but let's leave out the job part."

"You mean, you don't normally associate with women who work, or women who work in a tech capacity?" Emma knew what Dylan was insinuating, but for some reason, she wanted her to say it out loud.

Dylan sighed. "Let's just say the women I normally bring with me would never be an intellectual threat to anyone there."

"Is that what you prefer? Or is there another reason?" It was none of Emma's business why Dylan made the decisions she did, but that didn't stop her from wanting to know. She thought the reason would give her a little extra glimpse into Dylan. And professional distance be damned, she wanted as many glimpses as she could get.

Dylan looked over at her, but there was no anger in her eyes. She seemed to be a little surprised at the question. "It's not about what I prefer, although, no, it's not because I prefer their company. I bring them because it's easier for me to fit in, and if they aren't perceived as a threat, they're safe. They don't pay attention to the sometimes-coded language, and they never pass the information along. Say what you will about their capacity for understanding quantum theory, they'll never divulge what they see or hear."

Emma couldn't be sure, but she thought she might have offended Dylan. "I wasn't implying that they were less than. I'm sorry if it came across that way."

"It's okay." Dylan parked her car and leaned forward on the steering wheel, gazing up at the large house in front of them. "Stay close to me, but if we do get separated, just smile and nod. Remember to act like you aren't paying attention to anything. If they ask you a question about your past, keep it simple, easier to remember, and without much detail."

"Okay." Emma took a deep breath. "Should I leave my phone in the car, or take it with me?"

Dylan took it from her, turned it off, and tossed it into the glove box. "Let's not take any chances."

Emma got out of the car and took the arm Dylan offered her. "You look nice, by the way. I didn't tell you earlier, but you do."

Dylan smiled and kissed her cheek. "If this gets to be too much, let me know, and we'll get out of here."

Emma was caught off guard by the way her heart was thrumming in her chest. It could have been that they were drawing closer to the front door, or it could have been the way Dylan's breath had felt against her ear. It was warm, and the inflection in her whispered tone made Emma want to hold her there a bit longer.

She pushed the thought as deep down as it would go and focused on what would be happening inside the lion's den. She needed all her faculties about her. She couldn't afford the distraction Dylan brought when she was so close. Her entire job was to stay close to Dylan tonight, to learn what she could and be the team member they needed her to be. Whatever she felt for Dylan was irrelevant and dangerous. Tonight was about nothing but work.

Dylan forced herself not to look down when Emma intertwined their fingers. She couldn't remember the last time she'd held hands with someone. Trying to put the pieces together in her mind, she couldn't tell if it was a welcome feeling or one that had her petrified. She knocked on the door and decidedly put the thought away for later inspection. Right now, she needed to transform into Sasha.

Dylan took one last look at Emma before the door opened. "It's going to be okay."

Emma smiled at her. Her eyes said that she trusted Dylan, believed everything would, in fact, be okay. Dylan was grateful for the vote of confidence but terrified by what it could mean to let her down.

The door swung open; the house staff would need to know Emma's name to introduce her to the rest of the people inside. She flashed back to the night Tony and Emma had come to her apartment. She hadn't explicitly discussed with Emma that she'd use the same name from when she greeted her at the door, but she hoped she remembered and played along.

"This is Nada," Dylan said when the house staff studied Emma.

Emma squeezed her hand as they followed the staff into the main dining hall. She hoped it meant that Emma approved. It was the only name that came to mind when she'd looked into Emma's eyes. *Nada.* It meant hope in Russian, and Dylan thought they could use all the hope they could get.

Nikolai stood and greeted them after the staff had announced their arrival. He shook Dylan's hand and then looked Emma up and down as if he were going to devour her in one bite. *Perfect.*

Nikolai slid his hands up and down Emma's arms. "Sasha, you haven't brought this one around before. I would've remembered this face." He used the back of his hand to trace Emma's jaw.

Dylan flinched at their contact, but Emma handled it like a pro. She blushed appropriately and shyly smiled. She didn't pull away or act disgusted. Dylan was disgusted on Emma's behalf that she'd have to endure anything of this nature, but she was impressed by how she handled herself.

Dylan pulled Emma a little closer, wanting to make it clear that she was off limits. "Everything smells wonderful, Nikolai. Thank you for having us over."

Nikolai looked Emma up and down one more time but took a step backward and then slid into his seat. "Come, sit. The food will be out in a minute."

Nikolai went back into conversation with the man to his left, a man Dylan didn't recognize. That didn't necessarily mean anything. Nikolai often brought businessmen around to give them the full mafia treatment. This night would include expensive alcohol, excellent food, and then as many women as he could ever hope for. Nikolai was a savvy businessman who always got what he wanted. Dylan wondered what business this stranger was in and where Nikolai was testing the waters now. Her internal reflections were cut short when Emma placed her hand on Dylan's knee. There was no reason for them to still be in contact while sitting at the table, but Dylan figured Emma needed a little more security. Plus, it wasn't a sensation that she necessarily disliked. Her skin tingled where Emma rested her palm.

The waitstaff poured everyone at the table a glass of vodka and brought out the first course of dinner. Plates of oysters were passed to each of the table occupants, and Dylan felt her stomach roll. She'd never had much of a taste for oysters, but there was no avoiding them at these parties. She took every opportunity not to stand out, so she dutifully ate the shellfish. She spared a glance at Emma who was apparently enjoying the morsel and slyly listening to the conversation between the two men next to her even as she appeared to be engrossed in the food. Dylan made sure not to smile at her spy-like nature.

"Sasha, how are things going with your new project?" Bogdan asked from across the table. He held a similar position to her own within the mafia, but he oversaw human trafficking. She hated him. She hated the way he looked, the way he smiled, the way his face turned red at the first sip of vodka, everything.

"It's going well, Bogdan. You?" She didn't want to hear about the women smuggled in and out of the country for horny, disgusting men. Men who would do unspeakable acts to women, some children as young as seven years old, but it would be impolite not to ask.

Bogdan laughed, and his belly shook, hitting his plate in front of him. "Couldn't be better. We just shipped out a large order, lots of happy customers."

Egor leaned over Emma. "I hear your project may have some interference from America, Sasha."

If Dylan disliked Bogdan with everything in her, whatever was left over was reserved for Egor. She willed herself not to push him backward as his face lingered too close to Emma. "Nothing I can't handle. We're on the lookout for the trade inspectors, but no sign of them yet. If they show up, all the paperwork is in place."

Egor nodded and sat back in his seat. Dylan almost rolled her eyes at the ridiculousness of it all. They spoke in code, but it wasn't a complicated one. They used this coded language not to hide from their own government but from hidden eyes and ears of other countries. The Russian government all but officially sanctioned their actions, their behavior, their malicious intent. It was other countries they concerned themselves with. The irony was never lost on Dylan.

Emma removed her hand from Dylan's leg, and she had to force herself not to grab it and put it back where it was. She was enjoying the casual contact, the connection. It had been so long since she felt anything like it, and it surprised her when she missed it immediately.

Emma was sipping her vodka and working on the second course of dinner. Soup accompanied by bread, olives, and celery. Dinners like this would last for hours. They were events Dylan would slog her way through. She'd force herself to listen to men discuss the most heinous crimes humans could commit to one another, and all with a sense of pride in their voice. Emma was making it slightly more tolerable, and she didn't think that was possible. She reached under the table and took Emma's hand. She was pleasantly surprised when Emma squeezed her fingers. Dylan even smiled this time when she felt the tingling in her hand.

CHAPTER SIXTEEN

Emma had never eaten this much food in her entire life. It seemed to just keep coming out, cart after cart. She'd been researching Russia long enough to understand how their formal dinners worked, but nothing could have prepared her for the experience itself. When the coffee was finally served, she almost wept with relief.

She'd been listening to every conversation she could manage. Luckily, the men were arrogant, loud, and demanding. They wanted to ensure everyone heard about their accomplishments. Dylan was such a contrast to their brazen behavior. She didn't seek out approval, nor did she commend the others for their truly vile deeds. At first, Emma thought the difference might create distrust between her and Nikolai, but he seemed to appreciate her stoic behavior and took it at face value. Emma thought it might even act as a way to build trust between Dylan and Nikolai. If Dylan wasn't willing to boast about her endeavors in front of confidants, she absolutely wouldn't outside the safety of these walls.

Nikolai finished his coffee, stood, and motioned for the others to follow him. Emma let Dylan gently pull her from her seat. She immediately looked down and adjusted her skirt, worried she might inadvertently reveal too much and draw more unwanted attention. But unwanted attention wasn't what Dylan was giving her. The way Emma felt under Dylan's gaze was hypnotic. It felt as if Dylan was caressing her body with her eyes. Emma had never known a feeling like that was possible. She wasn't sure what to make of any of it, but she knew she wanted more.

She followed Dylan to a large parlor, separate from the main dining area of the house. When the doors slid open, Emma had to steel herself against Dylan from the surprise. A dozen half-naked women were lying in various positions across the long couches. There were bottles of alcohol and an assortment of powdery white drugs. The thumping of the music made Emma's heartbeat increase; it was like being in a club. Albeit, not a club Emma would ever want to visit. Nikolai and his men treated women as toys, something designed purely for their enjoyment and pleasure. It made Emma sick to think about what these women had to endure, especially after these men had indulged in their various party favors.

Dylan turned, pulled Emma against her body, and whispered, "Stay close and let me know when it's too much."

It was already too much. Emma had never so much as gone to a frat party much less something like this. She grabbed Dylan's hand tighter. "I will."

Dylan and Emma followed Nikolai to one of the couches farther from the commotion. He indicated that they should sit. "Sasha, tell me more about your new project. Is there anything I should be concerned about?"

Emma made herself look busy, staring around the room and letting her body sway to the music. She hoped she was giving off a sense of aloofness, to not draw any suspicion to her or Dylan. Dylan sat on the couch, and Emma made sure to stand behind her, not wanting anyone to think she was listening.

Dylan picked up a shot of vodka from the table and drank it without flinching. "It's an interesting project. She gave me the list of inspectors who should be coming to check on the goods, but they don't seem high enough in their department to be taking on something like this."

Nikolai pulled down one of the women walking by and kissed her. He ran his hand over her breast and released her. "Our manager is playing this one close to the chest. I know that she's critical to him and the company."

The same woman walked past Dylan and dragged her finger over Dylan's shoulder. Emma, not wanting to lose her position, or at least that's what she told herself, ran her hands down Dylan's arms, and kissed her cheek. She let her face linger against Dylan's for a moment. Dylan was flushed, warm to the touch. Emma wasn't sure if it was from their closeness, the alcohol, or the room itself. This whole situation was out of Emma's comfort zone. Maybe that was the reason she did nothing to stop her hands from sliding up Dylan's neck. She didn't stop herself from letting her fingers enjoy the softness behind her ear or the goose bumps she felt erupt underneath.

Emma was startled out of her trance by a possessive hand around her waist. She almost fell over in surprise but was held in place by Bogdan. He smelled of vodka, sweat, and cigars. If toxic masculinity had a smell, this was it.

"How about if you come and talk to me for a bit? Sasha won't mind." He spoke directly into her face, not even bothering to shield her senses from his grotesque nature.

Emma wanted to gouge his eyes and run away, but she just stared. She was unsure how she was expected to behave in this situation. She didn't want to do anything wrong or put them both in danger. A much softer hand slid into hers, and she knew it belonged to Dylan by the quick squeeze.

"Don't be an asshole, Bogdan. She's with me." Dylan pulled Emma from his grasp and put herself between them.

"Sasha, the night is still so young. Surely you wouldn't mind sharing with an old friend." Bogdan was talking to Dylan, but he kept his eyes focused on Emma.

Dylan motioned for two other women to come over. She put her arms around their shoulders and kissed their cheeks. "You'll be much happier with these two."

Bogdan squinted his eyes at Dylan. "I'll take what I want."

Dylan took a step closer to Bogdan, and Emma held her breath. She was grateful for Dylan's interference, but she was sure that toll would be paid with violence. She wanted to grab Dylan and get out of this horrible place.

"Bogdan, go somewhere else. Sasha and I are busy," Nikolai said with so much finality in his voice, Emma knew Bogdan wouldn't argue.

She'd been right. Bogdan raised a fist at Dylan like he was going to strike her, but walked away, women in tow.

"Come sit." Nikolai motioned to Emma and Dylan to rejoin him on the couch. "Ignore him. He only thinks with his dick." He lit a cigar and studied Emma. "Tell me, how did you meet Sasha?"

Emma felt her heart rate pick up. Then she steadied herself, ready to give the vaguest response she could muster. *Dylan is here with you; she'll help you through this.*

Nikolai's phone rang, and he pulled it from his pocket. He checked the screen, put his finger up, and answered.

Dylan was rubbing her thumb over Emma's hand. She was sure it was intended to calm her and bring her some reassurance, and to some degree, it did. Emma took a deep breath, preparing to answer questions. Luckily, it was all for naught. Nikolai hung up the phone and motioned for Egor to come over to him. Nikolai whispered something in his ear, and then stood to leave.

"I'll have to hear the story later." He took Emma's hand and kissed it. "I have to go, but please stay, enjoy." He leaned over and spoke into Dylan's ear, then patted her shoulder and walked away.

Dylan sat there, looking like a deer in headlights. Emma was immediately panic-stricken. Were they in danger? Was the team discovered? Did O'Brien escape? She had more questions than she knew what to do with. She rubbed Dylan's back, hoping for an answer that wouldn't mean complete upheaval for their team.

Dylan turned and looked at her. She leaned closer and whispered, "The pakhan is dead. Nikolai is now in charge, and I'm second in command." She brushed her lips closer to Emma's ear. "We need to get out of here. I have to regroup. This changes everything." She glanced around. "If I leave now, it will be too obvious. Bogdan has been watching us, and he'll have questions."

Emma pulled Dylan out of her seat and walked her over near the entrance. She slowly and as seductively as possible pushed Dylan up against the wall next to the door. She had no idea what she was doing. She had little previous sexual experience to help her navigate her actions. She let her instincts take over. She let herself touch Dylan the way her body screamed it wanted her to. She ran her hands up Dylan's arms and through her short hair. Her body felt like it was on overdrive. The only indicator of Dylan's surprise at Emma's behavior was the look in her eyes. The look of disbelief was quickly replaced by a flash of desire.

Emma pressed her body more thoroughly against Dylan. She enjoyed the way Dylan's breath changed at their contact and the way her breasts felt pressed against her own. Dylan slid her hands under Emma's jacket and up her back. Emma closed her eyes when Dylan's thumbs ran along the outside of her breasts. Emma could feel her heart pounding through every nerve ending in her body. The sensation was both electrifying and intoxicating. Emma felt like she was drunk, as if she were right on the brink of losing control. Her body and mind were teetering on the edge, and she didn't know where the bottom would be. Dylan put her lips to Emma's neck and her skin felt like it was on fire. Dylan moved her way up her jaw and then her chin. Dylan's lips were so close, there to take if Emma wanted. *Wanted.* Emma thought she knew what she wanted, what she needed, and it wasn't Dylan—it couldn't be.

Emma pulled away slightly. "I think we've given everyone here reason to believe you'll be occupied for the evening. Let's get out of here," she whispered.

Dylan stared at her, her eyes still a bit hazy with lust. "Okay." Emma stepped back, and Dylan pulled her close again to whisper against her lips. "I'm sorry if I overstepped. I didn't mean to offend you. I thought we were doing a bit."

A bit. Emma smiled. She could feel the sadness but hoped Dylan didn't notice. "We were, and you didn't." She kissed Dylan's cheek and allowed her mouth to linger next to her lips. "We should go."

Dylan moved away from the wall and looked across to Bogdan. He made a crude hand gesture and Dylan gave him a quick nod before pulling Emma out of the room with her. Emma let Dylan lead her out of the room and to the car. Her brain was cluttered with the conversations she'd heard that evening, the people she'd met, and Dylan. She wasn't sure what to make of her behavior around Dylan. She made choices and acted in ways she never had before. It'd be easy to chalk it up to being undercover and playing a part, but was that true? Dylan shot her a smile over the roof of the car before they opened their doors. Emma felt the heat rise through her chest and ears. *I'm in trouble.*

CHAPTER SEVENTEEN

Dylan turned in a circle inside her apartment, feeling more nervous than she ever had inside her own space. It could've been because she rarely, if ever, brought women back to her apartment. Her nerves could also be attributed to the fact that Nikolai would now be the pakhan and she'd be second in command. It would be career altering. Even as she thought it, she knew it wasn't any of those things. She was nervous because the woman in her apartment was Emma.

She ran a hand through her hair and motioned to the kitchen. "Do you want anything to drink?"

Emma pulled her jacket off and laid it on the couch. "Wine would be great. Then, I'd like to go through everything we each saw and heard tonight. I need to get it into the system."

Dylan stared at the wine in her fridge. *What is the right variety to serve to the coworker you almost made out with and definitely shouldn't have?* "White or red?"

"Whatever," Emma said as she sat at the table and pulled her tablet from the bag.

Dylan pulled her favorite pinot noir from its place on the shelf and busied herself with opening it. "What did you see tonight? Anything that wasn't in the files?"

Their fingers touched when Emma took the glass, and Dylan swore she saw Emma blush. "It's more what I heard." She took the glass and quickly went back to her tablet. "Nikolai isn't like the rest of them. He is controlled, savvy, and focused." She took a sip of her wine. "Do you think he had anything to do with the pakhan being killed?"

Dylan took a large sip of wine and walked toward her bedroom. "It's definitely possible. I wouldn't put it past him. I'm going to go change, but please, keep talking."

There was a long pause before Emma spoke again. "I pulled up everything I have on Nikolai Orlav. He was removed from the FBI's Ten Most Wanted list since the US doesn't maintain an extradition treaty with Russia."

Dylan laughed. "Yet, here I am." She pulled on a pair of running shorts and a tank top and then pulled out some of the same variety for Emma.

"His crimes run the gamut: wire fraud, mail fraud, racketeering, money laundering, securities fraud, aiding and abetting, falsification of books and records, false filings with the SEC, and conspiracy."

Dylan handed Emma the change of clothes. "I thought you might want to be more comfortable."

Emma absently took the clothes from her. "It also says that he's probably responsible for over one hundred contract killings."

Dylan continued to scroll through the information when Emma left to change. Law enforcement agencies throughout the world had been trying to prosecute him for over twenty-five years. But he had, in the words of one journalist, "a knack for never being in the wrong place at the wrong time."

Dylan leaned back in the chair and sipped her wine. Emma emerged from the bedroom, looking adorable in shorts that were too long on her and Dylan's favorite shirt. Dylan didn't realize she was staring until Emma spoke to her.

"This could be really big for you, huh?"

Dylan ran her finger along the rim of the wine glass. For a reason she couldn't quite put her finger on, she wanted Emma to understand why this was so important to her. She wanted Emma to understand her, to know her. She knew Emma could and probably already had read all about her, but she wanted to tell her story.

Dylan leaned forward, putting her elbows on the table. "I didn't know my parents. I don't say that because I want you to feel sorry for me, I don't. I'm telling you that because it's just part of the story. By the time I was eighteen, I'd been in fourteen foster homes. Some were unbearable, some were okay, and some I would've liked to make my forever home." Emma reached for her hand, but Dylan pulled away. She didn't want to be distracted. "I was lucky. I flew under the radar mostly and excelled in sports and school. I got a full ride to the University of Washington and was recruited to the CIA right out of college. The CIA suited me. I didn't need a place to call home. I didn't have any family or friends to lie to or to worry about me. I've been on the move in one mission or another since I was twenty-four. When I was chosen for this assignment, I was thrilled. It was going to be my career maker. I was going to get my first monumental tag at thirty. I was going to prove all the people in my life wrong, the ones who said I'd never amount to anything. I was going to prove I was worth something." She sipped her wine, pushing the old memories aside.

"I've been inside the Bratva for the last three years. I've had to do unspeakable things to gain my position as quickly as I have. Things I'm not proud of, things that keep me from being able to sleep. All to help dismantle one of the most dangerous criminal organizations in the world. Now, it's been practically dropped into my lap, and it may all be for naught. If we take O'Brien, Nikolai will have me killed. Even if I escape, I won't get to take him or the organization down. My cover will be blown. If we try to take him first, O'Brien will get away. I help you guys and I lose three years of the hardest work I've ever had to do. I don't, and one of the worst criminals in America gets away. It's a no win." Dylan sat back in her chair again.

Emma studied her, and Dylan waited for the barrage of positive reinforcement. Emma would tell her that it was all for the greater good, her sacrifices would matter, and that everything would work out in the end. Dylan was sure Emma had an overabundance of motivational phrases tucked away for something just like this.

Emma took her hand, even when Dylan tried to pull away again. "That must be so frustrating. I can't even begin to imagine how difficult this will be for you. And thank you for trusting me with your story. I know that probably wasn't easy for you."

Dylan couldn't do anything but stare. "You aren't going to lecture me about the bigger picture? Being a team player?"

Emma looked confused. "You've invested years into this assignment. Then, we show up out of nowhere and highjack it. No, I completely understand why you're frustrated. I also understand what it's like, feeling like you have to prove yourself. We have very different stories, but I know what that feels like. I can't fathom the position you're in."

Dylan watched Emma's eyes. There were different emotions swirling around in the tranquil blue, but what hurt Dylan was the sadness she saw. "Who hurt you?"

Emma let go of Dylan's hand and took a sip of her wine. "No one hurt me, not like they hurt you. I've just always been a bit of an outcast. I grew up with two siblings, my parents are caring and loving. But I never felt like I fit in anywhere. The only person who ever really understood me was my grandma, and when she died, I felt completely alone. I graduated high school at sixteen and college at nineteen. All the kids thought I was weird, awkward, or both. I've never had any real friends. Even when I thought I did, they were just using me for school. I was thrilled about taking this assignment. One, because it will be great for my career. But two, because I'll be able to show everyone that I can be part of a team, an important part."

"We're quite the pair," Dylan said, hoping to lighten the mood. "And, Emma?"

"Hmm?"

"I don't think you're weird or awkward. I think you're insanely smart, beautiful, and possibly the most authentic person I've ever met."

Emma blushed but met her eyes anyway. "Is that one of your lines?"

Dylan's body warmed. She wasn't sure how to manage what she was feeling. Women didn't often question her, only wanting from her what she wanted from them—nothing but a brief reprieve.

Dylan ran her thumb over the top of Emma's hand. "It wasn't a line."

Emma stared where their skin touched. "Dylan, I can't go down this road with you. I'm not built like that. I can't do flings. I'll fall, and you'll already be long gone."

Dylan heard the words but couldn't stop touching her. "How do you know I won't be there?"

"Because that's how you're built." There was no accusation or venom in Emma's words. She meant them for what they were, the truth.

Dylan felt a lump form in the back of her throat. Words were stuck there, choking her. She wanted to let them spill out of her mouth. She wanted to tell Emma that maybe she could be different. She wanted to tell Emma that she was lonely too. The realization caught her off guard, and she stood. Emotional entanglements weren't part of this job. Those could get you killed.

A knock at the door gave her the amnesty she needed from her unintended self-reflection. She wasn't surprised to see who was on the other side. His arms were the size of tree trunks, he had sunken eyes, and a five o'clock shadow that was more like a forty-eight-hour shadow.

"Nikolai wants you at his house at zero-nine-hundred tomorrow."

Dylan nodded. "You could have just called, Ivan."

Ivan shook his head. "I'm supposed to do a face-to-face. No phones until tomorrow." Ivan looked around her, his gaze landing on Emma. "Is that the same girl from tonight?"

"Yes."

Ivan looked like he was going to say more but changed his mind and turned to leave. "Don't be late, Sasha."

"I'm never late."

He waved as he disappeared down the steps.

She turned and faced Emma again. The mood in the room had changed. The closeness they'd shared just minutes before was gone. "I hate to do this, but I'm going to have to put you on a bus in the morning. We can't risk one of the team coming to get you, and I can't be caught leaving town until I know what's happening."

Emma gave her a faint smile, but it didn't reach her eyes. "I understand." She started walking to the couch. "I'm pretty tired."

Dylan wanted the closeness back, even if it was just for a moment. She made it to her and touched her arm. "I'll sleep on the couch. Please, I'd feel like an asshole if you slept out here. There're extra toothbrushes in the top drawer of my bathroom. Feel free to use one."

Emma crossed her arms, not making eye contact. "Okay, thank you. Why don't you go ahead and get ready for bed first? I'll use the bathroom when you're done."

"Emma, I—"

Emma shook her head. "Don't. Let's not do this. I'm tired, and we have a lot to do tomorrow."

Thirty minutes later, Dylan hit the pillow under her head for the sixth time. She was frustrated with her feelings, angry she couldn't articulate them, and disappointed that she hoped her pillow would smell like Emma when she went to bed the following night. She rolled over onto her side, hoping a different position would help her fall asleep. She should be planning her next steps. She should be figuring out how she could take down Nikolai and O'Brien, but all she could think about was the way Emma had felt pressed against her. The way her hair felt against her cheek and how she never wanted to be the cause of sadness in her eyes.

CHAPTER EIGHTEEN

I hate all three of you!" Jennifer leaned over and grabbed her knees. She coughed again and pushed Caden away when she placed a hand on her back.

"You did great." Tyler was trying to make her feel better, but the look Jennifer shot her proved it hadn't worked. "We ran five miles. You should be proud of yourself."

Jennifer flopped down onto the ground and put her arm over her eyes. "No, you ran five miles. I ran, walked, and cried."

Brooke laughed. "It's nice to see you haven't lost your dramatic flair."

"I'm going to take her back and get her cleaned up. We'll meet you down at control in a bit," Caden said as she pulled Jennifer to her feet. "You did great, babe."

"I hate you the most." Jennifer moaned as she wrapped her arm around Caden's waist, leaning on her as they walked to the main house.

"It's only seven. Stop worrying." Brooke grabbed Tyler's hand when she rechecked her watch. Brooke kissed her softly, smiling against her. "You worry too much. She's with Dylan. I'm sure she's fine."

"This is Emma's first assignment and we sent her into the lion's den. I'm going to worry." Tyler kissed Brooke again and then backed away to stretch.

Brooke mimicked her movement. "She's with a lion tamer. She'll be fine."

Tyler pulled her arm across her chest, enjoying the sensation of loosening her muscles. "Weren't you scared on your first mission?"

Brooke shrugged. "Not really. I was nervous, sure. But I had you there. I knew you wouldn't let anything happen to me."

Tyler shook her head. "I'm not a miracle worker and neither is Dylan. We can't stop everything. Some things are out of our control."

Brooke shrugged. "Exactly. Worrying about them won't make a difference."

"I'm going to worry. There's nothing you can do about that."

Brooke put her arms around Tyler's neck. "I know, and I'm going to tell you to relax. There's nothing you can do about that."

Tyler kissed Brooke softly. "Did you get around to reading that email from your mom?"

Brooke pulled her mouth away and stared. "That's the least sexy thing you've ever said to me." She turned and started toward the main house.

Tyler caught up and took her hand, relieved when Brooke didn't pull away. She knew if Brooke wasn't slightly pushed, she'd never get the information out of her. Not on this subject. "What did she say?"

Brooke sighed. "That she was open to having dinner with us."

"Hey! That's something!"

Brooke stopped walking and turned to face her. She crossed her arms and lifted an eyebrow. "I'm not interested in my mother's small acts of charity. She either accepts me for who I am, or not. I'm not going to be some check mark on a list of things she needs to do to fit in with her friends." She turned and kept walking.

Tyler let her go. She knew Brooke well enough to know when she needed a little space. The dynamics between Brooke and her mother were complicated, confusing, and messy. Brooke was as strong willed as they came, and from her brief interactions with Janice, she knew they shared that trait. Tyler wanted Brooke to have a good relationship with her mom, but she knew she couldn't force it. All she could do was be supportive of Brooke, even if Brooke acted like she didn't need it.

Tyler decided to head down to the control center. She'd shower a bit later. Right now, she wanted to check in with Tony, who'd handled the computers overnight, and see if there were any updates with O'Brien. She jogged over to Emma when she saw her walking up the path in the same direction.

"Hey," Tyler said when she got closer.

Emma ran a hand through her hair and smiled, but she didn't make eye contact. "Morning."

"How did everything go? Are you okay?" Tyler was a bit unnerved by the way Emma crossed her arms. She seemed on guard for some reason.

Emma's eyes fell to the hatch that led to their control center. "There's a lot to discuss. Are the others already here?"

Tyler pointed her thumb to the house behind them. "They're getting ready for the day. They'll be here soon." She gingerly put a hand on Emma's shoulder. "Are you okay? Is Dylan okay?"

Emma chewed on her thumb. "Dylan's fine." She finally met Tyler's eyes. "I just don't really feel like myself." She pushed her glasses up the bridge of her nose.

Tyler led her off the path and under the shade of a nearby tree. "Emma, did something happen to you? Did someone do something to you?" Tyler felt the panic crawl from her stomach into her throat.

Emma searched her face, and her eyes grew large. "Oh no, nothing bad happened to me. No one *did* anything to me." She smiled sheepishly at Tyler. "I'm sorry, I didn't mean to make it seem like that."

Tyler was relieved, but there was more to the story. "Do you want to talk about it?" Emma glanced up at the house. "Would you rather speak to Brooke or Jennifer?"

Emma stared down at the ground again. "No. It's just that...I think I may have feelings for Dylan."

"Oh," Tyler said and regretted she didn't have something more encouraging to add.

Emma continued before Tyler could think of something else. "I know that it's inappropriate and we're completely wrong for each other. She enjoys a surplus of women, she's on a long-term assignment, and I'm not one for anything temporary. Or anything at all, really. And yet, I'm just finding it rather distracting, a little confusing, and it has me off-kilter. I'm never off-kilter with work issues, and I've worked so hard to get where I am. The last thing I need is to make mistakes because my focus is misplaced."

Tyler laughed and patted Emma on the shoulder. "You know Brooke was in my class at the Farm when we met. Talk about inappropriate." She sighed. "I fought my feelings the best I could, but you see how far that got me."

Emma looked at her questioningly. "So, is it just because we're working together? Will this go away once we're apart?"

Tyler wasn't sure how she'd surmised that from what she said. "I don't know if it will go away or not, or why you're having these feelings. I guess that could be why, or maybe your feelings are genuine."

Emma rolled her eyes. "I need definitive answers. I don't function well in the gray."

Tyler smiled. "I understand. I didn't either. Unfortunately, that's not how this works. But I wouldn't worry about your focus or professionalism. I trust you to do what you need to do when things start to happen."

Emma's eyes focused behind her again. "Could we just keep this between us? I don't want it to become a thing."

Tyler nodded and turned toward the sound of the others joining them. "Of course."

"Thanks," Emma said and headed toward the control center.

Caden was beside her a moment later. "What was that about? Everything okay?"

"Yeah," Tyler said and moved toward the door that would lead them below. "Let's get to work."

Tyler didn't know enough about Emma to know what would come of her and Dylan. But she knew people. From what she could discern from Emma's body language, and the way she blushed, she was already in much deeper than she wanted to admit. Tyler had meant what she said to Emma. She trusted her judgment, but it wouldn't prevent Tyler from concerning herself with the outcome. Any kind of disruption in unit cohesiveness could spell trouble for all of them. She hoped Dylan knew what she was doing.

The server handed Dylan a cappuccino and placed a plate of blini on the table. She wasn't hungry, but she wanted to seem as relaxed as possible. She put a few pieces of fruit on top of the thin cake, folded it, and took a bite.

Nikolai was watching her closely. "Work up an appetite last night, Sasha?"

Dylan winked at him, unwilling to give him an answer. "What happened, Nikolai?" She slid her phone across the table to him. "It's my understanding we no longer need these."

He handed the phone to Ivan. "Our last pakhan made foolish decisions. It didn't turn out well for him. So, now it's my turn. Hopefully, my decisions are less foolish." He handed her a different phone. "You'll take my old position."

Dylan took another bite of her breakfast. "What about my old jobs? Who will do them now?" She made sure not to hold her breath, waiting for an answer.

"Bogdan will take your old position." Nikolai picked up a blini, dipped it in whipped cream, and shoved it in his mouth.

"What about my security job? Who will watch her?" Dylan sipped her coffee, keeping eye contact with Nikolai.

Nikolai waved his hand. "Roman cared for her. I do not. We have several countries interested in acquiring her. I'm selling her to the highest bidder at the gala. They'll pick her up from there."

Dylan willed her hand not to shake as she brought the cup up to her mouth. "Why not just sell her to the Americans? I'm sure they'd pay a hefty sum to have her back," she said and smiled.

"I don't want the Americans anywhere near my business. That's why we're getting rid of the problem as soon as possible." He took another bite of his breakfast.

"Do you need me to broker the deal?" Dylan hoped it might be her way out of the situation she suddenly found herself in, but she focused on the food as an attempt to look disinterested in his answer.

"It's already handled."

If there was a question in Dylan's mind as to whether Nikolai had been the one to get rid of Roman, it was answered then. There was no way Nikolai could have found a buyer and made arrangements for the sale of Carol O'Brien in ten hours. He'd been planning this for a while. He was watching her closely, probably trying to see if she'd put the pieces together. Nikolai may seem rather reserved, even soft-spoken to casual acquaintances, but Dylan knew better. Nikolai was as cold, calculating, and dangerous as they came.

"Good. One less thing to worry about." She held up her cappuccino cup in a sign of appreciation. She picked up her new phone and put it in her pocket. "Is there anything else you need from me right now? I'd like to get some sleep. Late night." She winked at him.

"Be at my house at eight this evening. We have things to discuss. And, Sasha..."

Dylan met his eyes and waited for him to continue.

"That girl from last night, you should bring her again. I liked her, and you seemed rather protective of her. But if you're done with her, I'm sure the others would like a shot."

Dylan nodded and headed for the door, not bothering to respond to the sickening remark. She knew there was more to it than sharing a nice piece of ass. He was fishing. She made her way through the busy streets to her apartment. She knew she needed to relay the information to the team, but there was no safe way to do it, not now. Nikolai might have promoted her, but he'd be keeping an extra close eye on her now. The whole situation just became significantly more complicated, more dangerous, and with a substantially more definitive timeline. She thought about Emma. Bringing her last night was to help her blend in, but now she feared she'd be in even more danger. Nikolai didn't take chances and it was what made him successful. He'd be looking for Emma, wanting to make sure she wasn't a loose end for him to tie up. Dylan tried to decide what would be more dangerous—keeping her close or out of sight. Keeping her close would put her in his orbit. On the other hand, if he couldn't find her at all, it would raise suspicion. *Shit.*

She picked up the phone Ivan had given her and sent a text to the burner phone they'd set up for Emma, just in case. *This is Sasha. I had to get a new phone, broke my old one. Thanks for last night. I have the afternoon off. Feel like picking up where we left off?* She pulled into her apartment complex and hoped she was doing the right thing.

CHAPTER NINETEEN

Carol eyed the overweight man standing in her doorway. His face was red, he smelled of stale alcohol, cigars, and body odor. He tried to fancy up his disgusting presence with a suit, but Carol knew this type of man. Hell, she'd been dealing with this type of man in one form or another her entire life. They thought they were the top of the food chain, untouchable, and deadly. His presence should have intimidated her, but all it did was enrage her.

"Where is Sasha? I want to speak to Roman."

He walked over to the counter and poured himself a glass of scotch. *Her* scotch. "You have me now. Trust me, you better off. Sasha is weak. I protect you. Roman gone. Nothing he can do for you." Even in broken English, he was arrogant.

She moved around behind her kitchen counter, wanting to be closer to knives if necessary. "What was your name again?"

"Bogdan." He sipped from the glass he'd so obnoxiously helped himself to.

"Well, Bogdan, I'm sure you're very good at your job, but I'm comfortable with Sasha. I'd like her back, please."

He smiled, finished the glass, and set it on the table. "You have me. Doesn't matter what you like." He walked back to the front door and opened it. "We pick you up next week for gala. Call if you have issue."

As soon as the door shut, she picked up her cell. *We have a situation.* She waited, annoyed at the amount of time that passed.

What?

She almost laughed at the response, so typical. *New boss in town. I'm afraid my time is limited.*

You need to relax. You're safe where you are. I'll see you soon.

She placed the phone on the counter before she picked up a glass and threw it against the wall. Through all the things she'd done, the lies she'd told, the people she'd outmaneuvered, she'd never felt like a sitting duck. Until now. Every day that passed was a day closer to those women finding her. That had always been her biggest fear. No matter who her friends were at the top, the women hunting her couldn't be turned, and they were too noticeable and connected themselves to simply disappear without it coming back to her. Once they were gone, there was no one else who would care enough to hunt her down. They were the only thorn in her side. Now, something worse might be on the horizon. In all the scenarios that she'd played out in her head, going down at the hands of an incompetent Russian mob boss wasn't one of them.

No, she wasn't going down without a fight, without a say. She wasn't going to be bested by men who could be bought and paid for like used cars. She picked up her phone again and sent a text message to Bogdan. *I'd like to speak to the new person in charge. Tell him I'll pay.*

CHAPTER TWENTY

Emma knocked on the door and held her breath. It wasn't intentional. She didn't even realize she'd done it until Dylan opened the door. Her smile was wide, and her eyes said she was genuinely happy to see her, but there was something else there. Fear perhaps? Dylan reached out and pulled her closer, but kept them slightly in the hallway.

Dylan wrapped her hand around her back and let it rest right above her ass. She leaned forward and kissed her cheek. "Hi." The now familiar smell of Dylan overwhelmed her senses. Emma didn't mean to take it in so fully, but it was compulsory.

The sensation momentarily startled Emma. Her body gave in before her mind had the opportunity to protest. She leaned into Dylan's cheek. "Hi."

Dylan pulled her inside and shut the door behind her. There was music playing again, just as there always was. "Sorry for that." She pointed to the doorway. "I'm not sure if Nikolai is having us watched."

Emma stared at her, not fully understanding. "Us?"

Dylan ran her hand through her hair and sat next to Emma at the table. "Nikolai is one of the most cunning men I've ever known. He requested that you accompany me tonight to his house. He's never done that before. He gave some bullshit reason about liking you, but I don't buy it for a second. Ivan must have mentioned that you were in my apartment. I never bring women back here. He wants to make sure you aren't a liability of some sort. That or he's angling to use you as leverage against me if I step out of line." She looked down at her hands. "I thought it was best to have you here with me. I didn't want him to send out anyone to look for you."

Emma pulled out her tablet and opened an encrypted video conference with the rest of the team. "I think you need to fill us in."

Dylan nodded and started to recount what had preceded their conversation. Emma said nothing as she watched Jennifer and Brooke in the background type as Dylan spoke. Tyler's expression never changed. Caden, the most animated of the group, started to pace.

When it was all said and done, Tyler spoke first. "My first instinct is to try to extract O'Brien before the gala. But, Dylan, you're the expert when it comes to these men. What do you think?"

Dylan was quiet for longer than Emma had ever seen when asked a question. "If we wait until the gala, you could get O'Brien, and I'd have the opportunity to identify all the major players here. We'll be able to put faces to names. Not just from Russia but from all over the world. I…*we* could put a major dent in some of the worst criminal organizations in the world."

Caden's face came into view. "We could also get killed. Remember, we don't know for sure who O'Brien's boyfriend is, and we can't just call this in. There will be security to the hilt at the gala. What are we going to do? Walk in and arrest them? We don't have jurisdiction there. Interpol relies on local law enforcement to make arrests, so they're useless to us. Even if we could find a sympathetic agency, we don't have time to fill them in or risk the chance of them making a mistake."

"I was never going to be able to do anything but identify them. Keeping track of these assholes, knowing who the players are? It's how we help stop human trafficking. It's how we prevent nuclear weapons from being bought and sold. It's how we keep the world a little safer." Dylan was trying to keep her voice low, but Emma could see her desperation.

Caden shook her head again. "If we wait too long, we could lose her."

Tyler leaned forward, her focus on Dylan. "How long would you need at the gala?"

Caden put her hands in the air. "You've got to be kidding me."

Dylan ignored Caden. "An hour, two at the most. If it looks like they're going to take O'Brien before that, we'll pick her up, call off the rest of it."

Tyler nodded. "Okay. Let's start working on the way to make this happen. This will be our primary objective unless something changes this week."

Dylan let her shoulders fall a bit, relieved. "Thank you."

"What am I supposed to do now? If Dylan thinks Nikolai might be watching me, or us, I can't lead him back to the team," Emma said, wondering out loud for herself as much as everyone else.

Dylan ran her hands over her face and sighed. "I think the best option is for you to stay here with me."

Emma's face ran hot with both annoyance for being in this position and at the possibility of staying with Dylan for a week. "With you here? At your apartment?"

Tyler nodded her agreement. "You'll be safest there. I'll have Tony create a dummy apartment for you somewhere out of town. If Nikolai has the resources to do a records search on you, you'll have an apartment listed under your name. I'm also going to have him put a more extensive background together for you than what he already did before the dinner last night. It should hold up in records searches if Nikolai is inclined to check."

"I guess it's settled then. Have Tony send me over the information once he's done, so I'm in the loop." Emma knew she sounded annoyed, but she'd never felt so out of control in any part of her life. It was unnerving.

"We'll check in later," Tyler said, and the screen went black.

Dylan touched Emma's arm. "I'm sorry about that. I just don't want to take any chances."

Emma looked at the hand on her arm and willed the thrumming in her head to stop. "I understand why the decision was made. I'm a pragmatic person. I just don't deal real well when things feel like they're out of my control."

Dylan leaned back in her chair and smiled. "I function better with a certain amount of chaos."

Emma scoffed. "What a pair we are."

"Do you want to go work out?" Dylan's question came from nowhere.

"What?"

"Work out. If we are being watched, I need to keep up with my everyday routines. I'd like to go for a run. Do you want to come with me? You can borrow some clothes." Dylan stood and headed toward her bedroom.

Emma was scared at the thought of going out in public. She'd never been tailed or watched before. But staying indoors certainly wasn't going to do anything but allow her imagination to run wild.

"Um, sure." Emma followed Dylan to her room.

Dylan handed her some clothes and headed into the bathroom to change. Emma dutifully pulled off her attire and replaced it with the workout outfit Dylan had given her. After changing, she went over to the full-length mirror. She took a deep breath and studied her face. She was surprised to see that worry and fear weren't etched between her eyes. She'd never trusted a team before, but the relief of having people on your side was something she could get used to.

Dylan came out of the bathroom. "You ready?"

Emma gave herself one final look in the mirror and nodded. "Sure, let's go."

Dylan didn't mean to stare, but keeping her eyes off Emma was proving to be more difficult than she'd imagined. Emma was using one of the park railings to stretch after their four-mile run, and Dylan was mesmerized. She'd been attracted to Emma since the first time she saw her, but the more time they spent together the surface attraction was shifting into something more real. She actually *liked* Emma. It wasn't just because Emma was effortlessly beautiful, even though she was. It was because Emma was intelligent, funny, and awkward in the most adorable way. Dylan couldn't remember the last time she'd thought about any woman this much, if ever.

"Are you okay?"

"Huh?" Dylan tried to buy herself a few seconds after realizing she'd just been caught gawking.

"You looked really deep in thought," Emma said, sounding a bit concerned.

"You're just really lovely." Dylan hadn't meant to be honest; it just slipped out. She wanted to take it back until she saw the blush creep up Emma's neck.

Emma shyly turned her head away. "I don't think anyone has ever looked at me with as much intensity as you."

Dylan didn't know how to maneuver this weird road of sudden onset honesty. She just knew she wanted off it before things got out of hand. "Do you want to go get something to eat? I know a place not far from here."

Emma agreed but still didn't meet her eyes.

Dylan requested a table toward the back of the café and sat where she could see everyone who was coming and going. She ordered a few of her favorite pastries to share. She wasn't trying to be presumptuous, but Emma had looked a little overwhelmed by the menu.

"Tell me about your siblings," Dylan said. She hoped it would help Emma take her mind off the chaos, but she also wanted to know more about her.

Emma waited for the server to put her cappuccino in front of her and took a sip. "My older sister, Felicity, is a teacher and a dance instructor in Texas. My younger brother, Sam, is a senior in high school."

"Okay, but what else? What did you all do for fun as kids?"

"Like I told you before, we aren't very close. My parents seemed to know what to do with normal kids. I wasn't normal, at least, that's what they said. Don't get me wrong, my parents are good people. They gave me every advantage they could. They put me in private schools when they realized that I was smarter than most. I went to science camps during every school break. They just had trouble connecting with me. It was never like that for my siblings."

"They sent you away every school break? What about your sister and brother? Did they get sent away too?" Dylan had never had a real family, but she'd seen enough television to understand what one should function like.

Emma shrugged. "They took them to the beach, to Disneyland, stuff like that. But yes, I was usually away at some camp or other academic activity."

Dylan's heart hurt imagining a tiny Emma always being sent away. "I'm sorry you went through that. It must have been very isolating."

Emma picked at the pastry in front of her. "They were trying to do what was best for me, to help me cultivate my gifts."

Dylan put her hand over Emma's. "You deserved to be a kid too."

Emma flinched at the contact but didn't withdraw. "It just seems silly to complain about."

Dylan squeezed her hand. "There's not an acceptable or unacceptable reason when it comes to loneliness. We feel what we feel, and you're entitled to those feelings. I hope you know that."

Emma nodded, and tears welled in her eyes. "I've been so lonely for so long. It just feels like my normal."

Dylan hated to see the sadness in Emma's eyes. She tried to think of anything to talk about that could take it away. "Any places on your bucket list?"

Emma smiled at this question. "Pretty much everywhere. I have pictures all over my apartment of countries, museums, landmarks. I want to see everything."

Dylan was about to tell her about her favorite places when a familiar figure walked through the door. He strode over to their table and pulled up a chair.

Dylan released Emma's hand and sat back in her chair. "Ivan, what can I help you with?"

He picked up one of the pastries and shoved it in his mouth. "Boss wants to see you."

Dylan took a deep breath and steadied her nerves. "You know I have a phone, right?"

He licked his fingers. "I was in the area."

It didn't surprise Dylan he knew where she was, but it did irritate her. She forced a smile. "Okay, let me take Nada back to my apartment, and I'll meet you there."

He shook his head and stood. "No, now. She can wait in the lobby during your meeting. I'll drive."

Dylan's stomach flipped, but she made sure to keep her face neutral. "Okay, let's go."

As they walked to the car, she surveyed the area. None of Nikolai's other guys were around, which was a good sign. She didn't think he'd send only Ivan if he intended to kill her. She grabbed Emma's hand as they walked, hoping to convey that they were in this together and she wouldn't let anything happen to her. She just hoped that was a pledge she'd be able to keep.

CHAPTER TWENTY-ONE

The drive wasn't a long one, but it felt as if it lasted hours. Dylan couldn't shake the feeling that something was very wrong. Some people would call it gut instinct or a sixth sense. Dylan knew it was neither of those things. It was merely the byproduct of having been around the worst humanity had to offer for as long as she had. These men traded on human life like it was part of the stock market; they'd buy, sell, or eliminate based on their whims. She had a feeling she was about to be on the receiving end of one of those whims. She might be walking into a predestined fate, but she'd do everything she could to save Emma.

"Did you ever call your mother and let her know you got here safely?" Dylan squeezed Emma's leg.

"No, I forgot." Emma put her hand over Dylan's.

"You should when we get there. I should only be a few minutes. I don't want her to worry. The reception on the back patio is best." Dylan knew Emma would understand what she was saying. If things went sideways, she needed to call Tyler.

"Okay." Emma's eyes were full of fear and concern, but she kept her expression calm. If Ivan were watching in the rearview, he'd never know how Emma was feeling.

Dylan's blood was on fire as they pulled up to the large residence. Every alarm bell was sounding in her head. If she'd been here without Emma, she'd take Ivan out and cut her losses. She didn't have that option, not with Emma in tow. She had a small firearm concealed in the back of her waistband, but it only held four bullets. It wouldn't be nearly enough if Nikolai decided she was expendable.

Once inside the house, Dylan pulled Emma to her. "Get out of here if things go bad," she whispered into her ear. She kissed her cheek. "See you in a bit." She walked away before Emma had a chance to say anything.

Dylan pushed the large doors to Nikolai's study open, ready to grab her weapon if need be. Her heart was pounding so quickly that her fingers tingled. She could feel the adrenaline burning in the back of her throat.

"Sasha, come in, come in. Shut the door," Nikolai said from behind his large oak desk.

Dylan scanned the room and almost fell over when she saw Carol O'Brien sitting in the high-backed chair across from the mob boss.

"Sasha, it's so good to see you. I've missed you." Carol smiled and ran a finger across her lips.

Dylan nodded her hello to Carol and turned her attention to Nikolai. "What can I help with?"

He motioned to the chair. "Sit, have a drink." He poured her a glass of vodka and handed it to her.

"Carol has given me some fascinating information." Nikolai smiled at Carol and raised his glass. He was speaking in English for Carol's benefit, so she'd do the same.

"Oh? Anything I can be of assistance with?" Dylan kept her breathing even and made sure her face showed her curiosity.

He slid a folder to her. "We have some visitors here from overseas. Captain Calvin Hart and the ones we'd discussed earlier."

Dylan opened the folder and flipped through the pictures of the familiar women, her team. "I knew about the women, but I didn't know they'd arrived. I was taken off this assignment before I had the chance to track anyone down." She looked back up at Nikolai. "Do you know where they are?"

Nikolai smiled. "Sasha, that's why I have you. I don't care about these women. Get rid of them. I'd like to have a face-to-face with this Captain Hart."

Carol leaned over in her seat, closer to Dylan. "There's an added bonus. I have a mole inside the CIA. He'll be here soon. If you all can work your magic and flip him, you'll be able to control most of the world. You could operate virtually unchecked."

Nikolai clapped his hands together. "How many men do you need me to give you for the task, Sasha? I want this taken care of before the gala."

Dylan closed the folder and took a large gulp from her glass. "I'd prefer to do it alone. I don't want to draw attention to his apprehension. It will give us more time."

Nikolai lit a cigar. "I don't need long with him. He's just to prove a point. I need to show this CIA man that I can get to anyone. Give him a reason to come to our side. After that, we'll fake an accident. Get rid of this Hart person."

Carol touched Dylan's arm. "I need these women dead. That's nonnegotiable. If I don't have proof by the gala, I won't give up my mole."

Dylan nodded. "I understand." She stood to leave.

"Do not disappoint me, Sasha. You know how upset I get when I'm disappointed." Nikolai smiled playfully, but Dylan knew his statement was a promise.

"Understood. I'll take care of it." She pointed behind her. "Can you please stop having your guys follow me around? It's more difficult to track foreign spies when I'm being tailed. Draws too much attention."

He studied her and finally nodded. "By Thursday, Sasha. I need it all handled. No exceptions."

"It was nice to see you, Sasha," Carol purred. "Looking forward to our next encounter."

Dylan opened the door, and Emma was beside her a moment later. She put her hand on her back and rubbed small circles to reassure her everything was okay.

Dylan smiled and took her hand. "You ready to go?"

Ivan stepped up beside them. "I'll take you back to your apartment."

Dylan wanted to protest, but she was trying to be as calm as possible. "Sounds good, Ivan. Thank you."

Emma smiled at him as well, and she was thankful to have the support. Whatever the next few days held, it was going to change all their lives forever. All Dylan could do was pray they'd all be there at the end.

Chapter Twenty-two

Tyler ended the video conference with Dylan and Emma. The silence in the room was deafening. She knew everyone was looking to her to have some words of wisdom or a brilliant idea, but at the moment she had nothing. *Four percent.*

"I say we take O'Brien now," Caden said.

"It's too late for that. She's going to be guarded by Nikolai's men now. We have to find another way." Tyler walked over to the large map of the area, needing to do something.

"Should we notify Captain Hart?" Jennifer asked.

"Not yet." Tyler didn't bother turning around to answer. "For all we know, Nikolai is having him tailed too. We don't need him to accidentally lead any of Nikolai's guys to us unintentionally."

"We have to warn him." Brooke sounded calm, but Tyler knew she was anything but.

"Jennifer, send him a message. Tell him I'll meet him at his hotel tomorrow afternoon at fifteen hundred." Tyler didn't want Brooke to have to play any part in this. "If you tell him I'm meeting him, he'll know it's important."

Brooke stood. "If he's being tailed, they could make you. What's to stop them from following you back here? What's to stop them from killing you in the street?"

Fair points. "Jennifer, rent me a room under a different alias than the one the CIA originally made for me. When I check in, I'll call and give you the room number and you can pass it along to the captain. I'll meet him there, talk to him, and we'll be gone before anyone knows what happened. If he is being tailed, the likelihood of the men being terribly sophisticated is pretty low. They aren't law enforcement. They won't be prepared to handle a quick sleight of hand. It will work." Tyler faced Brooke. "It will work."

Caden moved closer to the map and pointed to a third hotel. "Park at this hotel. It will throw them off if they're even slightly on to you."

Tyler nodded, still scanning the map. "Good idea."

Brooke still wasn't convinced. She crossed her arms and continued to shake her head. "You should send Caden. Her dark hair helps her blend in more. She's less likely to be noticed."

"I need Caden here. Deputy Director Martin is calling to give us an update on the mission at fifteen hundred tomorrow, the same time I'm meeting the captain. We need to see if Director Walker is on the call too. If he does have anything to do with this, I need to know that he won't be tracking the captain at that time. He'd want to hear firsthand what our status is and be able to ask questions if necessary. If he isn't on the call, then he probably isn't our mole, and isn't the one who sent us the original message. Martin has worked with Caden for years. They have a good relationship. He'll want to speak to her." Tyler knew none of this would help to ease Brooke's concern, but it was the most logical plan of action.

Brooke sat down behind her computer. "I'm going to map out the most direct routes and see if I can locate all the security cameras between here and there. You need to be as invisible as possible. You're also going to wear a hat and sunglasses. I want your face obstructed."

Tyler smiled. *That's my girl.* She sat at the desk as well and started creating a bullet point list of everything she needed to share with the captain. She couldn't take the chance of missing anything important.

Emma put her cards on the table and looked up at Dylan, finally allowing herself to smile. "Gin."

Dylan's eyes grew large as she looked between the table and her own hand. She groaned. "Do you have a secret life as a card shark?"

Emma marked down their scores. "Well, that's the eighth time I've beaten you. So maybe it's a profession I should consider."

Dylan tossed her cards on to the table and picked up her wine glass. "I'm not playing with you anymore. You must be cheating."

Emma started putting the cards back into their packaging. "This waiting around thing isn't so bad."

"Enjoy it while it lasts. As soon as we get the word, things will speed up with more ferocity than anyone is ever ready for," Dylan said.

"Is that how you like things?"

Dylan took a deep breath. "No. Believe it or not, I don't like it when plan after plan implodes. I like a certain amount of chaos, but not constant disorder." Dylan took their glasses and went back to the kitchen to refill them.

Emma chewed on her thumb, not sure where she was taking the conversation, even when she said it. "I just meant you seem to like intensity, danger, and adventure."

Dylan handed Emma her glass and sat next to her. "You've managed to make a lot of correct assumptions about me."

Emma let Dylan's statement bounce around in her head for a moment and watched Dylan take another sip from her glass. She couldn't stop herself from staring at Dylan's wine tinted lips. She wondered what her lips tasted like now. She made assumptions about Dylan because she couldn't stop thinking about her. She wanted to know everything. Emma wanted to know what made her sad, happy, and what kept her up at night. She wanted to know what Dylan was afraid of and how she pushed through the moments that scared her the most. She wanted to truly understand her. That was unprofessional, and terrifying, and so many other words she couldn't think of right now. So she stopped thinking.

She reached out and touched Dylan's hand draped over the back of the couch. She marveled at the way Dylan's fingers seemed to search for her when they grew close. Emma softly stroked the back of Dylan's hand, and she felt a jolt in her stomach when she saw the goose bumps travel up Dylan's arm. She looked up, and her eyes met the deep rich brown in Dylan's. Dylan's eyes were soulfully deep, and Emma felt herself start to get lost in them.

"Emma," Dylan whispered. "I don't think we should—"

"No." Emma stopped her. "I don't want to talk about all the reasons we shouldn't. I want to. I want this. I've never felt like this before." Emma had been battling with herself over her feelings from the start. There were plenty of reasons that the two of them shouldn't venture down this path. Valid, logical reasons that were based on facts. Emma didn't care about those reasons. She cared about the way she felt alive when Dylan was close. She cared about the way her skin prickled when they touched. She cared about the way her body seemed to be drawn to Dylan, like a magnetic force of some kind.

Dylan grasped her hand and pulled her closer. "You're feeling this way because you've never been in danger before. That sensation does weird things to people. You won't want this when it's all said and done."

Emma put a hand on Dylan's face, loving the way her cheek felt in her hand. The softness of Dylan's skin and the tightening of her jaw was hypnotic. "I'm not worried about then. For once, I just want to worry about right now."

Dylan looked like she was going to say something else, but Emma didn't give her a chance. She was done talking, done questioning, done playing it safe all the time. She was always a careful and predictable girl. She wanted to be something else entirely, even if it didn't mean forever. Even if all they had was right now, that would be good enough.

Emma leaned forward, and Dylan didn't back away. "Kiss me," Emma whispered against Dylan's lips.

If there was any hesitation in Dylan's response, it was swallowed whole with the fevered kiss Dylan gave her. Dylan was gentle, but Emma could feel the passion simmering below the surface. Emma pulled Dylan's bottom lip between her teeth and reveled in the moan that escaped from her. Dylan's breath was hot against her lips, labored and quick.

Dylan ended the kiss and put her hands on Emma's face. She kissed her forehead, her cheek, and then stood. Emma was about to protest when Dylan held her hand out. Dylan led her down the hallway to her bedroom. Once inside, Dylan kissed her again.

"Are you sure about this?" Dylan made her way up Emma's neck to her ear with soft kisses.

Emma wanted to scream that she was, that she'd never been more sure of anything, but her body was so consumed with desire all she could do was nod. Dylan slid her hands under Emma's shirt, caressing her back. Dylan's hands were so careful, so intentional that Emma was afraid she'd stop altogether. Her fingertips were like drops of water on a summer day. They left her wanting more and relishing in the momentary reprieve from thirst. Emma loved the way Dylan's palms felt against her. She wanted more, and she wanted it now.

Emma pulled her shirt up over her head and took off her bra. She wanted Dylan to know that she wanted this, wanted her. She couldn't form the words, so she hoped this would drive the point home. She left herself exposed, needing her to see that she was offering herself to her. She'd gladly take whatever Dylan was willing to give, and Dylan seemed to get the message. Dylan picked her up, and Emma wrapped her legs around her waist. She walked them over to the bed and let Emma fall onto it. She reached for Dylan, wanting her on top of her, needing her to be closer. Dylan removed her shirt and bra and crawled on top of Emma. She trailed her mouth down Emma's body, starting from her neck and moving to her shoulders and collarbone. Emma ran her fingers through Dylan's hair as she stopped at her chest. Dylan nipped and sucked Emma's breasts. It ignited every nerve ending in Emma's body. She felt like her skin was on fire, scorching under Dylan's mouth and touch. Emma had imagined what it would be like to be affected this way, to have someone pay such close attention to her body. But none of those fleeting musings did Dylan any justice.

Dylan's lips carved a path of heat and desire, leaving Emma wanting more. She felt like she needed the brief, intentional touches to sustain her. As Dylan kept moving down, Emma felt her already hot body flare again. Dylan ran her finger under the shorts Emma was wearing and slowly coaxed them off her hips. Dylan took off her underwear next with the same intensity and unwavering intention she'd done with everything else. The sudden cool air and the look of pure lust on Dylan's face caused her to shudder.

Dylan kissed the insides of her legs, taking her time. Emma could hear herself breathing, the noises escaping her lips. They weren't noises she'd ever heard herself make, and the realization of that ignited her body further. Dylan continued to lavish her sensitive skin with kisses and small nips. Dylan moved her mouth to Emma's center, taking her in. With each wonderful whirl of her tongue, Emma could feel the orgasm building. The sensation started low in her belly, moving its way up her body, a flood wanting to devour the landscape in its path. Dylan kept pushing her, urging her closer and closer until there was nowhere left to go. Emma dangled over the edge of a cliff of pure pleasure, wanting to prolong the sensation, while at the same time experiencing the guttural need of wanting to surrender. The orgasm washed over her, consuming her. The first wave made her gasp and call out Dylan's name. The second one was marked with quivering muscles and labored breathing she didn't even bother to try to control.

When it finally subsided, Dylan crawled up next to her. Emma wanted to explain what she was feeling, but her mind was an empty vessel. Dylan kissed her cheeks and wrapped an arm around her waist, pulling her closer. Emma stared into Dylan's dark eyes. They were heavy, still filled with lust and need. Emma wanted to make Dylan feel the way she just had. She wanted to show Dylan how much she wanted her. She had to stop herself from crying out in pleasure when she slid her hand down and found her eager wetness.

Dylan dug her fingertips into Emma's back as she slid inside her. Dylan was so close, it would be easy to push her over the edge, but Emma wanted to give her as much as she'd just received. Dylan was breathing and moaning in her ear, urging Emma to keep going. With each thrust of Emma's fingers, the intensity in Dylan's embrace increased. Emma turned her palm up, using it to massage Dylan's clit. Dylan's body tensed, the soft but powerful walls around Emma's fingers contracted, and Dylan cried out, her voice shaking.

Emma didn't move away immediately. She kissed Dylan's shoulders, enjoying the salty taste of Dylan's skin on her lips. Once Dylan's breathing was back to normal, Emma pulled her hand out from between them and wrapped her arms around her. She kissed Dylan's forehead and wiped the hair away from her eyes.

"I wasn't expecting that," Dylan said.

Her voice was quiet, and Emma wasn't sure if she'd meant to say it out loud. "What?" Emma kissed her chin.

"You."

Emma didn't want to move, worried that any change might disrupt or alter what they'd just shared. She listened as Dylan's breathing slowed and became rhythmic. She nuzzled a little closer to Dylan as she let herself drift to sleep. Her last lucid thoughts were that if this were a dream, she didn't want to have to wake up ever again.

CHAPTER TWENTY-THREE

Captain Hart sat on the bed. "I can't meet with Nikolai Orlav. Do you have any idea what that would look like? He could easily record the conversation and use it against the country. Or he could have me killed." He was probably saying it as much to himself as he was to Tyler.

"No one thinks it's a good idea," Tyler said. "But we need to do something. We're running out of time."

She hadn't been sure what to expect when she'd laid out all the information in front of him. She double-checked her list, relieved to see she'd covered everything. She knew Calvin Hart to be brilliant, a good strategist, and someone to be trusted. She also understood that his position opened him up to vulnerabilities the rest of the team didn't have to deal with. His presence in any given situation was an asset in the right situation, or a liability in the wrong situation.

"Let's approach this from a different angle. How would you handle it if it were Styles or me in your position? What would you advise?" Tyler tried to put an upbeat tone to her voice, wanting to snap him out of his haze.

He nodded, seeming to think about his response. "I'd say we need to put Nikolai off until the night of the gala. I'd say to stall him until we could get everyone in place. I'd have Prey convince him to meet somewhere else, divide his forces. Bring the mole to the other location with him when he comes to get me. That would be the only way we'd have a chance at grabbing O'Brien, catching the mole red-handed, and helping Prey either disappear or grab Nikolai."

Tyler sighed. "I figured you would say that."

He looked at her. "You don't like that option?"

Tyler shook her head. "I think it's our only option. It's just still not a very good one."

"No, it's not." Calvin pinched the bridge of his nose. "What did the others say when you ran it by them?"

"I haven't yet. Brooke isn't going to like it."

He patted her on the back. "She'll go along with whatever you decide."

Tyler wasn't sure how any of this would end. If she was going to say something to him, it had to be now.

"I'm going to marry her."

He looked a little surprised at first, but then a smile crept across his face. "I figured it would happen."

"You'll be there?"

He nodded and then walked toward the door. "I wouldn't miss it." He turned and looked at her. "I'll wait for your update. Until then I'll stay in heavily secured locations or in my hotel. I have a big day to attend. Let's be sure I'm around to get to it."

Once he left, she allowed herself a moment of relief. She'd never needed his permission to marry Brooke, but she wanted his approval. Now all that was left to do was ask Brooke. She wasn't sure which was more nerve-wracking, not knowing what Brooke would say, or not knowing if they'd all make it out of Russia in one piece.

Dylan did her best to push the previous night's activities from her mind while she sat in the control room waiting for Tyler to return. Emma sat across from her with the other computer analyst. She was hard at work, pointing to something on the computer screen with a pencil she'd just pulled from her hair. She kept seeing flashes of Emma's skin in her mind, the way she'd felt and tasted, the way she'd called out her name.

"Prey!" Caden kicked her chair, causing her to spin around.

"Yeah," Dylan said, trying to shake herself out of the daydream.

"What the hell, Prey? I said your name like five times." Caden cocked an eyebrow. "Everything okay?"

Dylan rubbed her face. "Yeah, just lost in thought. What's up?"

"When do you come back stateside?" Caden tossed a tennis ball in the air.

She felt Emma watching her now, but she didn't look. "I don't know. I don't know what my next assignment will be. Hell, it depends on how this one turns out. If by some miracle I'm not dead and my cover is still in play, I'll get to finish my mission. If not..." She shrugged.

Caden shook her head. "Man, I couldn't do what you do. I wouldn't be able to handle not knowing when I'm coming or going. Not to mention it makes it impossible to have any kind of real life."

Emma's eyes were still on her, but Dylan focused on Caden. "It has its challenges, for sure. There are also a few perks. I get to live in different places, learn new cultures, be a different person all the time." She hadn't meant to say the last part and hoped Caden wouldn't focus on it.

"Plus, there's no shortage of cute women at your disposal." Caden smirked and wiggled her eyebrows.

Jennifer threw a pen at Caden. "Ignore her, she's not housebroken yet."

Caden looked as if she was going to say something when the buzzer sounded, alerting everyone to someone being at the property. Brooke was visibly relieved and sank down into her chair when they saw that it was Tyler. Dylan looked at Emma. They hadn't discussed anything about what the future might or might not look like for them. They'd woken up, had sex again, then went about their day. They'd eaten, worked out, showered, and come here. Dylan had been expecting a significant discussion. She'd expected Emma to want answers to establish expectations. But neither of them initiated the conversation, though the silence hung heavy between them. Dylan would typically have been thrilled. This was exactly how she liked things—comfortable, with no expectations. She should be relieved, but instead, she felt sad. Dylan searched Emma's eyes, and they held the same uncertainty she was feeling. They needed to have a conversation, but it would have to wait. Their attention turned to Tyler when she came through the door.

Dylan watched Brooke again. Her eyes raked over Tyler, not out of lust, but confirmation she was okay. When she seemed satisfied, she sat back in her chair and let out a long breath.

"I have a plan I think will work, but it's going to take some manipulation on your part, Dylan." Tyler threw the baseball cap she'd been wearing onto the table and removed her sunglasses.

"My job usually does," Dylan said. "What's up?"

Tyler grabbed a marker from the table and went to the whiteboard. "Step one, convince O'Brien and Nikolai that we're dead. Step two, convince Nikolai that you've arranged for Captain Hart to meet you under the premise that you haven't killed Brooke, but instead have her captive. Step three, tell Nikolai you can't get him there before Thursday evening without raising suspicion within the military ranks. Hart has dozens of meetings he's scheduled to attend and people would question where he is. Step four, have Nikolai bring the mole with him so he can watch Captain Hart be flipped. Step five, we get the mole, Nikolai, and O'Brien. O'Brien will still be at the party. This will divide his personal security, making her easier to access. This will also give you an opportunity to actually take Nikolai. He wants to flip Hart, but you were hoping to flip Nikolai. We'll outnumber him, and you'll never get an opportunity like this again." She capped the pen and turned to look at the room. There was plenty left to figure out, but the bones of the plan were clear.

The room was so quiet that Dylan thought she might have momentarily lost her hearing. If it wasn't for the soft humming of computers, she could've convinced herself of it.

Caden spoke first. "I don't know if you should be promoted or if you're going to get us all killed."

Tyler put her hands on her hips. "Yeah, it will definitely be one of those two outcomes."

Caden shrugged. "Well, I'm in."

Tyler looked at Dylan expectantly. "You know Nikolai. Will this work?"

Dylan pushed her chair out and walked to the whiteboard. She uncapped a pen and started making notes next to the outlined steps. "I'll need to take pictures of each of you as proof of death. Next, I'll need some kind of note from Hart, in his handwriting, dictating where and when to meet. I'll give that to him Wednesday afternoon. He'll send guys there ahead of time, so we'll need to be prepared for that. Nikolai won't want to draw needless attention to himself, so he won't make a move on Hart before the agreed upon time. You'll have to take O'Brien near a service exit. We'll need blueprints of the hotel."

"I'll get the blueprints." Emma started typing furiously on her computer.

"How many guys will he send ahead of time?" Tyler was staring at the words on the whiteboard as if the answer was already there.

Dylan wrote next to the step. "Five, maybe six. He won't take any chances if he's going out in public like that."

"There you go." Emma pointed to the large screen next to the whiteboard.

Caden came up between Dylan and Tyler. She pointed to a service entrance that led to the parking garage. "How do we get O'Brien here without sounding any alarm bells?"

"I can do it," Emma said. Everyone turned and stared at her, but she continued. "I'll make sure she sees me with Dylan before then, so she'll recognize me. I'll find a way to get her there."

Dylan pointed to the map. "It's too risky. There'll be armed security coming and going from the service entrance. They check in every fifteen minutes. That's a tight time frame. There's no way you can get rid of all four of them and get O'Brien there without raising suspicion. Not without being spotted and taken out. They've got your pictures, after all."

"But I can," Brooke said. There was a short intake of breath from Tyler, but Brooke continued. "I'll handle the men on the garage side first, then take the two inside. They won't see me as a threat, so I have the element of surprise. Emma can get O'Brien to the door, and we'll toss O'Brien into the van and get the hell out of there."

Tyler turned and stared at Brooke. Her jaw muscles were clenching, and she rolled her shoulders. "Okay." Tyler turned her attention to Dylan. "That leaves me, you, and Caden at the meeting location with Nikolai."

Emma pointed to the screen again. "Here. There's a shipping facility a half mile from the hotel. I saw in Nikolai's work-up that he uses this place for business. He'll be comfortable there. It will cause him to be less suspicious."

Dylan nodded. She'd been there before.

Caden crossed her arms, still staring at the screen. "Tyler and I should be able to take out Nikolai's guys. Captain Hart will need to get Director Walker talking, and the captain will have to record it." She turned and looked at Tyler and Dylan. "This will be your one chance to get Nikolai."

Dylan chewed on her lip. "If we can flip him to our side, we'll have an inside track on some of the world's most heinous criminal activity. It would be an absolute game changer. If he refuses, I'm sure the CIA can drop him in a hole somewhere. No one will be around to witness us taking him, so no one will be looking for him. He'll know that. He values his own life above anything else. Nikolai would rather be a CIA asset than die alone and forgotten."

Caden moved closer. "Do you think we can pull it off?"

Dylan ran her hand through her hair. "We have to try. We may never get an opportunity like this again."

Dylan could hear the confidence in her voice, but it didn't reach her stomach. If this didn't go as planned, it could very well mean the end of her. It could mean the end for all of them. She had this one glimmer of opportunity, a chance she'd never thought she'd get, and she had no choice but to take it. She looked at Emma, who had turned a ghostly shade of white. She wanted to tell her everything would be okay, that she'd be okay. Instead, she said nothing. It wasn't a promise she could make in a game with stakes this high.

"So, we know for sure Walker is the mole?" Tyler asked Caden.

Caden snapped and pointed at her. "That's right, you weren't here. Yeah, the call with Deputy Director Martin only lasted a few minutes. We told him that we'd stood down and have been waiting for further instructions. Walker was all up in the mix though, asking who we were working with over here, if we had any assets, if we'd made any contacts. It was super weird and totally out of the norm. Even Martin looked confused." She chuckled. "For being head of the CIA, he sure isn't very sneaky." She pointed to Dylan and Emma. "We made sure to keep them out of the frame. He doesn't know we're working with anyone else. He also thinks we're at a safe house northeast of here. We made sure of it. Emma doctored a few of the computer files to make it seem legit if he were to go poking around. He expects us home next week, after we've done some sightseeing."

Dylan walked back over to the desk and picked up her phone. "Are any of you really good with makeup?"

Brooke raised her hand. "I am."

Dylan pointed to them. "Good, I need you to make some really convincing corpses."

Dylan did her best to push down her unease. This was a good plan, or at least it was the best option they had. If it all worked out, it would be a win all the way around. So why did it feel like a massive loss?

CHAPTER TWENTY-FOUR

Emma felt sick to her stomach as she looked at the four women lying across the compound in various poses. Dylan was snapping pictures of their bodies. They used ketchup on either their chests or backs to try to replicate gunshot wounds. She wondered if O'Brien would believe that Dylan had managed to kill all of them. All these years, she'd played cat and mouse with these women, and now it would be over. Assuming everything went to plan. *Of course, she'll believe it. She wants it to be true, so her mind will fill in the gaps.* She watched Dylan. Was that what Emma's mind was doing? Did she want things between them to be real so badly that she was filling in the blanks?

Emma shook her head, pushing away the thoughts. She couldn't think about any of this right now. These next few days would require her full attention. They couldn't afford any mistakes. Emma was going with Dylan to Nikolai's house tomorrow. Carol would be there, and Dylan wanted to make sure she saw her again. It would be easier to lure her away during the gala if she recognized her.

"Damn! We really do look dead!" Caden laughed and pointed to the pictures on the phone.

Jennifer slapped her arm. "It's not funny. This is terrifyingly realistic."

"It's just a picture, Jen." Caden wrapped her arm around Jennifer and kissed the top of her head.

Emma was still watching the casual intimacy Jennifer and Caden shared when Dylan snapped her out of her reflection.

"You ready to go?"

Emma nodded because she didn't trust her voice at that moment. She walked toward the others to say good night.

"You okay, Emma?" Brooke looked concerned.

"Me? Yes, just mentally preparing."

"Okay," Brooke said, but her eyes indicated she wasn't convinced. "We'll see you in two days. If you want to go over anything before then, just call."

"Thank you," Emma said. She didn't know if she should hug Brooke, so she didn't.

She said the rest of her good-byes and walked with Dylan to the bus stop. From there, they'd get the car and go to the apartment. Emma's stomach tightened at the thought of being in Dylan's bed again. It wasn't that she didn't want to be in Dylan's bed again, she did. She just didn't know if that was a path they should continue down with all the uncertainty surrounding their lives. She wanted to talk to Dylan but didn't know how. She'd never been in anything like this. She wouldn't even know where to start.

They made idle chitchat for the next hour, biding their time until they were in the safety of Dylan's apartment once again. When they finally got there, Dylan turned on music and went to the fridge, retrieving the wine they'd previously started.

Dylan handed her a glass. "Here's to hoping this works and we don't die."

Emma clanged the glass out of habit. "Do you really think one of us could die?"

Dylan sat on the couch and motioned for Emma to do the same. "You do know how serious this all is? How dangerous these men are?"

Emma sipped her wine. "Yes, of course. I just don't like to think about it."

Dylan shrugged. "Thinking about it helps me stay focused. If I understand the worst outcome is a real possibility, I can prepare."

"Does that just go for your work or your personal life too?"

Dylan scooted back, putting some space between them. "Do you want to talk about what happened?"

"I think we should." Emma decided she'd be completely honest in this conversation. Not just because it was how she preferred to do things, but because she might not get another chance.

"I don't regret what happened," Dylan said.

Emma raised her eyebrows. "Good to know."

"No, I mean—" She sighed, seeming frustrated. "Damn it, I'm not very good at this. I don't regret what happened because I like you. I like being around you. I like the way you talk, the way you smell. I like the way you laugh, how smart you are, and how you're a little awkward yet surprisingly brave at the best moments."

Emma felt her body tingle, a reaction she was growing used to when it came to Dylan. She touched her hand. "You like me?"

Dylan laughed. "Yes, Emma, I like you. I wish we could be more. I wish we'd met under different circumstances. I wish things could be different. But the truth is, when this is over, I'll have to disappear. Even if we don't flip Nikolai, the next pakhan will be looking for me. He'll want answers. If we do flip Nikolai, I'll need to get as far away from him as possible. The CIA will tuck me away somewhere until they need me again. It's not fair of me to start something with you when I know that I can't be there for you after this."

Emma's first instinct was to pull her hand away, but she left it there despite the hurt she felt. "Are you even going to ask me what I want?"

Dylan picked up her hand and kissed it. "It doesn't matter either of us want. It can't happen. Not beyond this mission. That's the life I accepted when I agreed to this job."

Emma knew Dylan was making sense. Everything she was saying was true. Unfortunately, the message wasn't being received by her body. Her hand was still warm from where Dylan had kissed it. Her fingers ached to trace Dylan's strong features. Her body wanted Dylan, regardless of what her mind said.

"I understand our limitations. I'll take what I can get. If it's only for this limited time, I'm okay with that." Emma ignored the voices in her head, warning her to stop talking. They were screaming advisories, trying to protect the heart her body had no issue betraying.

Dylan's features softened, and she moved closer. "Are you sure? I don't want to hurt you."

Emma leaned closer, her mouth so close to Dylan's she felt the hitch in Dylan's breath. Her mind screamed one more warning, but she ignored it. She closed the finite distance between their mouths. She heard herself groan with the relief and excitement her body felt from their contact. She sought Dylan out greedily, wanting to feel every part of her. She wanted to memorize every inch of her. She wanted it all seared into her memory. Every curve, every muscle, every scar, she'd keep them with her. She wanted to be able to play back these feelings, these sensations, the smells, the noises, at a later time. She'd need them to be able to get through. She needed to know she'd have them later, when she no longer had Dylan.

Tyler watched Brooke wipe the remainder of her makeup off in the mirror. Seeing the pictures Dylan had taken left a pit in her stomach. She knew they weren't real, but she couldn't dispel the images all the same. They needed O'Brien to believe Brooke was dead. She wouldn't play ball with them otherwise. Carol believed they'd lie to Brooke's father, pretending she was alive to draw him out, only to reveal she was dead in order to prove they could get to anyone. Tyler was glad it was Dylan and not her that had to keep all of this straight. Pretending had never been one of her strong suits.

Brooke pulled on her tank top and came to sit next to her on the bed. "What's going on in that mind of yours?" Brooke ran her fingers through Tyler's hair.

Tyler chose her next words carefully, not wanting to give the impression that she didn't have faith in her. "Taking out four guys can get a bit squirrely. What's your plan?"

Brooke stroked Tyler's cheek. "You asking as my girlfriend or the ranking officer on this mission?"

Tyler kissed her palm. "Both. I'd ask anyone on my team what their plan was if the odds were four against one."

"We'll take in a delivery van as cover to get into the parking garage. I'll wait until the fifteen-minute mark when they check in to allow myself the most time. I'll hop out of the van to show them what's in the back. When one of them is turned to open the back, I'll use the succinylcholine to take out the first guy and administer a dose to the next one before the first even hits the ground. I know that I have to inject it directly into their necks for it to work in under a minute, so I'll need to be fast and careful. It will completely paralyze them for approximately six minutes." Tyler nodded her approval, and she continued. "I'll drag the bodies to the side, then knock on the door to the hotel. I'll move outside his peripheral, forcing him to step into the garage. When he does, I'll paralyze him too. The other guard will follow suit and he'll be met with the same outcome. Then, hopefully, Emma will have O'Brien in place and we'll paralyze her too. Then we'll throw her in the back of the van. We drive straight to the empty field in Moskovskaya Oblast, sixty-five klicks south of Moscow. It shouldn't take us more than one hour and fifty-two minutes. We'll be picked up by a Sikorsky UH-60 Black Hawk. That transport will take us to Poland, and we'll go home from there."

Tyler traced her thumb over Brooke's palm. "And how long do you wait for us before you go?"

Brooke stared at her, tears starting to fill her eyes. "Eight minutes."

Tyler placed her finger under Brooke's chin, forcing her to make eye contact. "You can't wait longer. That helo can hide from radar, but it's not invisible. If anyone notices it, they'll call it in, and eight minutes is the response time. If you're not out of there, we're done."

"I know." Brooke wiped a tear away from her eye. She sighed. "You and Caden will start firing on the meeting. Dylan will return fire as if she's protecting Nikolai from the attack. She'll shove him into the car by himself and take him to the alternative safe house. Once they arrive, CIA reinforcements will meet her there and work on turning him into an asset. Dad will take Walker into custody and bring him to the embassy in the car he drove to the meeting location. Jennifer will stay behind and run surveillance through the city, hotel, and street security cameras. She'll also monitor their communications, keep us abreast of everything that's happening and their whereabouts. She'll leave immediately after we board the helo for the US Embassy in Moscow. Once she's there, she'll be put on transport to head home and meet us back in the States." She looked down at her hands. "So, there're only about one million things that could go wrong."

"You know I'll always find a way to come home to you, right?" Tyler had told her this dozens of times before, but she wanted her to remember it now more than ever.

Brooke nodded. "Yes."

Tyler slid off the bed and knelt in front of her, placing her hands on Brooke's knees. "We met during one of the most confusing times in my life. After being hurt in Iraq, I didn't know what I was going to do with my life. I'd never known anything but military service. I didn't know what my direction would be, and I felt helpless. Then I met you. You were smart, fierce, and were so full of tenacity, it caught me off guard."

Brooke kissed her. "You tried to play hard to get."

"I did. You were off-limits. More than that, I thought you deserved better than me. I was a mess. But you've always felt like home. I don't thank you for that enough." She pulled the ring from her pocket and almost laughed at the way her hands were trembling. "I can't promise you that I'll never make mistakes. I can't promise that I won't do things you don't understand or that won't upset you. I *can* promise that I will never hurt you intentionally. I promise that I'll love you every day, for the rest of my life." She took a deep breath and looked up at Brooke's smiling face. "Brooke, will you marry me?"

Brooke covered her mouth with her hands and started to cry. Her hands were trembling with so much force, Tyler had to hold her left hand steady as she slid the ring onto her finger. Brooke grabbed her and kissed her, mumbling her acceptance to the proposal against her lips over and over again.

The elation was all-consuming. Tyler felt grateful, joyous, and so filled with love she thought she might explode. Brooke would be her forever, and there was nothing she had ever wanted more.

Chapter Twenty-five

Dylan and Emma waited in the entryway for Ivan. He'd gone to announce their arrival to Nikolai, leaving them with a few moments to themselves. Emma had her face tilted up, admiring the large stained glass windows. The different colors were reflecting off her face, and Dylan got momentarily lost in her admiration. Emma must have felt her looking because she dropped her eyes, settling on Dylan.

"You're beautiful." Dylan mouthed the words, wanting to keep the moment private.

Emma blushed and turned her attention to Ivan, who was coming back down the hallway full of purpose.

"Sasha, Nikolai will see you." He turned toward Emma. "You can wait in the parlor with me."

Dylan took several deep breaths as she headed for Nikolai's office. She needed to pull this off. She needed to be convincing. She needed this to work. Not just for her sake, but for the rest of the team. This was the first domino in a long line necessary for their success.

Dylan entered Nikolai's office and was surprised to see Bogdan sitting next to Carol. He shot her a look that left no room to question his feelings about her. He detested Dylan as much as she did him.

"Sasha, where is your little whore?" Bogdan smiled when he said it, but she could tell from the look in his eyes, it was meant to be a dig.

"I haven't seen your wife in ages, Bogdan. You should check with your brother." Dylan made sure not to smile when she spoke. She had no need to hide her feelings. She didn't work for him.

"That's enough, you two," Nikolai said as he drained the brown liquid from his glass. "Sasha, where are you with locating those women?"

Dylan opened her phone and pulled up the pictures she'd chosen as the most realistic. "It's handled."

Nikolai picked up the phone and scrolled for a few moments. "Where were they?"

Dylan and Tyler had already agreed to give him some information but not the truth. The CIA had another safe house in a different part of the countryside. One that hadn't been used in quite a few years, but would work perfectly for the cover story.

Dylan sat in the chair closest to Carol. "Safe house northeast of here. I left a message at the location for Calvin Hart. He'll go there when he hasn't heard from them." She made sure Nikolai met her eyes before she continued. "I told him the only way he'd see his daughter again was to meet with us and that I'd be in touch. I also explained that if he notified anyone else, it would be the end for him and his daughter."

"You should have brought him to me, Sasha. The sooner the better."

"I couldn't drag him in off the street. He's in a very visible position. You wouldn't want me to attract any undue attention. It would be terrible for business." Dylan cocked an eyebrow. She hoped her expression would articulate that he should already know what she was saying. Making someone feel foolish worked well as a gag. If they didn't kill you for it.

Nikolai didn't seem pleased with the last bit of information. His eyes crinkled, and he frowned. "What assurances do you have that he isn't on the phone with Langley right now, setting us up?"

Dylan cocked her head. "Your mole would tell you, wouldn't he?"

Carol took the phone from Nikolai and scrolled through the pictures. At first, her face was contemplative, and then it split into a wide smile. "I spoke with him yesterday. He was in contact with the women a few days ago, but they haven't spoken since. He did tell me about the safe house location, in case we had trouble finding them. It seems to match where Sasha says she found them." She handed the phone back to Dylan, giddy with excitement. "Where are the bodies? I'd love to see them."

Dylan forced herself not to recoil in disgust over Carol's excitement. "The river. I dumped them there immediately after."

"Pity. I would've loved to spit on them," Carol said.

The smile on her face told Dylan that she meant it.

"I am curious, though, how you managed to get to them. Many people have been trying for years without success."

Dylan knew this was a potential question and was glad she'd prepared. "They felt safe where they were comfortable. I hit these two first." She pointed to Caden and Tyler. "While they were out for a run around the property." She opened the pictures of Jennifer and Brooke. "These two were inside, typing away on their computers. They never saw me coming."

"Where are the computers now?" Carol leaned closer to Dylan.

"In the river with them. I didn't want to take any chances. Who knows what kind of software was loaded on there? I didn't want to lead anyone back here, to Nikolai." Dylan forced herself to remain in the same spot, despite her mind and body screaming to increase the space between her and Carol.

"There you go." Nikolai hit his desk and pointed at Carol. "Now, you bring me this mole. I need him to secure the deal with Calvin Hart. I want to make sure I have these men in my pocket before we start the next stage of our operation."

Carol dipped her head in acknowledgment. "I'll speak to him. He gets into town soon. I'll arrange the meeting."

Dylan's ears were burning, but she didn't want to seem too anxious. "What next stage?"

Nikolai shot Bogdan a look and pointed to the door. "Carol, let me know when your contact arrives. Help yourself to some pastries before you go."

Carol stood and headed for the door. When she walked past Dylan, she placed a hand on her shoulder and squeezed. "Thank you."

Dylan acknowledged her with a nod but said nothing. A moment later, she was alone with Nikolai and Bogdan. Bogdan pulled a cigar from his jacket pocket and lit it. Smoke started to billow in the room as he brought the cigar to life, and Dylan focused all her attention on not choking.

Nikolai walked over to the bar in the corner and poured everyone a drink. "We have a large shipment of girls coming into town over the next few days. I need to get them turned over within a week. I already have buyers for them but need to get them shipped." Nikolai handed both her and Bogdan a glass. "Bogdan is taking care of the shipping arrangements, but I need you to find a place to store them until they're ready to go."

Dylan tried to ignore the words he was using to describe human beings. "How many?"

Bogdan snorted. "What does it matter?"

Dylan glared at him, aggravated by his stupidity. "I need to know how many women I need to accommodate to do my job."

Nikolai took a sip from his cup. "About thirty. They're all between the ages of nine to fourteen. So, they won't need much."

Dylan felt her stomach tighten at the descriptors. These weren't women, these were children. Children who were being sold into sex slavery. Perhaps they were born into a family without means or lost their parents. Maybe they'd been stolen, victims of being at the wrong place at the wrong time. It didn't matter. They didn't deserve this, no one did. Human beings were traded like commodities and being sold to the highest bidders. She hated that she'd never been able to rid the world of men like them.

Emma tried to ignore the way Ivan looked at her while she busied herself getting a cappuccino. He watched her like it was a game. The intensity in his stare was unnerving, and she contemplated how she'd ended up here. She wasn't trained to be doing things like this. Hell, she wasn't prepared to do a whole lot except break open encrypted communication and develop software to eventually replace her at work. She'd figured out in her first few days on this assignment that she needed to be flexible in order to succeed. It pushed her out of her comfort zone, made her deal with her anxiety differently, and brought out skills she didn't know she had. Unfortunately, it took coming here and falling for Dylan to make her think she could actually do these things. *Wait. Fall for Dylan?* Had she fallen for her? She closed her eyes and focused on the cappuccino in her hand. *November eighth is National Cappuccino Day. Kopi Luwak is considered to be the rarest and most expensive coffee in the world. It is grown in Indonesia, and is fifty dollars a cup. The first use of cappuccino in English was recorded in nineteen forty-eight in a work about San Francisco.*

Her internal meditation was interrupted by Carol O'Brien strolling into the room as if she owned the house. Her arrogance was obnoxious at best. Emma also understood that it was arrogance that would likely take her down. Carol's belief that everything should simply fall into place because that was how her life had always worked was her blind spot. Carol couldn't possibly imagine being outmaneuvered in the end; her brain would never allow that to process.

Carol waited for the cappuccino to finish filling her mug. "I'm sorry, I don't think we've ever been introduced. I'm Carol." She stuck out her hand.

Emma begrudgingly took her hand. "Nada. I'm here with Sasha."

"Oh?" Carol pulled her mug from the machine and took a seat next to Emma on the couch.

"I must say your English is excellent." Carol crossed her legs and turned toward Emma. "How do you know Sasha?"

"My nanny taught me English." Emma sipped her beverage and reminded herself that she needed Carol to like her enough to trust her. She smiled. "I'm a very good friend of Sasha's. I've been staying with her for the last few weeks."

"Have you now?" Carol's question was rhetorical. Emma could tell by the flatness in her voice. "Will you be attending the gala with her?"

"I hope so." Emma didn't want to sound too committed to any plan they might have. She knew Carol was smart and didn't want to give her more information than necessary. "Will you be attending?"

Carol picked up a pastry from the plate in front of them and took a bite. "Were you with Sasha a few days ago? When she went to the countryside?"

Emma noted that Carol evaded her question and now seemed to be trying to subtly figure out precisely who Emma was. "I was with her a few days ago, but I didn't go to the countryside. What was she doing there?"

Carol tilted her head slightly. "I haven't decided whether or not I believe you."

Emma felt the heat in her body rise. "Which part?"

Carol put her cup down on the table. "Any of it."

Emma could see this conversation was going off the rails quickly, but she wasn't sure how to recover from it. She replayed the last several minutes in her head. She'd done something to make Carol suspicious, but she couldn't pinpoint what that would have been. She was going to ask Carol to explain further, but she was saved by Dylan's entrance into the room.

Carol's expression changed, a smile replacing the scowl from a moment before. "Sasha, I want to thank you again for handling my situation with such precision." She stood and walked to Dylan, taking her hands. "I wish I'd known you years ago. You'd have saved me an awful lot of grief and a great deal of money."

Dylan smiled back at her, but it didn't reach her eyes. "You're welcome. Is there anything else I can do for you?"

Carol cocked an eyebrow and ran her hand up Dylan's chest to her neck. "Are there parameters regarding my request?"

Emma felt an unease spread through her body. Watching the way Carol touched Dylan, the way she looked at her, made Emma want to come across the room. Emma tried to swallow, her mouth suddenly dry. She was jealous. The sensation was unnerving the first time she'd felt it, but this time, the sensation was like a firebrand in her stomach.

Dylan moved around Carol and grabbed Emma's hand. "Have a nice day. If you need me, you have my number."

Carol's face indicated that she was less than thrilled with Dylan's rebuff. She stared after Dylan, looking confused. Emma assumed it was probably because no one ever turned her down. She had an overwhelming desire to stick her tongue out at her but thought better of it. She needed Carol to listen to her at the gala. Aggravating her wasn't going to help make that happen.

It felt good to be the one Dylan chose, even if it was for show. Emma couldn't remember when anyone had ever chosen her above anyone else, except for in the world of academia. Dylan held her hand with so much possessiveness, she almost let herself believe they were a couple. She let herself get lost in the idea of them being together, of them having a future together. She forced the thought from her mind when they got in the car and Dylan released her. Dylan wasn't hers. They'd share a few nights, a few stolen glances, and that would be it. She'd go home with a heart full of memories and nothing else to show for it.

CHAPTER TWENTY-SIX

Carol held her breath as she waited for Steven Walker to finish. He'd been thrusting on top of her for the last two minutes, but it felt like hours. Sweat from his face dripped onto her chest, and all she wanted was to push him off and get in the shower. He stunk like cologne and travel. He'd never been particularly attractive, and that was never clearer to her than in this moment. Soon, she'd no longer have any use for him, and she could finally end their ridiculous relationship.

He finished with a heavy sigh and rolled off her. "Bet you missed me?"

Carol moved off the bed so he wouldn't see her roll her eyes. "I'm going to take a shower."

Steven propped himself up on his side. "Want some company?"

"No." Carol didn't bother looking back at him. The thought of his skin touching hers again made her want to shiver in disgust.

Carol scrubbed herself with as much force as she could bear. She wanted his scent off her. She didn't want any remnants of their exchange clinging to her skin. *How long have you been doing this?* She leaned back against the shower wall, realizing the answer was, always. She'd been using her body, her sex, to get what she wanted for as long as she could remember. She hated herself for it. But more than that, she hated men like Steven. Men who traded sexual favors to allow women a seat at the table. It had been going on long before Carol and would continue long after she was gone. She had never had any aspirations to change the system; she just wanted it to work to her advantage.

She got out of the shower after she pulled herself together, dressed, and went out to the living room. Steven was lounging on her couch in sweats, reading his tablet, and having a drink.

He pointed to the table. "I poured you one." He put his tablet down. "Why don't you get me up to speed."

She picked up the glass, finished the contents in one gulp, and poured another. "Monroe, Styles, Hart, and Glass have been handled."

His back stiffened. "What do you mean?"

"Sasha, Nikolai's right hand, she took care of it." Carol sat down but kept the space between them abundant.

"Well, then that solves your problem. You can take off to Tahiti or wherever it was you wanted to spend the rest of your days," Steven said.

Carol ran her finger around the rim of the glass. "I had to give them something for the job. It wasn't money, and you won't like it."

"What could you possibly give them besides money?"

She took another sip of the alcohol, enjoying the way it warmed her chest. "You. Nikolai wants to speak with you." She almost laughed at the way his face turned red. "Well, you and Captain Calvin Hart."

Steven looked like he was going to come unglued. The veins in his neck bulged, and he vigorously wiped his hands over his face. "What the fuck, Carol? I'm here to meet with Hart. We have several meetings with diplomats over the next few days. He couldn't have possibly agreed to this. That man doesn't have a dishonest bone in his body."

She shrugged, enjoying his anger. "He thinks Nikolai has Brooke, that she's still alive. Is there a bigger motivator than your daughter?"

"What does that have to do with me?" He was up off the couch now, pacing.

"Nikolai is going to use you to convince Hart to work with him."

He moved quickly, grabbing her arm with such force, she knew it would leave a bruise. "And when he finds out his daughter is dead? Then what? This is the stupidest fucking plan you've ever hatched, and there have been some doozies."

She pulled her arm away and refrained from slapping him. "If he doesn't comply, his wife and sons will be next." She stood and got in his face enough for him to know she was serious, but not so much that he'd be inclined to strike her. "I don't understand what your problem is. You've done far worse to people. You've given orders to make people disappear. You've held people captive for longer than what's allowed. Hell, you've had people tortured. Now, what? You've suddenly grown a conscience about working with the Russians? Spare me, Steven." She took a step closer to him. "Don't forget, you knew about my plans to take out the president and vice president. You didn't care then. You knew I was breaking into the CIA training facility. You didn't care then, in fact, it got you your current position. This is how the world works. Stop acting like you don't know that. You helped create it for Christ's sake."

"I'm not going to work for some Russian mob boss. Hart isn't going to work for a Russian mob boss. You're so blinded by your need to get away that you haven't thought any of this through."

She pushed him backward, wanting distance between them. "You're a child. Agree to work with him, let me get away, then take him down. You'll be a damn hero, and I'll be free. Don't forget, if I go down for this, you do too. How do you think you'd fare in prison the rest of your life for treason? That is, if you aren't sentenced to death for treason. You don't have any other options."

He put his hands on his hips, leaning toward her. "Do you really think I'll let you dictate what I do?"

She allowed herself to laugh. "Now you have a small glimpse, just a passing knowledge, of what it's like to be me. Men like you have been dictating my entire life."

"I didn't realize you were such a victim, Carol." He stalked to the bedroom and came out dressed. "I hope you get everything that's coming to you, bitch."

"I'll text you with the time and place to meet."

He slammed the door without saying another word. If he weren't such a petulant child, she'd find the whole situation amusing. Everything was working out better than she could've ever hoped. She was so close to being free. She'd never take her place of power like she'd wanted, but a beach sure beat prison. She had no misgivings. She didn't think Hart would actually turn; it just wasn't her problem. Hart could turn Walker in for all she cared. In reality, she hoped that was exactly what happened. He could wail and proclaim her misdeeds from the rooftops for all she cared. She'd be long gone. Far out of the grasp of anyone who could touch her. Walker belonged behind bars, but she sure as hell didn't. She picked up her glass and finished the drink. A few more days and she'd finally be free.

CHAPTER TWENTY-SEVEN

Dylan knocked on the door to the hotel room. When Calvin Hart opened it, he popped his head out and looked up and down the hallway and pulled her inside.

"How do you know you weren't followed?" Captain Hart whispered like his room was bugged.

"There're a few guys following you, but they expect me to make contact. It doesn't matter though. They're in the lobby, and I took the service entrance. They don't know I'm here."

He nodded and took a deep breath. "Okay, what should I be expecting?"

Dylan pulled out the chair in front of the desk and sat down. "Nikolai is convinced I killed Tyler, Brooke, Caden, and Jennifer. He wants you and Walker to act as double agents of some kind. Keep him protected, look the other way, don't interfere with his affairs, that kind of thing. Nikolai believes that I've left a message for you at a different safe house, indicating that I have Brooke captive. He plans on using her to get you to meet with him. That's why I'm here. I need you to write a note saying that you agree, but it can't be until Thursday night." She pulled out her phone and showed it to him. "Use this address as the meeting location. Tyler, Caden, and I will be there for backup."

He did as he was asked. "What about O'Brien?"

"We have it worked out." She didn't want to tell him that Brooke would be going into the gala to help extract O'Brien. He didn't need to worry more than he already was. "I can't stay here long. You're going to have to trust me."

He handed her back a piece of paper with the words she'd requested. "I can't believe Walker has been working with O'Brien. I mean, I never liked the guy, but this is treason."

She put the note in a hotel envelope, sealed it, and put it in her pocket. "The only thing that is never surprising to me about people is how truly horrible so many of them are." She stood to leave. "You need to make sure you get this meeting recorded. One of the first things Nikolai is going to do is have you searched for weapons and recording devices. Tony designed this about a month ago." She handed him a pen. "It's a voice recorder, captures everything in a twenty-foot radius."

He took it. "Thanks." His voice was laced with frustration.

"It won't be detected if Nikolai scans you for listening devices, but it only lasts for about thirty minutes, so be cognizant of when you use it. Caden and Tyler will start firing down at the meeting, and I'll return fire so Nikolai will use me for protection. When his security has been neutralized, I'll push him into the car and take him to the other safe house. Merrick and a few of my other associates will be there waiting. During the commotion, you need to take Walker into custody. I assume, since you're a naval officer, you'll be able to handle this aspect. From there, take him to the embassy in Moscow. Jennifer will meet you at the embassy approximately an hour later. You and Walker aren't worth Nikolai losing his life, so he won't try to fight for either of you. Tyler and Caden will escape to another location and be evacuated with Brooke, Emma, and O'Brien."

"Do you think we'll pull this off?"

She stopped at the door and turned to face him. "I don't know." She smiled at him. "But we're going to give it a helluva try."

"The rest of the team, they're safe? They're doing okay?" He was searching her eyes, and she felt his desperation.

"They're fine. They're smart, detail oriented, and ready. Just let Caden and Tyler do their jobs." She rolled her shoulders, wanting to ask a favor, a feeling she wasn't accustomed to having. "I need you to do one more thing for me. There is a shipment of girls coming into town, about thirty of them. Nikolai plans on having them shipped all over the world. Sex slaves. It's my job to stash them until their ship date, which is next Tuesday. Before you leave Moscow, I need you to use your influence to stop this. I'm not sure if you notify the United Nations, Interpol, whoever, but they need help. I just want to make sure this is handled in case something goes wrong. I need to know these girls have a way out aside from me." She handed him a card with the address the girls would be at. "Please, don't leave without helping them."

He took the card from her. "I promise."

"Thank you." She hoped she'd done enough. She didn't want to leave something as crucial as this up to someone else, but she didn't have another choice. Sure, there would be more girls. There would always be more girls. But these girls, she could help.

An hour later, she found herself in Nikolai's office again. She needed to convince him that tomorrow was an acceptable time to meet. She needed him to believe her when she said she thought this was the best option. She needed to rely on the trust she'd built with Nikolai and the relationship they'd forged.

"I hope you have good news, Sasha." Nikolai pushed open the door and came to sit behind his desk.

Carol's voice came into the room next, followed by a man's she didn't recognize. She didn't have to recognize it to know who it was; she knew Director Walker would be sitting next to her a moment later. Her heart thumped in her chest, and she did her best to steady her face and body language. This was it, if she failed now, the whole mission would be over before it really started.

He held out his hand to Dylan. "Steven Walker, nice to meet you."

"Sasha." She didn't bother taking his hand, nor did she look at Carol. "I have news." She slid the envelope across Nikolai's desk.

Nikolai opened it and took a deep breath, clearly irritated. "He doesn't give orders. I give orders." He leaned forward and stared at Steven. "It seems Calvin Hart will not meet with me until tomorrow evening, and he even gave me an address. Tell me, Steven, am I being set up?"

Steven took the letter from Nikolai and read it. "I haven't heard anything about you from any of my guys. I assume he wants to meet tomorrow because we have a full day of discussions today with your government. If he didn't show up, it would raise suspicion."

Well, Steven is more helpful than I could've ever hoped for. I might not have to do much convincing. Dylan kept her expression impassive, like she had nothing to lose or gain from whatever the fallout there was.

"He believes we have his daughter, but he isn't interested in getting to her? He's willing to put it off? Doesn't make sense. Now I'm supposed to miss part of my party to accommodate him. Seems unusual for a desperate man." Nikolai crossed his arms, frustrated with the information.

Steven spoke before Dylan had a chance. "If he came now, he'd have to answer to quite a few people who are much higher ranking than he is. I think he's being careful to help his daughter."

Dylan added on to his sentiment. "If we meet him at this time, during the gala, it's also a good cover for you. Everyone will have seen you there for almost a full hour before. If for some reason things don't go well and we end up having to kill him, you'll have an alibi."

"What do I need an alibi for?" Nikolai glared at her.

She shrugged, wanting to seem as nonchalant as possible. "Two dead Homeland Security agents, two dead CIA computer analysts, and a dead US Navy captain. You don't want to be implicated for that, not that I think the bodies will ever be found. It could hurt business. People won't want to work for you because you'll have too many eyes on you."

Nikolai rocked back and forth in his chair. "Fine. You and Ivan will come with me. Send out a crew an hour before we get there. If something seems fishy, I want to be notified. I'll call the whole thing off."

Dylan nodded and stood. "I'll take care of it." She turned to leave.

"Sasha," Nikolai called as she was walking out. "Don't be late tomorrow evening. I need you here."

She drove back to her apartment, her body humming with excitement. She'd done her part to put the plan in motion. Hopefully, everything would go as smoothly as it did back there. This was going to be huge for her career. Her momentary excitement was tamped down by the thought of what the end of the mission would also mean. She wouldn't see Emma again. The thought made her sick to her stomach. She wasn't sure how she'd allowed herself to develop feelings for Emma, but she had. Dylan was normally good at compartmentalizing her life, but she'd failed in this instance. She thought about Emma all day long, no matter what she was doing. She lived for their quiet moments together. She couldn't imagine what it would feel like to have her taken away so quickly. She shook her head, trying to throw the thoughts from her mind. It didn't matter how she felt about Emma, there were more significant issues. They were making a real difference, and that's what mattered.

CHAPTER TWENTY-EIGHT

Tyler watched Brooke arrange her hat in the mirror. Tony had brought them a van and a delivery uniform earlier in the day. Tyler and Caden had gutted the insides, needing to remove anything that O'Brien could potentially use as a weapon once she was inside. She wouldn't stay in her paralyzed state for long, and O'Brien was terribly resourceful. Now, with only a few hours to go, everyone was making their final preparations. A night that was years in the making was finally upon them.

Tyler ran her hands up and down Brooke's arms. "You ready?"

Brooke grabbed Tyler's hands. "Definitely."

Jennifer clipped communication devices to the three of them. "I'll be tracking all of you from back here. If you get separated or need an update on Nikolai's location, let me know. Once you're safely on board the helo, I'll shut everything down and head to the embassy."

"Don't wait for us to get there. As soon as Brooke and Emma have O'Brien loaded on, you get out of here in eight minutes as well. Nikolai has guys everywhere, so you can't take any chances. It will only take him fifteen minutes to get back to his house, and he'll have a forty-five-minute head start on you," Caden said.

Jennifer's eyes filled with tears. "I need to know you're safe."

Caden kissed her forehead. "Please just follow protocol. Tyler and I will be fine. You have to trust us. I need to know you're safe."

Jennifer hugged Caden, burying her face in her shoulder. "This never gets any easier."

Brooke kissed Tyler. The kiss was slow and soft, and it brought all of Tyler's feelings to the surface. She felt lucky to have found Brooke and was terrified of losing her to circumstances out of her control. She didn't have the words to convey the swirling emotions in her chest, and she hoped the kiss would do just that. It wasn't enough; it would never be enough.

"You come home to me," Brooke said, her forehead pressed against Tyler's. "We have a wedding to plan, and you aren't getting out of it."

Tyler smiled against Brooke's cheek. "I'll always come home to you." She felt Brooke's hot tears on her lips, making her stomach lurch. "Don't ever forget how much I love you."

Brooke kissed her again. "I won't."

Tyler looked at Jennifer. "Is there anything else you need from us?"

Jennifer sat behind her computer. She wiped the tears from her eyes and took a deep breath. "Your bags are in the car for me to take to the embassy. Your comms are up and working. Brooke has eight syringes of succinylcholine. We received confirmation from Dylan and Emma." She put her earpiece in place. "Caden and Tyler will move into position. Brooke will leave an hour later. Let's get this done and get home."

Tyler and Caden headed up the stairs to the car. They'd watch from the storage site next to the meeting place while Nikolai's guys swept the area. When it was clear, they'd move into position and wait.

The drive to the block of storage warehouses wasn't particularly long, but it unnerved Tyler. She didn't like being in the open for longer than necessary. She was fully aware of the difference a single witness could make. She didn't like taking chances, especially where the lives of other people hung in the balance.

"How you feeling about this?" Caden looked out the window.

"Four percent," Tyler said.

Caden nodded. "Better than one."

Tyler turned into the storage facility and parked the car inside an empty shipping container. They crawled out onto the top of one of the other containers. Tyler pulled out her binoculars and scanned the site next to them.

Caden pushed her comm button. "We're in position. A clear line of sight to meeting location. No sign of Nikolai's men yet."

There was crackling in Tyler's ear before Jennifer's voice came on the line. "Roger that. Update me when they arrive. I'll get a thermal tag on them so we can follow their location after."

"Copy," Caden said and then turned her attention to Tyler. "We didn't bring any snacks."

Tyler pulled a protein bar from her pocket and handed it to her. "Here."

Caden unwrapped the bar. "You're the best."

Tyler finished adjusting her binoculars, wanting to make sure the image was as clear as possible. "I need you to promise me that you won't do anything crazy."

Caden finished the bar and stuck the wrapper in her pocket. "Me?" She let out a hissing sound. "I would never."

"I'm serious, Caden. Stay low, stay quiet, and stay out of sight. I'm not going to lose you to something stupid."

Caden patted her on the back. "I knew you loved me."

"Fuck off."

Tyler focused on the task in front of her. She needed to clear her mind to be aware of her surroundings and push all other thoughts out of the way. She gave herself one last moment to picture Brooke. Brooke was the driving force for her need to be careful, aware, and the best operative she could be. That's how she'd get home to her.

Emma stared at herself in the mirror. She'd never worn such an expensive article of clothing. The black shimmered in the light, giving it the look of purple or navy blue as she moved. It hugged all the curves and valleys of her body, leaving very little to the imagination. She felt beautiful.

"You look incredible," Dylan whispered against her ear. Her voice was husky, intoxicating.

Emma turned, wanting Dylan's arms around her. "Thank you for getting it for me."

Dylan's eyes traveled over her, and it felt like she was being touched with feathers. "I'm so glad I did."

Dylan wore a fitted black tuxedo. It pulled perfectly at her shoulders, showing off her toned physique. The dark colors of the clothing made her green eyes shine in a way Emma never thought possible. Her cropped dark hair fell loosely into her eyes. Dylan always had an aura of confidence about her, but it seemed more pronounced tonight. Emma hoped that boded well for their evening.

Emma kissed Dylan's cheek. "You look amazing." She let her mouth linger next to Dylan's lips. "I wish we were going somewhere else tonight. I wish things were different."

Dylan turned her head, capturing Emma's lips. "Me too. I wish we'd met somewhere else, under different circumstances."

Emma pressed her face against Dylan's, loving the jolt of arousal she felt whenever they were near each other. "No regrets."

Dylan ran her hands over Emma's back, pulling her closer. "Me either." Dylan's phone vibrated, and it broke the trance. "The car's here."

Dylan held her hand through the car ride. Emma tried to think about what the night would hold, what she'd need to do, and how she needed to behave. So many people were counting on them to get this right, to not make any errors. She looked down at the hand entwined with her own. Dylan made her feel safe. How would she feel tomorrow when all this was over? Regardless of the outcome, tomorrow, there would be no Dylan. She felt suddenly nauseous. She wanted to freeze time like that girl from the television show she watched as a kid. She wasn't ready for it to be over. She wasn't prepared to say good-bye.

"Are you okay?" Dylan sounded concern.

Emma eyed the driver in front and chose her words carefully. "Yes. I just wish I had more time with you. I'm sorry I have to go back home tomorrow."

Dylan kissed the top of Emma's hand and pressed it against her face. "I know."

The car slowed to a stop. They were out of time. This was the last moment they'd ever be truly alone. There were so many things

Emma wanted to say, so many feelings she needed to get out, but they were stuck in her throat, a marble she couldn't dislodge. The car door opened, and a swell of noise filled the space. That was it. Their time had come to an end. Emma had missed her chance to tell Dylan how she felt, and now she'd have to live with that forever.

❖

Dylan scanned the large ballroom. The men in this space represented the worst parts of humanity. She thought briefly that the world would be better off if someone took the whole place out in one swoop. They dressed themselves up in expensive suits, drank expensive alcohol, and patted each other on the back for profiting from the worst impulses of men. Before she'd come to work for the CIA, she'd never fully believed that some people were born evil. It didn't take her long to discover that those were childish impressions that had no place in the real world.

She noticed Carol across the room, talking to Steven Walker. He looked angry, and she looked bored. It was amusing that neither of them had any idea what was in store for them tonight. She saw Nikolai speaking with a general from North Korea. Her stomach turned, imagining the vast topics they could be discussing and what it could mean for the world.

"You need to relax," Emma whispered.

Dylan kissed her cheek. "I'm the spy, remember."

Emma's eyes were sad, and Dylan wished she could take the statement back. "I'm very aware."

Dylan led Emma through the ballroom. "Hello, Nikolai."

Nikolai smiled and kissed Emma's cheek. "Nada, it's lovely to see you again. Thank you for coming."

Emma returned the kiss. "Thank you for having me. Everything looks exquisite."

"My wife lives to throw a party." Nikolai lifted his glass in the direction of his wife on the other side of the room. "I'll introduce you later."

"I'll find you in half an hour," Dylan said to Nikolai.

He took a sip of his champagne. "Please do."

Dylan led Emma over to a table, swiping two glasses of champagne on the way. She handed one to Emma. "Here you go. We're less suspicious if we have these and no one will try to force a drink on us."

Emma played with the stem of her glass, rolling it between her fingers. "Be careful tonight."

Dylan should have told Emma how much she cared before they'd arrived at the gala. She should've told her she'd never be able to get her out of her mind. She should've told her that if she'd met her before this mission, she'd consider giving it all up for her. She should have said all these things, but now there was no point. She wouldn't burden Emma with that knowledge. She'd be better off moving on and forgetting Dylan altogether. Emma didn't deserve to be bogged down by what-ifs and maybes. She deserved happiness. She deserved someone who could be there with her every day. She deserved to be loved properly. She deserved more than Dylan could give.

She put her hand over Emma's. "I will. You too." It wasn't enough. It would never be enough. But it was all she could give. "I'm going to go find Ivan."

"Sasha," Emma said.

"Yeah?"

Emma looked down at the ground, unable to make eye contact now. "Nothing."

Dylan walked away because if she looked at Emma for one more second, she'd lose herself. She couldn't bear to see the hurt in Emma's eyes or the way it broke her own heart to know she put it there. This hurt Emma now, but it was for the best. She just needed to keep telling herself that every day, for the rest of her life.

CHAPTER TWENTY-NINE

"Thermal targets approaching. Three minutes out," Jennifer said over the radio.

Tyler clicked her comm button. "Roger." She looked at Caden. "You ready?"

Caden looked down at Captain Hart, who was waiting in a car. "Think he's ready?"

"We're about to find out." They bumped fists. "Head on a swivel."

"I know, little cat." Caden got up and moved quickly and silently to the other side of the storage facility.

They'd have them covered on both sides. This formation would be easier for an aerial attack, and it would also help them see if someone was coming up behind either of them. Tyler wished they had about twenty more agents at their disposal, but there was no point in hoping for the impossible. They'd gotten into this together, and they'd get out together.

Tyler watched as the car pulled to a stop. Before this moment, she could feel every thump of her heart in every inch of her body. Now, she felt eerily calm. She was focused, determined, and ready. Nikolai sent three men out of the car. Two to flank the rear and one in front. Next, Dylan and Ivan exited the vehicle, each looking around, surveying the tops of the storage containers. She knew Dylan saw her because she paused for just a millisecond longer than necessary. Ivan, on the other hand, was oblivious to Caden's whereabouts.

Nikolai and Steven finally got out of the car when Ivan and Dylan told them it was safe. Captain Hart was already waiting outside his own car, watching the gathering in front of him. Tyler sent up one final prayer that Hart would be able to pull this off convincingly. Any chink in his armor could alert Nikolai and ruin the whole thing.

One of Nikolai's guys walked over to Hart and patted him down, looking for any hidden weapons. When he didn't find any, he pulled out a small electronic device and ran it over his body. It started beeping at Hart's pocket, and he pulled out his cell phone and handed it to the bodyguard. The large man turned around and nodded at Nikolai.

"Director Walker? What are you doing here? Do you know where Brooke is?" Hart shielded his eyes from the headlights. To his credit, he managed to look and sound surprised.

Walker took a step forward. "Captain Hart, I need you to listen to Mr. Orlav. He has a proposition for you, and I think you should consider it."

"If it doesn't involve me getting my daughter back, I'm not interested."

Nikolai motioned to Dylan to hand him the phone. "I want you to come and work for me, Captain Hart. It won't require a lot on your part. I just need you to make sure that your government doesn't focus on me. I will pay you handsomely. It won't be something that you regret."

Hart shook his head. "You want me to betray my country? That will never happen." He took a step toward Walker. "Is that what you're doing here with him? You're working for Russia? You've got to be kidding me."

"It's not something that I wanted to do. They left me with very little choice," Walker said in a pathetic attempt to defend himself.

"Bullshit. You always have a choice." Hart practically spit his words onto Walker.

Nikolai handed Hart the phone. "It's true. We know about Mr. Walker's involvement in trying to kill your president and vice president."

"That has nothing to do with me," Hart said.

Nikolai shrugged. "True, I have something much worse on you." He pointed to the phone and waited for Hart to look at the picture. "I had your daughter killed. Next, it will be your sons, then your wife. So, you're right, Captain Hart, you always have a choice. Now is the time to make yours."

This was their cue. They had all the information they needed to put Walker away. Tyler glanced across the grounds to Caden. She needed to hear Caden say she was ready before she made the first move. They needed to do this in tandem.

Her radio crackled, and she felt the surge of adrenaline pump through her body. "Take him."

Tyler and Caden hit the men at the back of the car first. Two clean shots through the back of their heads. The vibration of the shots ricocheted off the steel containers as Nikolai headed for the car, Ivan draped over him like a wet rag. Hart grabbed Walker and wrestled him to the ground. Dylan and the man at the front of the car stepped forward, firing shots up at Tyler and Caden.

The other bodyguard had exceptional aim. Tyler gritted her teeth as the bullets whizzed by her head, causing her to break her concentration. She rolled over and took aim at the bodyguard again. It took three more shots for Tyler to finally take him down. Dylan fell to the ground. Ninety-six percent flashed in her mind. Dylan was hit, but it couldn't have been her or Caden who'd made the mistake. Something had gone wrong. Fear and fury pumped through Tyler as she watched the pool of blood spreading out beneath Dylan.

Tyler came down from the top of the storage container just as Caden did the same. She turned her attention to Hart. "Get him out of here!"

Hart threw Walker into the car. "No, I'm not leaving you." He pointed behind them where another car had pulled up.

"Follow the plan. You're no good to us dead," Tyler yelled at Hart who reluctantly got in the car. "You have to go. There's no more time." Hart started the engine and drove away.

Tyler wove in and out of the containers. She needed to get to Dylan. She needed to get her to safety. She needed to regroup before whoever was in the second car had her in their sights. The fog that had started to crawl its way out of the river added a little more coverage, but not enough to make her feel comfortable. She was only a few feet away when she saw Caden come up behind Dylan.

Caden grabbed Dylan under the arms and dragged her behind one of the containers. "This wasn't part of the plan," Caden said into the radio.

"No, shit. Glass, what's the status on O'Brien? Nikolai is headed back." Tyler held her breath, waiting for an answer.

Gunshots started to bounce off the metal containers around them. "No word yet," Jennifer answered.

Tyler dropped to her knees and fired low around the corner, hoping to hit a few of the bodyguards in the leg, or better yet, the kneecaps. She heard one yell and hit the ground. "Styles, get Prey into the car and get out of here."

Another round of bullets rained down on them. The sound of metal tearing against metal pierced her ears. "I'm not going anywhere, Monroe."

Tyler fired back, drawing their attention away from the area where Caden was nestled with Dylan. When they fired back in Tyler's direction, they were hit by Caden. This was a maneuver they'd practiced a dozen times, and they excelled at its execution. The bullets that came next were less than before. They'd taken down at least two of the five guys.

"Get her out now while I lay down cover. We don't know how badly she's hurt," Tyler ordered over the radio.

"Then let's get these guys and get out of here. Together."

Tyler moved to the next storage container. Small shredded pieces of steel that had been knocked loose from bullets scraped Tyler's legs and arms. She managed to take another one down. *Two left.* The shots stopped, and rapid footsteps came toward her. She had one of the men in her sights. She took aim and fired and watched him fall to the ground.

And then blinding pain started pulsating from the back of her head.

Tyler turned around, unsure what had happened. Another blast of pain, this time from her nose. She tried to aim her gun, but it was knocked from her hands. She took a swing at him but knew it wouldn't land. She was dizzy, her vision blurring, and there was blood in her eyes. It didn't matter; she wasn't going down without a fight. Another punch to the side of the head, heaving her against the storage container. She felt herself fall to the ground. Small pieces of asphalt and rocks found their way into her mouth. Finally, a shot fired. The bodyguard fell to his knees, then landed face-first onto the ground beside her.

"Aren't you glad I didn't leave?" Caden said from somewhere behind her.

Tyler rolled onto her side. Everything was so fuzzy. "We need to get Prey out of here." In her head, that's what she said, but she couldn't be sure that's how it came out. Her jaw throbbed, and her tongue felt too big for her mouth.

"Can you walk, or do I need to carry your sorry ass?" Caden's voice didn't hold the sarcasm she was trying to convey. It was filled with fear and concern.

Tyler put her hand out. "Just help me up."

Tyler clung to the storage bins, trying to make it to the car as she stumbled and shook. She saw Caden carrying Dylan and knew she needed to hurry. There was blood dripping from Dylan's body as Caden moved her. Her face was ashen and her limbs were limp. Tyler finally made it to the car, the pulsating sensation dulling her ability to move or act correctly. Caden pulled off her jacket and used the arms to tie a tourniquet around Dylan's shoulder. Tyler tried to put the pieces together while watching Caden work. *Left shoulder, not good. Blood flowing from the wound, good. Heart still pumping.*

Caden jumped into the driver's seat. "Glass, change of plans. We have injured. We'll meet you at the embassy. Call ahead, tell them to have medics waiting."

Jennifer responded immediately. "Not advised, police on the move. They have your description. You need to make it to the helo. There's a paramedic on board. I'll tell them you have another passenger coming."

Dylan coughed from the back seat, finally coming around. "No embassy. Take me to the helo."

Caden started the car and skidded out of the storage facility. "Both of you better pull through this, goddamnit. I'll kick your asses if you die on me." She pressed the comm. "What's the update on O'Brien?"

❖

Emma pretended to sip her champagne as she looked around the ballroom. People were laughing, dancing, drinking, acting as if they didn't have a care in the world. She could practically taste the money that oozed from their skin. *Blood money. All of it.* These people profited off the cruelty, despair, and fear in the world.

Carol passed by her, and Emma checked her watch. She felt her skin prickle and sweat started to form on the back of her neck. She rolled her shoulders, trying to get the sensation to go away. It was time.

Emma walked up to Carol and put a hand on her shoulder. "Have you seen Sasha?" She made sure to slur her words a bit, wanting to give Carol the impression that she was inebriated.

Carol's face said she was disgusted that Emma would even think to touch her. "No. Why would I know where Sasha is?

Emma shrugged. "I saw her go off with Steven and Nikolai."

Carol exhaled loudly to articulate her annoyance. "They had an errand to run."

Emma shook her head. "No, they're back from that. They went off together again five minutes ago. But I'm bored. I want her back now."

Emma knew Carol wouldn't be able to help herself. The idea that the three of them could be working together without her knowledge would drive her crazy. She'd want to know if it had to do with her. Carol wasn't one to be left in the dark, and this would be no exception.

"Never mind. I'll find them." Emma clumsily patted Carol's shoulder again. "Thanks for your help."

Emma walked slowly out of the ballroom, pretending to look around as she went, making sure Carol was following her. She glanced down at her watch when she turned to the final hallway. Two minutes.

Carol was still about fifteen feet behind her, pretending not to care what Emma was doing.

"Sasha, wait," Emma yelled when she made it halfway down the hall. Emma slowed her pace, wanting Carol to see where she was turning.

Emma turned into the small maintenance area, surprised to see Brooke already there. Brooke put her finger up over her lips, indicating that Emma should be quiet. When Carol finally came around the corner, her face turned a shade of white Emma had only seen on paint samples the moment Brooke stepped out of the alcove behind her.

Brooke smiled and something flashed in her eyes. "Hello, Carol." Brooke pushed a needle into her neck before Carol had a chance to respond and held her against the wall by her throat until the drug took effect and she stopped struggling. Before Carol fell to the floor, Brooke had thrown one of Carol's arms around her shoulders. "Help me get her out of here."

Emma got under Carol's other arm, and they moved as quickly as they could to the service entrance. They pushed open the door and dropped Carol into the back of the van. Brooke secured her wrists behind her back with zip ties. Emma climbed in after her, stepping over Carol's inert body as she moved through the van. Brooke started the vehicle, and Emma quickly changed out of her dress and into clothes that were much more suitable for climbing onboard a helicopter in the middle of a field.

"Is it wrong of me to say that I thought that would be a little more difficult?" Emma buttoned the pants Dylan had given her, pulled on a black shirt, and secured the radio in her ear.

The squeal of tires sent a chill up Emma's spine. She looked in the side mirror and saw a black SUV gaining ground on them.

"You jinxed us." Brooke hit the gas, practically flying out of the parking garage. "Glass, we have O'Brien and a tail. What's the status?"

"Monroe, Styles, and Prey are on their way to the helicopter," Jennifer said.

Why is Dylan with them? She was supposed to be halfway to the CIA safe house by now. "Everyone in one piece?" Emma braced as Brooke took a hard left onto a side street.

"There were some issues. I don't have details." There were several seconds of silence before she came on the line again. "Hart, take the third route we discussed. That should help you lose the guys behind you. I don't have anyone in sight on that route."

Brooke made a hard right. Tires screeched behind them again. The sound of gunshots came next, a few coming through the back of the van and out through their windshield. The car behind them was closer to the ground and handled the turns better than their vehicle, which bounced off cars as they drove down some of the narrower streets.

"Do you want me to fire back at them?" Emma asked as she clung to the door of the van, her heart in her throat.

"No. This isn't a movie. If you poke your head out of that window, you're going to get shot." Brooke's knuckles were white as she gripped the steering wheel.

"Glass, can you put me through to Styles and Monroe?" Emma wasn't sure how she and Brooke were going to get out of this, but she wanted to know if Dylan was okay. It didn't make sense that she was in the car with them.

"Negative, Quinn. No distractions, just get to the pickup location. Brooke, take the left turn six hundred feet in front of you and then an immediate right."

Brooke pulled on her seat belt, making sure it was secure, so Emma did the same. The shots were coming in more rapid succession now. Two more went through the windshield from the back, and Emma willed herself to breathe. They rammed the back of their bumper, and the vehicle jumped forward.

Brooke took the left turn at the last possible second, causing two of their tires to come off the ground. Emma felt her butt lift off the seat and then slam back down as the van leveled out. Brooke took the immediate right, and the tires came up again. Metal scraped against metal like the world's most massive aluminum can was being crushed. There was yelling and car horns, and more gunshots.

After a few moments, all the sound started to drift away. Emma glanced over at Brooke, who was still focused intensely on the road in front of them. She hadn't reduced their speed and took several more turns. Emma assumed it was to put more distance between themselves and their assailants, on a path they'd never think to take.

Emma grabbed her radio and Brooke shook her head. "Don't."

Emma looked at her, confused.

"Don't do that to yourself. The what-ifs will kill you. We'll be there soon, and you can see for yourself."

Emma decided Brooke knew better than her in this instance. She busied herself by going into the back of the van and checking on O'Brien. Her pulse was good, but she'd have a few nasty bruises because of the car maneuvers, though it was amazing she didn't have any bullet holes in her, given that the rear door looked like Swiss cheese. At least something good had come out of the chaos. Carol deserved much worse than a few bruises. If Dylan was hurt, she'd kill Carol herself.

Dylan. A myriad of possibilities ran through her head. If she was with the other two, something had gone terribly wrong. *Four percent.* The number flashed behind her closed eyes. They all knew the risks when they'd gone down this path, and the success rate was low. Emma had just assumed they would beat the odds. She felt the hot tears start to stream down her face. She could tell herself the tears were a byproduct of the stress she'd just endured, but she knew that wasn't true. No, her tears were from the possibility that Dylan wasn't okay. She put her hand over her heart, hoping it would still be in one piece tomorrow.

CHAPTER THIRTY

At first, the bouncing around in the car made Dylan want to cry out in pain. She hadn't immediately realized she'd been shot. She saw Ivan's arm coming down as he fell to the ground. She saw the fire explode from the end of his weapon and felt the searing pain in her chest immediately after. At first, she thought she'd fallen on something. She tried to get up, to move off the object that was obviously lodged in her back. When she'd finally forced herself to roll over, she realized she hadn't fallen on something. The pool of blood underneath her and the waves of heat and agony that came from her chest proved to her that she'd been shot. Blackness threatened, and the world around her was nothing more than a pinprick of blurry images and far-off sound.

Caden had grabbed her and pulled her behind something metal. *Storage containers.* Yes, she'd been in a sea of storage containers. Time was messy now. Black spots were consuming her memory like small insects, carrying their food away. Voices were traveling through her mind. Directions on where to go, how much time they had, where to meet. *Who are we meeting?*

More darkness. More pain. More confusion. Staying awake was becoming more difficult with each lucid spell. Her legs were getting cold. She just wanted to curl up under a nice warm blanket, next to a fire, and have Emma stroke her face. Emma. She'd been so worried she'd never see her again going into tonight and now she was almost certain that would be true. She'd never again hear her laugh, taste her skin, feel her touch. *Emma.*

"What happened?" Emma's voice broke through her haze.

More talking. Another car. Nikolai. Escape. She wanted Emma's voice back. She wanted to listen to her lull her to sleep. Sleep. All she wanted to do was sleep. Now she was being lifted. Vibration, wind, and choppy noise. Someone was pulling off her shirt. Shouting.

She wanted to tell Emma that it didn't hurt anymore, that she felt much better now. She wanted to tell Emma not to worry. She wanted her to know she'd be okay. She couldn't feel the hole in her chest. Nothing hurt, anywhere. There was an absence of sensation, of feeling, of anything. The crystal clear absence should have been concerning, but it wasn't. She was floating and grateful for the reprieve. She didn't want to feel anymore. She was so tired. So cold. She wanted to let go, to release herself. She wanted to be free.

"Don't you go anywhere, you hear me?" Emma again. "Don't you give up on me."

Dylan tried to move her hand. She wanted to touch Emma, to feel her. She wanted her to know that she could hear her. The blackness came again, but this time, it swallowed her whole.

"We're going to have to make an emergency landing in Estonia. She's not going to make it farther than that. Call it in." The paramedic was yelling at the pilot.

Emma racked her brain, trying to file through all the information she had on Estonia. She knew that they wouldn't be landing somewhere that would put them in danger, and it made her feel better to be doing something. *Estonian's official languages are Estonian and Russian, but many speak English, German, and Swedish. It's made up of a parliamentary government. Estonia uses the euro as currency.*

"Quinn!" Brooke shook her.

Emma was finding it difficult to breathe. She looked at Brooke, unsure how long she'd been trying to get her attention.

"You need to get off of her. They're trying to stop the bleeding," Brooke shouted.

Emma looked down. There was blood on her hands, arms, coating her clothes. Not her blood, Dylan's blood. She'd draped herself over her and was speaking into her ear, urging her not to give up. She moved away from Dylan but didn't release her hand. She understood what was happening, but it was like she was watching it from somewhere else. *How could this be happening?* The medics were attaching bags of fluid to her hands. *What is the right word for that?* They pulled Dylan's eyelids apart, flashing lights into them. They were applying pressure and bandages to where the blood continued to seep from her body. Dylan's hand twitched in her own, forcing Emma to refocus.

Emma leaned next to Dylan's head again, making sure to stay out of the medic's way. "Dylan, baby, I need you to stay with me. Listen to my voice. I need you to focus on my voice."

It was an hour flight. That's what Emma heard the pilot say. But Emma didn't measure the passing moments in seconds or minutes. Time blurred and she couldn't find a point of reference. Time was being measured by the depth of the color of red. Time was now the way the bandages on Dylan seemed to darken to a crimson color Emma had never seen. Time was being measured by the small gasps of air Dylan was taking through the oxygen mask. Time wasn't relevant if it meant Dylan couldn't be saved.

Someone was rubbing her back, and it didn't make sense. Brooke was kneeling over Tyler, putting an ice pack against her face. Jennifer wasn't there.

"They're going to do everything they can." Caden was talking to her, trying to soothe her. That in itself was surreal.

Emma didn't want to be soothed. She wanted to know why this had happened. She wanted to understand what went wrong. She wanted someone to tell her why she'd spent her life being lonely only to find someone she could never have. She wanted to know what she'd done, and if she could take it back. She'd take it all back to save Dylan.

They were landing. Dropping onto the ground from a helicopter would've been something she'd like to see, but not now. She wanted someone to fix Dylan. It was taking too long and she was mad at herself for not being able to do anything but watch. Finally, there were people jumping out and others jumping in the helo. Caden grabbed her and pulled her away from Dylan. Instinctively, she fought against the hold. She didn't want Dylan to be alone.

"They need to get her into the hospital. They'll take care of her." Caden again. Voices seemed far away and echoed off her panic. She knew Caden was standing next to her, but she seemed somewhere else.

Emma watched as they wheeled Dylan into the building and away from her. "Can we go with her? We have to go with her. She won't know where she is."

Caden nodded and put her hand on her shoulder. "Let's go talk to the nurses."

Emma followed Caden inside. It wasn't a hospital but rather a makeshift area for medical emergencies sustained during a military accident. There were only a few chairs inside the building, and the front desk wasn't much more than a table with some files and a phone. A doctor ran in from another area and disappeared behind another door.

There were men and women in uniforms she didn't recognize. She wanted answers, but she didn't feel like she could move. She couldn't see Tyler or Brooke, either. Her feet were stuck and she stared around the room, numb and lost.

Caden sat her down in one of the chairs. "Wait here, I'll be right back."

Emma listened to the beeping instruments coming from somewhere else. Personnel were yelling to one another. Giving directives, she assumed, in a language she didn't understand. She covered her face with her hands, finally letting herself cry.

CHAPTER THIRTY-ONE

Tyler thanked the officer who'd allowed her to use the phone. She wasn't comfortable with the idea of powering up her cell phone until she knew what was going on back in the States. Her wounds had been superficial, but a minor concussion was causing her head to throb.

"Do you have a room I can meet with my team in?" She rubbed her brow. She knew it wouldn't get rid of the pain, but she tried all the same.

"Of course. We're happy to help, however we can." He stood. "Follow me, and I'll direct the rest of your team where to meet you."

Tyler sat in one of the empty seats and chugged down the bottle of water on the table.

Brooke looked like she wanted to check on her again when she entered the room but sat next to her without saying anything. Right now, all their focus had to be on the mission. Caden and Emma came in next. Emma was looking over her shoulder as if she could see the hospital from a building on the opposite side of the base.

Tyler pulled out her notepad and flipped it open. She needed to make sure she covered all the information she'd received from their superiors. "I was able to speak with Deputy Director Martin. I informed him that we have O'Brien in custody and that she's being held here in Estonia until we get transport back home. One of the Marines who escorted us on the helicopter is guarding her now. Captain Hart and Director Walker made it to the embassy without issue. Glass made it safely as well. They'll be sent back to the States on a military transport tomorrow evening. Walker is being charged with treason, conspiracy against the United States, and conspiracy to assassinate the president and vice president. I'm sure there will be more." Tyler took another sip of her water. "They want O'Brien back as soon as possible. We're scheduled to be transported to Germany, and then to the States. Obviously, the helo had to leave without us, but we'll get another ride without a problem."

"When?" Emma's voice was void of emotion.

"Tomorrow night," Tyler said.

"I'm not leaving Dylan here alone." Emma crossed her arms.

"I don't feel good about it either, but they want O'Brien back. They want us all debriefed, and they aren't keen on us staying here. Estonia is one of our allies, but we don't know Nikolai's reach, and the longer we stay here, the more dangerous it is for everyone." Tyler knew none of that would matter to Emma. Brooke had told her that Emma had become single-minded after Dylan had been shot.

"We don't even know if she's going to pull through yet. We can't just leave her here alone." Emma was growing more agitated with each word.

"The Marine with O'Brien right now will stay with Dylan until she can be transported to Germany to fully recover." Tyler kept her voice calm, hoping her words would sink in.

"Then what? Where will she go when she's healed?"

"I don't know. That won't be up to me. That will be up to the CIA, just like it was before this went down," Tyler said carefully. She didn't want Emma to misconstrue her words as condescending. "Emma, they weren't giving us an option as to whether or not we were going. It was an order."

Emma pushed her chair away from the table. "Fine. If you want to give me any more orders, I'll be over at the hospital unit." She walked out before Tyler could respond.

Caden watched her leave and then turned her attention back to Brooke and Tyler. "I don't blame her. I think it's wrong to leave Prey here. Germany maybe, at one of our bases, but here? How do we know Nikolai won't get to her somehow?"

Tyler shared their feelings, but it wasn't her job to make these calls. "Look, Estonia shares a literal border with Russia. The longer we're here, the more we risk ourselves, and the people here. Everyone will be safer the sooner we're gone, including Dylan, and he most likely thinks she's dead anyway. It doesn't matter what any of us think. They're bringing us back. It's not up to us."

Tyler didn't like this part of the job. She hated having to disappoint members of her team, and she hated leaving one of them behind even more. The wheels of the government left microscopic room for human compassion or understanding. The powers that be had one single focus and that was getting O'Brien back into the States before anything could derail the effort. She understood it to an extent, but it didn't make it any easier.

❖

Dylan could hear the machines beeping. *Well, you're not dead.* At least she hoped not. It would be a cruel joke to create an afterlife that beeped at you incessantly. She tried to move, and a wave a pain enveloped her body. *No, definitely not dead.* She managed to open her eyes, the harsh light of the room making her want to shut them again. She must have moaned because someone was stroking her face immediately after.

"Dylan. Try not to move too much. There're a ton of lines hooked up to you," Emma said.

Dylan was so relieved to hear her voice that she almost cried. "Emma? How long have I been here?"

Emma rubbed the top of Dylan's hand with her thumb. "You got here about twelve hours ago. You took a pretty nasty shot through your shoulder. You were lucky, though; it didn't hit anything major."

"Did we get her? Did we get O'Brien? Did Nikolai escape?" Dylan's throat was dry, and she was consumed by the need for water. She pointed to the plastic cup next to her bed.

Emma held the cup and put the straw in her mouth. "Yeah, we got her. She's in a holding cell now. A Marine is with her, and we're waiting for transport out of here. No one is sure where Nikolai is right now."

Emma took the straw away too soon, but she didn't have the energy to fight her. "Where am I? Germany?"

Emma stroked her face. "Right now, you're in Estonia. Your injury was too serious to go any farther, and there was an emergency med base here. When you're stable enough, they'll send you to Germany."

Dylan nodded and then regretted it. The motion made her head pound and she felt dizzy. "Is everyone else okay?" She didn't think she'd be able to stay awake much longer, but she needed the basics.

"Everyone is fine. You need to get some sleep. I'll be here when you wake up."

Dylan let the words settle in her mind as she drifted back into the darkness.

When Dylan woke next, it wasn't only Emma sitting by her bed. The team was waiting, and Dylan could tell by the bags in the corner that they were there to say good-bye. She must have been administered more painkillers because now where there was once excruciating pain, there was only an obnoxious throbbing.

Dylan tried to sit up, but Emma put her hand out. "Let me help you." Emma helped her shift in her bed so she felt more like a human being.

Caden leaned over her, pretending to inspect her face. "Yeah, I'm still better looking than you."

Dylan tried to laugh, but the burning in her chest wouldn't allow it. "You wish, Styles." She put her hand over Caden's. "Thank you for saving my ass. I owe you."

Caden squeezed her hand. "You don't owe me anything, except maybe a beer or two."

Dylan managed a half smile. "Take care of Jennifer. She's too good for you."

Caden laughed and moved aside for Brooke. Brooke kissed Dylan's forehead. "I'm sorry we have to leave. Thank you for everything. Please let us know when you're safe."

"I will," Dylan said. She felt tears forming in her eyes and was surprised by the sudden onslaught of emotions. She'd never grown attached to anyone she'd worked with. Not to this extent, anyway.

Tyler was furiously writing on a piece of paper. When she finished, she put it on the table next to Dylan. "I wish we could see this through with you. None of us want to leave you here—"

"Orders," Dylan interrupted.

Tyler nodded. "Yeah. There's all our contact info." She pointed to the note on the table. "Whenever you're able, please keep in touch." She patted the top of her hand and then ushered Caden and Brooke out of the room, leaving Dylan with Emma.

Emma pulled up the chair and sat next to her bed.

"Don't you need to go?"

Emma took her hand. "I'm not leaving you. I'll find my own way back to the States. I don't care if the NSA fires me."

The words were like a warm fuzzy blanket. Emma had been the only thing she thought of when she'd known her time was up. All she'd wanted was to be touched and loved by Emma. When she'd woken up the first time and saw her sitting there, she'd known she wanted to wake up to Emma every day. She also knew that wasn't possible.

Dylan pulled her hand away, and it almost broke her heart when she saw the look in Emma's eyes. "You have to go with them. You're part of their team. You need to go back to the States and get debriefed."

"I don't care about any of that. I need to stay with you, to make sure you're okay."

Dylan gritted her teeth, attempting to keep the tears at bay. "You can't stay with me. It's not safe. We don't know how much Nikolai knows or where he is. And as soon as I've recovered, I'll have to disappear. The CIA will assign me somewhere new, change my identity. Nothing has changed, Emma."

"I'll change mine too. No one is better at hacking than me. I'm not going to leave you, Dylan. I just found you. Then I almost lost you. I can't do that again."

Despite her best efforts, Dylan felt the hot tears stream down her cheeks. "We'll be much easier to find if there's two of us. I can't put you in that kind of danger. I won't risk you."

Emma's face went through a series of emotions, finally settling on anger. "So what? That's it? You're done with me?"

"It's what's best for both of us. It's not what I want, but it's what we have to do. I can't ask you to wait around for what could be years. I never wanted to hurt you, but we knew the choice we were making. Now we don't have one." Dylan heard how clichéd her words sounded and hated herself for saying them. Emma deserved more, but she didn't have anything to give.

Tears were streaming down Emma's cheeks, but she wasn't sobbing. Her face was like stone, her expression set. "There's always a choice, Dylan. Is this yours?"

Dylan closed her eyes because she couldn't bear to see the look on Emma's face. "Yes."

She didn't open them again until she heard the door shut. Dylan covered her mouth, a sob falling from her lips. She'd just watched the only woman she'd ever really cared about walk out the door. The pain was far worse than any gunshot wound she'd ever have to endure. This would be an injury she'd never recover from. The mark that Emma had left on her heart was far greater than any scar she'd ever have.

Chapter Thirty-two

Emma reached over to the table next to her bed and turned off her alarm. She pushed herself upright and forced her legs to carry her into her bathroom. She turned the shower on and stepped into the cold spray. She didn't bother waiting for it to get warm. It was the same thing every single morning since she'd returned to the States eight weeks ago. She'd wake at the same time, to the same alarm, and take the same cold shower. She'd drink from the same coffee pot and eat the same yogurt. Every day, she'd wake up with the same hole burning in her chest, the only proof she had of Dylan's existence in her life.

Dylan had contacted Tyler and Brooke to let them know she was in Germany, and then again when she was leaving. Emma only knew about it because she heard the whispered conversations between her friends, neither of whom wanted to upset her by saying Dylan's name. She'd spent the first several weeks back barely able to function. She got through work and did her tasks, but just barely. She'd done the debrief in a daze, the weight of her grief making it hard to tell the story. She couldn't shake the feeling that something had been stolen from her. The part she couldn't let go of was that nothing had been *stolen*. Dylan had chosen this. Deep down, she knew that wasn't fair, but she couldn't help feeling that way just the same.

Emma stared at herself in the mirror. She'd lost weight, unable to eat anything of substance. Her cheeks were sunken and her skin was pale. She turned her head, wondering what Dylan would think of how much bluer her eyes looked now that her skin had lost so much of its color. The thought brought on the tears again, and she cursed herself for being so damn predictable.

"Hello?" Jennifer's voice came from the living room of her apartment. "Emma?"

"I'm back here." Emma stood and blinked, trying to get rid of the tears before Jennifer made it the forty feet to her room.

Either Jennifer or Brooke had taken to stopping by every day to check on her. Emma had grown tired of answering the door and finally surrendered keys to both of them. She wasn't sure what to make of their sudden involvement in her life since they'd returned. Emma had never had many friends and absolutely none who seemed to worry about her the way these women did. If she was being honest, she'd grown to rely on their support and loved them for giving it so willingly. They gave her a small sense of normalcy that she so desperately needed.

"You've got to get dressed. We're going to be late." Jennifer went to her closet and pulled out jeans and a sweater. "If we aren't on time to go dress shopping with Brooke, she'll kill us both."

This had been the one activity Emma had been looking forward to. She was disappointed with herself for not being able to pull it together to give a minuscule amount of support to someone who'd given her so much. She decided at that moment that today would be different. This was a big day for Brooke, and she wouldn't be the one to bring them down.

Jennifer came back into her room with a cup of coffee in a travel mug. "Did you sleep any better last night?"

Emma took the coffee. "Let's not talk about Dylan today. I want to focus on Brooke and finding her the perfect wedding dress."

Jennifer laughed. "Brooke will look perfect in anything. We need to focus on making sure Brooke doesn't kill her mother."

Emma hurriedly dressed and was looking at her hair in the mirror, trying to figure out how to look put together in under three minutes. "What's the deal with that, anyway?"

Jennifer sat on her bed and crossed her legs. "Jesus, where would I even start? Let's just say that Janice Hart doesn't approve of Brooke being a lesbian."

Emma twisted her hair up in a bun and turned her face from side to side. *Good enough.* "Is that seriously what it is? My parents would be over the moon if I brought someone home like Tyler. But then again, my parents would be over the moon if I was Brooke."

Jennifer walked with her to the door. "The world is full of crazy people, and you're about to meet one of the craziest. I think the only reason either one of them agreed to this was because they both told Brooke's dad they'd give it a chance. But in my opinion, it won't end well."

❖

They walked into the small boutique, and Brooke practically tackled them both. "Thank God you're here. Did you bring me booze? A valium? Anything?" She waved her hand in her mother's direction. "She is insufferable."

"I can hear you, dear." Janice Hart walked over to them and put her hand out for them to shake.

Emma could see the resemblance immediately. Janice was Brooke twenty-five years from now. But where Brooke wore jeans and a blouse, Janice was in a tailored pinstriped suit. Janice's makeup, hair, and manicure were flawless. Emma didn't know whether to shake her hand or curtsey. She'd never even met someone who demanded so much respect with just her presence. It was fascinating.

"It's nice to meet you, Mrs. Hart," Emma said, thinking Janice would ask to be called by her first name. She didn't.

A squeal came from behind Brooke's mom, and she rolled her eyes as the shrieking newcomer moved past her to hug Jennifer. "Honey, you look fantastic! I missed you. I need you to catch me up on everything."

Jennifer hugged the woman with a substantial amount of adoration. Then she turned in Emma's direction. "Claire Monroe, this is Emma. Emma, this is Claire, Tyler's aunt."

Before Emma had a chance to get a word out, Claire was wrapping her in a warm embrace. "It's so nice to finally meet you, Emma. Brooke and Tyler have told me so much about you."

Emma couldn't help but smile. Claire was warm and full of life. Her clothes told Emma that her roots could probably be traced back to hippie, and Emma loved it. The contrast between the two maternal figures was stark, and Emma wondered how these two managed to raise women who fit so perfectly together.

"It's so nice to meet you, Mrs. Monroe." Emma didn't let go of her because Claire seemed determined to hug her as long as possible.

"Oh, sweetie, call me Claire." She rocked her back and forth a few times before finally releasing her.

"Is Nicole Sable coming? She was the only woman I enjoyed from that terrible training place you were at." Janice was walking back to the sitting area where mirrors were placed in a large semicircle.

"She couldn't make it because of work, but she and Kyle will be at the wedding. I'll let her know which bridesmaid dress to get. She'll take care of it." Brooke's tone was clipped; she seemed annoyed by her mother's question.

"Kyle seems like a nice young man." Janice poured herself a glass of champagne.

Brooke poured herself one too and swallowed it without taking a breath. "You've never met him. You're just saying that because he's a guy." She poured another glass.

"Is there something wrong with marrying men now?" Janice sat on the couch and crossed her legs.

"There is if you're a lesbian, Mom. And I am. A lesbian." Brooke waved to the young woman at the counter, clearly wanting to get this started.

"Brooke, you don't need to use such foul language." Janice shook her head as if she'd just heard a dirty word.

Claire leaned over and whispered, "Not what you expected when you heard you were going to meet Brooke's mom, huh?"

Emma took a sip of the champagne Jennifer handed her. "Not at all."

Emma had been so honored when Brooke had asked her to be a bridesmaid that she'd said yes without hesitation. Brooke wanted her to be part of the most important day of her life, despite her behavior in recent weeks. Brooke had sat with her when she cried and asked the rhetorical question of "why." Brooke had talked to her late into the night while she stayed awake, worried that Nikolai would find Dylan. Brooke, Jennifer, Caden, and Tyler had all become such an essential part of her life in the last several months, it was hard to imagine what it was like before them. She allowed the warmth of friendship to eclipse her feelings of loss for the moment. She knew it wouldn't last, that the loss of Dylan would resettle in her chest without warning, but she'd take these moments when she could and appreciate the reprieve they brought.

Merrick dropped Dylan's bags in the apartment. "Here you go, don't say I never did anything to help you."

Dylan looked down at her arm in a sling. "You helped someone with one working arm carry their bags. You're quite the hero."

He did a short lap through the apartment, taking everything in. "I don't know how long you'll be here for, but I'll keep you updated." He put his hands in his pockets. "We're trying to find out how much Nikolai knows. We're keeping a close eye on him, but so far, it's business as usual. Although we're sure you dealt his business a pretty hard blow when we were able to extract those girls you tipped off Hart about." He rocked forward on his feet. He was probably feeling uneasy for giving her anything even slightly resembling a compliment. "You should be safe here. We're working on getting you back to the States, but we want to make sure all the breaches in the CIA are shored up first so you don't become a target again."

She walked to the window and looked down on the street. "There're worse places to convalesce than London. Plus, I've always worked in Europe. I'm sure I'll be reassigned soon."

He placed a laptop and a large envelope onto the table. "You'll be good as new in no time." He reached into his jacket and pulled out a cell phone.

She took the phone. "Thanks for everything, Merrick."

He patted her good shoulder. "I'm glad you didn't die." He gave her a quick awkward smile and then left.

She opened the envelope and dumped the contents onto the table. A passport, cash, and background information. Everything she needed to take on her new persona and start the process of becoming someone else. She wanted to be someone else, anyone else. She wanted to be someone who hadn't hurt Emma. She wanted to be someone who hadn't done the unspeakable things she'd had to do. She wanted to be someone who could fall asleep at night without the horrors of her job scratching at the edges of her psyche. She thought she'd made the right choice when she asked Emma to leave. She thought she was protecting her, keeping her out of the way of the mission that had gone a little sideways. But as the days stretched into weeks, she wasn't so sure. The painkillers she'd been prescribed would never be strong enough to dull the pain she felt every time she thought of Emma. She thought of the different outcomes that could have played out instead of the one she'd chosen. They could've come up with a plan to run away together. They could've gone into hiding. Spent a year or two on an island where no one would ever find them or ever bother them. But she couldn't do that to her. A life on the run, always looking over your shoulder, was no life at all. Plus, even if she'd made the decision to run, there was no guarantee Emma would accept her—all of her. If Emma knew the truth of all she'd had to do throughout her undercover years, she would never look at her the same. She sighed when the familiar pang of loss started in her chest and made her stomach turn.

She opened the laptop, hoping to shake off some of her melancholy by reading about some of their success. It wasn't hard to find information about Carol O'Brien or Steven Walker. Their faces and bad deeds were splashed across every news outlet in the world. They'd either spend the rest of their lives in jail, or they'd be sentenced to death. Dylan hoped for the former. A lifetime spent having to relive your bad decisions seemed much more painful than death.

She opened a link on the news article. It seemed O'Brien and Walker were rolling over on whoever possible to garner even the slightest bit of favor. Major players in the National Socialist Movement were being arrested in swaths. Apparently, loyalty had no place in their circles. The forces of good were winning, at least for today.

She went over to the small bag of groceries she'd picked up on the way to her apartment and pulled out a salad. She struggled to open the packaging with only one good hand. Yet another reminder of how alone she really was. When she first came to work for the CIA, the allure of a solitary life was the most appealing aspect. She loved the idea of depending on herself and no one else. She relished the thought of leading different lives and blending in anywhere she went. What had changed? She knew the answer. *Emma.* Emma had changed everything. She finally got the plastic container open, despite her shaking hand. She told herself it was from the strain of trying to do things with one hand, but that wasn't true. The loss of Emma had crippled her far more than any injury she'd ever sustained.

CHAPTER THIRTY-THREE

Director Ericson is ready for you." Anne, Ericson's assistant, hung up the phone and pointed to the closed door.

Tyler and Caden stepped into the office and waited for him to tell them to sit. "Good morning, Director," Tyler said.

"I don't know why the CIA has such a hard-on for you two, but I'm getting really tired of having to share my agents." He took off his glasses and pinched the bridge of his nose.

"Sir?" Caden looked between Ericson and Tyler.

He slid a folder across the desk in their direction. "You're temporarily assigned. Again. I don't have all the details. The CIA classifies damn near everything as Top Secret. Go talk to Deputy Director Martin, get your assignment, and get this wrapped up. I need you two back."

Tyler took the folder and opened it. Most of the information had been redacted, but she recognized the name at the top. Nikolai Orlav. She showed the papers to Caden.

"Did Deputy Director Martin tell you when he wanted to see us?" Caden asked.

Ericson looked incredulous. "I don't know, Styles. Apparently, I don't need to be in the loop. Why don't you go find out?"

Tyler turned toward the door and Caden followed suit. "We'll report back as soon as this is over."

He waved them off. "Don't embarrass us."

"He seems like he'd be fun at parties," Caden said as they made their way to the elevator.

"What do you think this is about?" Tyler asked, ignoring Caden's comment.

Caden shrugged. "Your guess is as good as mine."

The drive from DC to Langley only took about twenty-five minutes. The process of getting inside took about just as long. Once their credentials were accepted, they were escorted to one of the secure rooms.

"This must be big," Caden whispered to Tyler as they were escorted through the hallways.

"It always is when we get called over here," Tyler said.

The agent escorting them entered a code into the panel next to the door and waited until it beeped before he left them. Tyler wasn't surprised to see Brooke and Deputy Director Martin sitting inside. She was surprised to see Emma.

Martin must have noticed the look on Tyler's face because he answered her unasked question. "Quinn is on loan to us from the NSA."

"You guys really have a thing for poaching other agency agents, huh?" Caden laughed at her own joke, but Martin didn't seem amused.

"Play the recording," Martin said to Emma.

There were several minutes of idle chitchat between Nikolai and the guy named Bogdan. Tyler was beginning to wonder why any of this was relevant when she finally heard it. "I'll be in DC for about a week. My daughter is graduating from Georgetown."

Emma slid folders to both Caden and Tyler. "We weren't aware that Nikolai had a daughter. So, we ran the student database to find out what Russian citizens were attending. We came up empty, so I had to do some more digging. It turns out Nikolai's daughter is Ashley Lloyd, who is an American citizen. We were able to find a connection between Nikolai and Ashley's mother, Rachel Lloyd, in the summer of ninety-six. Rachel took a backpacking trip through Europe the summer before college. These two had a whirlwind relationship that ended with Ashley. As far as we can tell, Nikolai has sent money to Rachel over the years but has no relationship with either of them."

Tyler flipped through the pictures. "What's changed? Why is he coming now?"

"We aren't sure. We couldn't find any correspondence between Nikolai, Rachel, and Ashley. It's safe to assume he's kept an eye on his daughter and knows her happenings. We don't think Rachel and Ashley know he's coming," Brooke said.

Tyler directed her attention to Martin. "It was Prey's intention to flip him, and she was nearly there when the mission went sideways."

Martin smiled. "It seems we've been given another chance to help make that happen."

Tyler shook her head. "There's no time. Even if we could get past his security, we'd never convince him to talk to us. It would cause too big of a scene. He's never in public without a full entourage, and even in private he has a full security force. An asset is no good if people know they're an asset."

Martin held up his hand for her to stop. "I've put in a request to bring someone in who can get to him. You're all familiar with Agent Prey. She's being flown in tomorrow to help with this mission, given her knowledge of everything to do with Nikolai. You four will help with support. Prey is already familiar with all of you, and we need expediency with this mission. Glass won't be joining you this time. She's on another assignment, which is why I asked for Quinn."

Emma turned a ghostly shade of white. She clearly didn't know about the full scope of the mission until this moment. Tyler couldn't begin to imagine what she was feeling, and she wished there was some way to make it better. Emma had been a wreck when they left Dylan almost nine weeks ago. It was only in these last few days she'd seen any improvement. She couldn't imagine what it would do to her emotionally to be thrown back in with the source of her pain.

Martin stood. "Be here, thirteen hundred hours tomorrow. We only have a few days to get this wrapped up."

Martin left the room, and for a full minute, no one said anything. Finally, Emma broke the silence. "I'll pull everything I have on Rachel and Ashley. That way, it will all be ready for Prey when she gets here." She looked at Tyler and Caden. "I was able to figure out where Nikolai will be staying. Can you two please figure out the best place to try to corner him with the least impact? I want to make sure Brooke and I have time to find out schedules of employees if necessary and run backgrounds on them. I want to make sure we know which people are Nikolai's."

Tyler nodded and watched Emma walk out the door. There'd been such a shift in her since they'd met a few months before. She'd gone from being quiet, awkward, and nervous to giving them orders. Emma's time in Russia had been good for her. But at what cost?

❖

Emma stood in the doorway with her gift. She didn't want to go inside. All she wanted to do was go home and drink an entire bottle of wine. She took a deep breath. She reminded herself that wasn't an option and she owed it to Tyler and Brooke to be here. It didn't matter that she'd have to see Dylan tomorrow. The world didn't stop turning just because her world hadn't quite gotten back on its axis.

"Emma? What are you doing out here?" Jennifer sounded concerned.

Caden appeared by her side and put her hand on the doorknob. "I'll be inside if you need any of my expertise."

Jennifer rolled her eyes. "Doubtful. We'll be in soon."

Jennifer pulled her to the corner. "I heard about Dylan. How are you holding up?"

Emma wanted to say that she was fine. She wanted to tell her that she was over Dylan. She wanted to say that they'd shared a lovely time together, but now that it was over, she was ready to move on. That's not what came out of her mouth. "I don't know what to say when I see her."

Jennifer rubbed her arm. "I'm sorry. I know this must be terribly difficult for you. At least it's only a few days, right? Plus, it will be all work. That will be a good distraction."

Emma knew Jennifer was trying. In truth, there was nothing she could say that would make it better. She appreciated that she had friends who tried. Emma closed her eyes and focused on the importance of this evening. Two people who were meant for each other were celebrating their union with a bridal shower. Well, a bridal shower that was more like a BBQ. She decided she'd focus on the people she cared about, instead of the one she'd lost.

"You ready to go inside?" Emma gave Jennifer a forced smile.

"We can stay out here as long as you need."

Emma nodded toward the door. "No, this will be good for me."

When Emma opened the door, she was hit with a wall of laughter and chatter. People were wandering around, talking, drinking, and laughing. Hugs were being exchanged, and music flowed through the house. The room was overflowing with love, and Emma let it wash over her.

Claire greeted them with a hug. "Emma, Jennifer, it's so good to see you both."

Emma stuck out the present she'd brought. "Where should I put this?"

Claire smiled and took the package. "You know they'd tell you that you didn't have to do that, but I'm sure they'll appreciate it. Brooke and Tyler are somewhere over there. Make yourselves at home."

Brooke's expression when she saw them was genuine and full of love. "You made it! Thank you for coming." She handed Emma a glass of wine.

Emma took a sip. "Thanks for inviting me."

Brooke laughed. "Emma, you're a bridesmaid, of course you're invited. Is there anything I can get you?"

Emma held up her glass. "This was all I wanted."

Brooke rubbed her back. "Well, help yourself to anything you see. I have to go greet some more guests." She hugged her again. "Thank you for coming. I know today was hard for you."

Making the best of the evening was much easier than Emma had expected. Everyone Brooke and Tyler had invited was warm, vivacious, and genuinely nice. There were several times throughout the evening where she was so caught up in conversations, she didn't think about Dylan at all. It was the first time since she'd left Estonia that she thought she might make it through. No, her heart would never be the same, but she'd be all right.

Tyler and Brooke were a sight to watch. Their love for one another permeated everything they did. Their subtle touches and long glances were proof that true love existed. Emma felt lucky to witness something so extraordinary. She hadn't realized until Dylan that she wanted something like this too. She wanted someone who looked at her like there was no one else in the room. She wanted to know that someone would risk it all to be with her. She wanted a relationship where they'd put aside their own insecurities because their relationship was more important. She'd foolishly thought that person could be Dylan. Now that she knew better, she wouldn't make the same mistake again.

CHAPTER THIRTY-FOUR

Dylan sat in the cold, harshly lit room. She'd been surprised to hear about her summons back to the States but was excited at the prospect of seeing Emma again. Since her arrival in London, she'd spent the entire time scouring potential job openings that could get her back to this area, back to Emma. It had taken plenty of lonely nights, a lot of tears, and hours of soul searching to realize what a colossal mistake she'd made. At first, she pushed Emma away because the prospect of something happening to her was too much. She couldn't bear the responsibility of keeping Emma safe, or worse, what it would do if she failed. Finally, she realized those had been excuses. She'd run from Emma because she'd been scared. Emma had been so overwhelmed with emotions that Dylan had to make the final break. They had discussed what the outcome would be and Emma thought that had changed because she'd gotten hurt. Emma didn't want to see the danger they were still in and what that could mean. She needed to talk to Emma and clear things up between them. Her reasons had been valid, but so had their emotions.

Tyler and Caden entered the room first, and both greeted Dylan with a hug. Brooke followed next, holding the door open for Emma. Brooke greeted her warmly, tossing questions at her about her injury. Dylan couldn't answer because she wasn't paying attention to anything but Emma. Emma was a bit paler and much thinner than the last time she'd seen her. Dylan had a feeling the transformation had nothing to do with illness and everything to do with the way she'd ended things.

She wanted to go talk to her. She wanted to say anything to erase the dark circles from under her eyes.

Deputy Director Martin interrupted any plans to get Emma alone. "Agent Prey, thank you for coming back. I assume you read the brief overview of what we'll be doing here?"

Dylan forced herself to pull her attention from Emma. "Yes, I understand the objective."

"Did you hear any whisperings about a daughter during your time with Nikolai?" Brooke held her fingers over the keys on her laptop, ready to take notes.

"No, he never mentioned anything to me, and I never overheard anything about her."

"Here's the plan," Tyler said and put a map up on the screen in the room. "Nikolai arrives tomorrow afternoon. He has a reservation for dinner at seven that evening. The next day is his daughter's graduation, and then he leaves fourteen hours later. We can't pick him up at graduation. Our only opportunity is his restaurant outing."

"It won't be easy to get to him. He always has a personal driver and at least two security guards with him. Even if he were going to use the restroom, at least one of the men would accompany him," Dylan said.

"We expected that. We'll have minimal opportunity to grab him and bring him in. So, we're going to get him to come to us." Caden smiled and continued. "When he walks out, you're going to hand him a note. The note will say that he must meet you, alone, or you will go after his daughter. We don't have any record that he knows you're CIA yet. So, we assume he'll believe your threat."

Dylan watched Emma. She was clearly uncomfortable with the situation, and she still wouldn't look at her. "And if he ignores the note and brings some of his guys? What if he refuses to flip and then knows I'm CIA?"

"If he brings his men with him, we will neutralize them. He won't refuse to flip. Emma has put together his extensive criminal activity, and we'll threaten to expose it to his daughter. I have a pretty good feeling she's the key we never knew we needed." Tyler sat back, obviously waiting for Dylan to offer feedback.

Dylan ran her one working hand over her face. "This is a rushed plan. It's clear you've only had a few days to put it together."

Caden leaned forward. "So, is that a yes?"

"Of course, I'm in," Dylan said. "Having Nikolai as an asset will be the difference in dismantling some of the worst criminal activity in the world. It's worth the risk."

Caden smacked Tyler. "Told you she'd do it."

Martin stood. "Whatever you need equipment wise, you got it. I'll be at the safe house waiting for your arrival. Monroe and Styles will run backup for you. If things get too hairy, they'll extract you. Quinn and Hart will be your eyes and ears out there. They'll be able to track and see everything Styles and Monroe can't." He shook Dylan's hand. "Thanks for doing this. I know you aren't cleared for duty yet. It won't be forgotten." He walked out of the room without another word.

"I'd invite you to stay with us, but I know you have to stay hidden here until the mission starts. Rain check for when this is all over?"

Tyler was genuine, and Dylan appreciated the sentiment.

"Absolutely." Dylan watched them all stand to leave. "Emma, can I talk to you for a second?"

Emma closed the distance between them. Dylan was caught off guard by the fury in her eyes. "There's nothing to say, Dylan. Let's just get this over with and then we can both go back to our separate lives."

Dylan didn't care that the others were still in the room. Emma clearly didn't mind doing this in front of them, so she wouldn't either. "I don't want separate lives. I thought that was what would keep you safe. I thought I was doing the right thing. I was following the rules we'd already set, and at that time, we did what we had to do. But things are different now. We can find a way to make this work."

Emma's face flushed. "It's too late. I spent months crying myself to sleep over you. I checked my phone and email hundreds of times a day, hoping you'd reach out to me. Spoiler alert, you didn't. You contacted Tyler and Brooke, but not me. I get that we set rules, and that we had boundaries. I understand why things ended the way they did. But you've been out of harm's way for months, Dylan.

You've had thousands of minutes and even more seconds to pick up the phone and call me, but you didn't. Now, you've decided that we can make this work. I can't go through this again. Losing you once was enough."

Dylan tried to reach for Emma's hand, but she pulled it away. "Emma, I'm sorry. I think I love you."

Emma glared at her. "You *think* you love me? Jesus, Dylan. You can't even make your mind up about that, but you want me to risk my heart again. For what? For you to change your mind in a few weeks? No thanks." Emma left before Dylan could say anything else. The others followed her out, and Tyler threw her a look of commiseration before closing the door softly behind her.

Dylan flopped into the chair after the door shut. Emma was much angrier than she'd anticipated. She was right; she should've called. Dylan's own insecurities had prevented her from taking that step. But she was wrong about losing her. Emma had never lost her. Dylan was playing by the rules they'd agreed upon. She was following through because Emma hadn't been in a space where she could. But now that things were going to be different, Dylan needed to prove to Emma, through her actions, that she wanted to be part of her life. And somehow, she'd figure out a way. Then, if Emma didn't want her, at least Dylan would know she tried.

Emma paced furiously in Tyler and Brooke's living room. "I never should've gotten involved with her. I can't believe I was so foolish. I never do things like that, and this is exactly why."

Brooke watched her from her place on the couch. "Why did you?"

Emma looked at her but didn't stop pacing.

"I mean, if it was out of character for you, why did you decide to get involved?"

Emma's curt laugh was incredulous. "It wasn't my original intention. I know how Dylan is wired. Christ, we even discussed that this couldn't possibly last beyond Russia. But then she got hurt and I realized exactly how I felt about her." She pointed at Brooke. "I know what you're thinking. You think it's my own fault. We made clear boundaries, and I knew the outcome before I went down this path with her. Believe me, I play those exact sentiments over and over in my head, every day."

Brooke grabbed Emma's hand and pulled her down onto the couch. "That wasn't what I was thinking." She gave her a half smile. "I was thinking that despite your intention to keep this in some nice little box, you fell in love with her. I know she hurt you in Estonia, but I think she was scared, and she was doing what she's programmed to do—follow the plan. That's what we're all taught to do. She's here now, and it seems like she wants to give you two another chance."

"None of that matters." Emma closed her eyes. "I'd never felt pain like that before, and I can't imagine going through it again. I'd accepted what happened as something that was out of her control. I know she was trying to do the right thing. But then, she never called me. She spoke with you and Tyler, but never me. If she really missed me, if she really thought we could be something, she would've called."

Brooke looked at the engagement ring on her finger and pushed it around with her thumb. "You know, Tyler tried to keep me away at first, too. She thought she was protecting me." She quietly laughed and shook her head.

"Not everyone is you and Tyler. You two are lucky."

"How do you know that you and Dylan aren't like Tyler and me?" Brooke took Emma's hand again. "Emma, you're going to have to decide if the pain of not being with Dylan is greater than the pain of potentially getting your heart broken again. Once you figure that out, you'll know what to do."

Emma tried to hold back the tears she felt forming. She understood what Brooke was saying; she just wasn't sure if she was strong enough to endure the loss of Dylan all over again. The idea of getting close to Dylan, sharing herself with her, just to have it ripped away again was too much to bear. Because that was really what it all came down to, wasn't it? All this anger she was feeling was coming from a place of fear. She understood why Dylan did what she did, so why couldn't she get past it? Even the premise of Dylan not calling her as her source of anger was nothing more than a shield against the pain. Emma knew the answer but couldn't bring herself to say it aloud. It didn't matter how much her heart longed for Dylan. She'd listen to her head this time like she should have when they first met, so she'd never have to feel like this again.

Chapter Thirty-five

Dylan pushed her earpiece. "Testing."

Brooke's voice was in her ear a moment later. "Roger, we hear you loud and clear."

"We have a visual on you, too. If anything goes sideways, we'll pull you out," Caden said.

Dylan adjusted her baseball cap and continued to lean against the lamppost. She checked her watch. It wouldn't be long now. She thought about Emma sitting next to Brooke, their computer screen scrolling with various images they were abstracting from all the public cameras available. Emma wasn't talking to her, but it felt good knowing she was there.

The front door to the hotel opened and Nikolai strolled out, a man on each side of him. He gazed up at the sky, waiting for his car to pull around. Dylan took a deep breath and darted across the street. She knew the men would stop her when she approached, so she wasn't surprised when one grabbed her shoulder before she got too close. She pulled away, not liking the contact.

"Sasha?" Nikolai's expression shifted from surprise to anger. "Or what is it that I should call you? I know you aren't who you say."

Dylan handed him the note and hid the shiver of fear she felt at his words. Her cover was blown, then. Now she knew. "No, I'm not." She waited for him to finish reading it. "Follow those instructions, and your questions will be answered."

Nikolai balled up the piece of paper, but he put it in his pocket instead of dropping it. "You dare to threaten my daughter? I should take care of you here and now."

"But you aren't going to do that, Nikolai. I finally found your one weakness and you have no idea who else I've told. You have something to lose." One of the men grabbed her by her injured arm, but she resisted the urge to cry out.

Nikolai's neck turned red and the color crawled up to his face. "Let her go." He opened the car door and got in without saying another word.

Dylan watched the car pull away and wasn't sure if her nerve endings were registering pure terror or relief. The ball was no longer in her court. Nikolai would either become a CIA asset, or he'd be dropped into a hole and never be heard from again. Either way, her mission was over. She thought of Emma, and for the first time in her life, she was looking forward to what came next in her life.

Emma rubbed the rosary in her pocket. The adrenaline pumping through her body had her on edge. The feeling was disorienting, making her feel a little dizzy, and she wasn't convinced that she wouldn't vomit. She had pulled all the information Martin had asked her to retrieve. It was on the table, in full display for Nikolai to see. She chewed on her thumb and did her best to ignore Dylan sitting a few feet away. Her face was pale, and Emma fought the urge to see if it had anything to do with her arm.

"Target is on his way. He appears to be alone," Tyler said, her voice crackling in the earpiece.

Emma rubbed her hands over her face. "I don't know how you've ever gotten used to this feeling."

Brooke made a few more keystrokes. "I'd like to say that you do, but I'd be lying."

"Sit down, Quinn," Martin said as he took his seat. "You're making everyone nervous."

The buzzer to the door sounded and Caden pulled it open, her weapon drawn and ready. Nikolai noticed immediately and put his hands up, showing he wasn't carrying anything. Caden quickly checked his waistband and ankles, then directed him to the table in the center of the room. Emma watched as he glared at Dylan, anger radiating from his body. The way he looked at Dylan, clearly wanting to kill her, sent a shiver up her spine.

"I'm Deputy Director Martin of the CIA." He put his hand out, but Nikolai took a seat without acknowledging him.

"What do you want from me?" Nikolai turned to look at Dylan. "What have you done?"

Martin pushed the papers forward. "We know exactly who you are and about all the things you've done, Nikolai. I'm here to offer you a deal. We want you to become an informant."

Nikolai was quiet, and then his body started shaking. It started in his belly and moved its way up, guttural laughter taking hold of him. "You think I'd betray my county for America?" He snorted out between laughs. "Why would I do that?"

Martin didn't so much as crack a smile. "Because if you don't, we'll reveal exactly who you are to your daughter. We know she believes her father was some kind of war hero who died before she was born. We'll tell her the truth. We'll tell her everything about you."

Nikolai picked up a picture from the table. He looked at the small girl in the photo, touching her cheek. "What makes you think that would matter to me?"

"Because you kept her a secret. Because you know she's the only good thing you've ever created. Because you know that if she discovers the truth about you, the only remaining part of your humanity will be gone," Dylan said. There was no emotion in her voice or her face. "Or worse, we'll let your enemies know exactly who she is, and where she can be found. Do you want that hanging over your head? Are you willing to put her in danger?"

"What is your real name?" Nikolai turned his full attention to Dylan. When she didn't answer, he continued. "You think you're better than me? You think you ascended to your position in my organization because of good deeds? No, dear girl. You got there because of your ruthless instincts. You got there because you did whatever I asked, without fear of consequence or conscience. Now you sit here in judgment of my humanity? Have you forgotten the people you helped make disappear? Have you forgotten the blood, the carnage?"

Dylan picked up a more recent photo of his daughter and held it up to him. "If your enemies discover who she is, she will be hunted every day for the rest of her life. Do you want that on your conscience?"

Nikolai took the picture and stared at it. "Do you want it on yours?"

Martin nudged Brooke, and she turned the computer screen toward Nikolai. "You can see here that we have access to your international bank accounts. We have copies of your emails from all your business deals. You can either work with us or we'll shut it all down. We'll dismantle your remaining relationships one by one. You've already taken a major blow in human trafficking. We can make things much harder than you could ever imagine. Or better yet, we'll drop you in a hole somewhere and let you imagine what we're doing."

Nikolai looked surprised by the information on the screen. "Even if you get me out of the way, there will be another. We're too big to fail."

"We aren't all that interested in your business. We're much more concerned with the Russian government." Martin was deliberate with his words, taking his time.

Nikolai smiled. "I see you're not really all that different from us after all. You're not as concerned with the people affected by my business as you are with my government. Politics before people, always."

Martin pulled a folder from his bag and placed a piece of paper in front of Nikolai. "We consider it part of the greater good. We're willing to look the other way regarding your indiscretions if it's beneficial to us and to the world overall."

Emma felt a lump form in the back of her throat. She knew how dangerous Russia was, there was no denying it. From their interference in US elections to their rocky relations with the international community. But the US was willing to trade on the lives of human trafficking, drug trafficking, and money laundering to have an inside edge on the Russian government. She understood intellectually what the CIA was trying to accomplish, but it didn't make her feel any better about her role in it.

Nikolai stared at the paper. "You'll leave my daughter alone? You'll leave her relation to me a secret?"

Martin nodded and pointed to the dotted line. "As long as you keep your end of the deal. And you'll leave Agent Prey alone. If you violate any of the conditions…well, we have ways of making people disappear, too."

Nikolai looked at Dylan. "Prey?" He waited for her to make eye contact with him. "In my experience, you've been much more the predator than the prey."

Dylan crossed her arms and shrugged, her expression inscrutable. "I did what I had to do."

Nikolai picked up the pen and signed his name. "See, we're not all that different. I need assurances that my government will not find out. Your threats pale in comparison to what they'll do to me if they find out I'm here with you."

Martin pulled the papers away and handed them to Brooke. "We'll make sure you have good cover from our end. Remember, as long as this stays mutually beneficial, you're worth more to us alive than dead."

Martin and Brooke explained to Nikolai how he would report, what channels to go through, and how they would be in touch. It was all background noise to Emma. Dylan looked defeated in a way she hadn't expected. This was a win. It would be good for her career. Emma wanted to run her hands over her face and soothe away the pain Emma saw flash through Dylan's eyes when she looked at Emma. She wanted to kiss her until all Dylan could think about was the good that existed in the world. She wanted to remind her of all the things worth fighting for. But she stayed in her seat and let the possibilities of what could have been play in a loop in her mind. Once something was broken, it could never be put back together the way it was before.

CHAPTER THIRTY-SIX

Tyler did her best to remain calm, more for Brooke than herself. She knew Brooke needed her to be steady now more than ever. She wanted her to understand that no matter how this night played out, they would be okay.

"I'm not having this conversation with you again, Mother." Brooke's voice was steady, but Tyler could feel the impatience bubbling below the surface.

"It has nothing to do with Tyler, Brooke. She seems nice enough. I just think it's too soon. You've never really given any man a chance."

Brooke squeezed Tyler's hand under the table. "I'm not going to keep doing this with you. Even if I didn't know Tyler, I wouldn't end up with a man. I'm gay. As in, only attracted to women. I don't know why it's so hard for you to understand."

Janice sipped her wine, undeterred by her proclamation. "It's just not natural, and it's embarrassing."

"I'm sorry I'm such an embarrassment to you," Brooke said sharply.

"Oh, don't be so melodramatic, Brooke. You know what I mean. Look at your brothers, they all turned out perfectly normal. I don't know what I did to you to make you behave this way," Janice said.

Brooke put her fork down, trying to gain her composure. "Not everything is about you. Why don't you understand that? This is who I am. It doesn't matter to me if you think it's normal or not. I'm going to marry Tyler on Saturday. You can either be there or not, I really don't care." She raised her hand for Janice to stop when it looked like she was going to interrupt. "But if you *are* going to be there, it has to be because you support me. Us. I don't want to hear your flippant remarks, and I won't tolerate your disdain, especially on the most important day of my life, among my friends who would be equally offended by your narrow-mindedness. I love Tyler, and I'm going to spend the rest of my life with her. It's up to you if you want to be a part of that or not. But I'm done trying to play nice with you."

Captain Hart looked between his wife and his daughter and took a deep breath, focusing on Tyler. "Tyler, you're one of the finest people I've ever met. I'll be proud to call you my daughter-in-law. I'll be there to walk Brooke down the aisle whether my wife is in attendance or not." He looked over at Janice. "Sweetheart, I never tell you how to feel or behave. You've given me a wonderful life and four wonderful children. But in this instance, you're simply wrong."

Janice threw her napkin on the table and stood. "If you want to watch our daughter throw her life away, that's your prerogative. I've been supportive. I went dress shopping, and we even bought them a gift. But do not expect me to remain silent when I see, as clear as day, that this is wrong." She left the restaurant, never bothering to look back.

Brooke's father swirled the scotch in his glass, staring at the dwindling ice cubes. "I'm sorry—"

Brooke shook her head. "Don't. Don't defend her actions like you always have. Don't try to make what she said okay. Don't try to make me feel better about this. You're my parents. Your love is supposed to be unconditional."

He nodded and sipped his drink. "You're right. When Tyler told me she intended to marry you, I was overcome with joy. I'm embarrassed to say that feeling was quickly eclipsed by dread, knowing your mother's reaction. I know it's hard to believe, but she does love you."

Brooke got out of her chair. "You're right, it is hard to believe. She wants to love a version of me that doesn't exist. She doesn't love the real me." She glanced around. "I'm going to go freshen up." She shook her head when Tyler went to get up too. "I'd prefer to go alone."

Calvin watched Brooke walk away and took a deep breath. "They're more alike than they realize, you know."

Tyler sipped her wine, choosing her words carefully. "I'm sure that's true in many aspects, but there is one glaring difference—Brooke is fearless. She isn't bogged down by differences in people, or how that may reflect upon her. She loves with a ferocity I'm lucky to be on the receiving end of. So, while they may share similar features and even a propensity for stubbornness, they're very different."

Calvin wrapped both hands around his glass and continued to stare at the liquid. Tyler knew there were no answers there, but it seemed to be a habit of his when he was thinking. "When Brooke was a little girl, I remember thinking she'd be a force to be reckoned with as an adult. There was no obstacle too big, and no challenge she wouldn't meet head-on. Her need to prove herself, to prove her independence, is hardwired into her. I'd tell my wife how it was going to take an equally strong man to make her happy." He looked at her and smiled. "You may not be a man, but you're worthy of my daughter. She met her match with you."

Brooke returned to the table, and he stood to kiss her. He hugged her for longer than Tyler had ever seen. He rubbed her arms, and it looked like he was fighting back tears. Tyler stood, and he hugged her as well. The embrace seemed to more of an apology than a farewell.

"See you on Saturday?" Brooke seemed to need reassurance.

He picked up his jacket from the back of the chair. "I wouldn't miss it."

Tyler wasn't sure if Janice would make an appearance at the wedding or not. Her gut told her that her stubborn streak would keep her away. If that was the case, it would be for the best. Tyler didn't want anything to ruin their day. She didn't want it tainted with Janice's dirty looks or mean comments. She'd thought she and Calvin had made some progress, but not all relationships could be saved.

Carol made use of every square inch of her small cell. She could make it around the room in twenty paces. She'd done it over two thousand times. It had become a habit of hers, to count her steps in this small room. The simple task helped to clear her mind and settle the pit that was growing in her stomach. She'd made her request almost sixteen hours ago, but it didn't seem that anyone was in a hurry to accommodate her.

Finally, she heard a clanging at the door and a voice telling her to put her hands through the small hole at the front of her door. This whole process was ridiculous. She was going to be shackled at her hands, then her feet in some bizarre effort to keep her from hurting anyone, including herself. She also knew it was to prevent her from running away. But where would she go? They'd shoot her before she was within a foot of the gate.

The large, hulking man told her to stay close against the wall, to not look around, and to keep her mouth shut. She did as she was told. It was a weird feeling, to suddenly feel so submissive, so willing to bend to the whims of others. But Carol was a survivor, and she'd do whatever was necessary. The guard used his keycard to access another room and pushed her inside, slamming the door behind her.

She shuffled over to the metal table and took a seat. "Thank you for coming."

"What is it you want, O'Brien?" Caden's arms were crossed, and there was a fury in her eyes that Carol assumed was reserved for people she truly hated.

Tyler leaned forward on the metal table, intertwining her fingers. "You have ten minutes."

"I want a reduced sentence. I'm going to give you something that neither of you has in exchange for the death penalty being taken off the table."

Caden laughed. "Do we look like prosecutors to you? We can't give you that, and even if we could, I'd never make a deal with you."

"I want to testify against Walker. I'll give you everything I know." Carol wished she still smoked. A cigarette sounded wonderful right about now. She'd given up the habit two decades earlier but might take it up again now.

Tyler pointed in Caden's direction using her thumb. "Like Styles said, we're not the right people to talk to about this."

"Aren't you, though? Hasn't this always been about us? Who will win? Who will lose? You two know me better than anyone else. You know me well enough to have finally caught me. So, you know that I'm not lying when I say that I'll give you everything. I'll give you the inner workings of the white nationalists, everything. I'll give you the people they haven't found yet. The people who remain hidden in the system. Think of what that would do for your careers."

Caden snorted. "This isn't a game. No one has won or lost. You've built an entire organization with the sole intent of igniting hate and fear. You tried to have the president and vice president murdered. You've tried to have each of us killed on more than one occasion. Now, you think you can call us in here and we'll help you?"

Carol shrugged. "People do funny things when they're backed into a corner." She tried to smile, but she knew she wasn't nearly as charming in her orange jumpsuit. "I've done some pretty horrible things, I know that. I can't change any of that now. I know it doesn't make sense to either of you, but I did what I had to do to succeed. There was no other option for me."

Tyler looked at her with so much disgust in her eyes, Carol had to look away.

"There is always a choice. Countless people have been hurt or killed because of you. You ignited a brand of fear in this country that we haven't seen since the Civil War. Spare us your musings about your feminist roots. You hurt more people than you will ever know. You've endangered more people than you will ever know. Now, you have a rare opportunity to do the right thing, and you want something in exchange. It's not good enough for you to finally do something right, there has to be something in it for you. You make me sick."

Carol admired Tyler's resolve. If nothing else, the girl had spunk. "Oh, please. Your naiveté may work on your girlfriend, but it doesn't work on me. You think I created the hate in this country? You think I personally put a pitchfork in their hands? I may have given those people a direction, but they never needed a purpose. They were raised with hate in their hearts, I didn't do that. I know it's easy to blame me. It makes you more comfortable to point at a single person, to lay the entirety of the issue at their feet. But be realistic, if it weren't me, it would've been someone else. People hate people who are different because it's easy. It's easy to look at your shitty life and blame a force that you don't understand. We've made it easy in this country, and that didn't start with me, and it won't end when I'm gone."

Caden leaned against the wall on the other side of the room, apparently wanting as much space between them as possible. "You may not have given it to them, but you capitalized on it. You found illness in the hearts of people, and you sold them a fake cure. Your charlatan ways hurt more lives than we'll ever know."

Carol sighed. Their belief that they were better than her was irksome. "I did. I saw an opportunity, and I took it. Now, I'm going to give you the tools to fix it."

Tyler checked her watch. "You unleashed something that can't be put back in the bottle. Putting you on trial, seeing you pay for your decisions, won't erase the hate in anyone's heart. We know that. But what it will do is show people that it won't be tolerated. At best, you'll spend the rest of your life in jail. Your legacy will be one of evil, corruption, and hate. In thirty years when kids read about you in history books, your story will be one of warning." Tyler knocked on the door, signaling they were done. "That will be the only way you're remembered."

Carol watched as they both moved toward the door, to leave her alone, once again. "You know what?" She waited until Tyler turned to face her. "They *will* remember me."

CHAPTER THIRTY-SEVEN

Dylan looked herself over in the mirror one last time. She'd bought the suit two years prior but never had an occasion to wear it until now. She ran her fingers through her hair and took a deep breath. She was looking forward to the day's festivities. It'd be the first step she took toward fitting back into normalcy. The last few years had been a whirlwind. Drugs, money, death, and mayhem had been her way of life with the Russians. Now she'd have the opportunity to know what it was like to live outside the eye of the storm.

She was looking forward to this transition, as scary as it felt. She had so many things she wanted to say to Emma. So many things she needed to say. She still wasn't sure if it was going to be good enough. She knew that if she didn't take the chance, she'd always regret it. She'd turned in her request for transfer, something she never imagined doing. Being someone else, being invisible, no longer appealed to her. Even if Emma didn't take her back, she'd awakened something in her. Dylan wanted something different from life now, and she'd always be grateful to Emma for that change.

Dylan's phone buzzed, and she picked it up to check the text message. A few minutes later, she was getting into Tony's car. "Thanks for coming with me."

Tony ran his hand down the front of his chest, adjusting his tie. "I don't get invited to many weddings. I'm happy to go with you."

"How long are you here for?" Dylan wanted to engage in casual conversation, an attempt to tamp down the anxiety she felt growing in her stomach.

"I can't tell you." He smiled at her. "You're not on my team anymore."

"I'll always be on your team, Tony." Dylan patted his leg.

"You beat the odds this time. I was sure you'd be killed." Tony flipped his turn signal as if he'd just said the most mundane sentence possible.

Dylan couldn't help but chuckle. She enjoyed Tony's straightforward approach and no-nonsense summaries. "Yeah, I wasn't sure there for a while myself. It was a close call."

Tony pulled up to the valet. "Well, I'm glad you're still alive."

She opened the car door and got out. "Thanks, Tony. Me too."

They walked into the venue, and Dylan was overwhelmed by the beauty of the area. The flowers and lights were a beautiful touch and added a sense of elegance mixed with casual warmth. The view overlooking DC was the real showstopper. Dylan walked over to one of the large windows and looked down on the Potomac River and the Washington Monument. It was breathtaking. She smiled, happy to be here to share this day with people she had grown to count as friends.

All that was left to do was lay her heart bare to Emma. She wasn't sure what the outcome would be, or how she'd leave her tonight. She'd never been in a situation like the one she was in with Emma. She'd never found anyone worth fighting for, or worth showing herself to. This was uncharted territory, and she should be terrified. But that isn't what she felt. She was going to lay it all out there and hope Emma would see the truth on her face. It was all she could do. She was ready to take the leap.

Emma and the other bridesmaids watched as the hairdresser put the final touches on Brooke. The day had already been filled with laughter, tears of happiness, and a few glasses of champagne. Emma searched her mind trying to come up with a better word than "stunning" to describe how Brooke looked, but that's what she was, stunning. Brooke was beautiful, there was no denying that. Today, there was something else that made her exquisite. She was exuding happiness, contentment, and love. Watching Brooke smile when she thought no one was looking brought Emma a sense of warmth she couldn't quite explain.

Nicole handed Emma her flowers. "It's time for us to line up."

Emma took the flowers and peeked around Nicole. "Still no Janice?"

Nicole glanced at Jennifer, who was shutting the door. Jennifer shook her head. "I guess not."

Brooke walked over to the three of them and gathered them up like a bundle of sticks, hugging them as a group. "Thank you all for being here today. It means everything to me."

Nicole beamed at her. "I'd kiss your cheeks, but I don't want to ruin your makeup."

"I'm so glad you and Kyle made it." Brooke kissed Nicole's cheek.

"We wouldn't have missed it."

There was a knock on the door, and a moment later, Captain Hart stuck his head through. "You ready, sweetheart?"

Brooke hugged them all again. "I'll see you all in a minute."

Caden was the first in line. She looked amazing in the black tuxedo that seemed to match her hair perfectly. The deep ebony color of her suit set off the color in her eyes perfectly. She stuck her arm out to Jennifer after kissing her cheek and whispering something in her ear that Emma couldn't hear, but it made Jennifer laugh and blush. Nicole took Kyle's arm behind them. Emma watched as Nicole ran her fingers through his hair, ensuring that he looked perfect.

"You're with me," Patrick said to Emma. He stuck out his arm for her to take. The boyish charm Brooke had described flowed out of him effortlessly. "You all look incredible."

She'd only recently met Patrick but already knew she liked him. "Thank you." She leaned closer to him. "Are you nervous?"

He covered her hand with his own. "I just hope I don't trip over my own feet and take you down with me. Tyler would be very disappointed to discover her training sessions with me at the Farm didn't alleviate my klutziness."

Emma squeezed his hand. "We'll help balance each other."

Emma heard the music start, and her heart started thumping in her chest. She had no idea why she was so nervous; this was Brooke and Tyler's day. Maybe it was the thought of having people watch her move down the aisle, or maybe it was the thought that she might trip and fall. As the door opened, she knew exactly why her heart was pounding in her stomach, why her hands were tingling, and why she could feel the blood pumping in her ears. Dylan.

Dylan watched her with so much intensity it felt like she was actually touching her. Emma's skin felt like it was on fire as Dylan's eyes tracked her. She felt her body shudder under her gaze, and she forced herself to take several deep breaths to stay focused on the task at hand. She finally made it to the front and took her place. The room stood as Brooke and her father crossed the threshold, every set of eyes focusing on the bride. But Dylan, Dylan continued to stare at Emma. The longing on her face and the love in her eyes almost brought Emma to her knees. She thought she'd feel the familiar pang of loss when she saw Dylan, but that's not what was there. Loss had been replaced by a need she hadn't anticipated.

Chapter Thirty-eight

The amount of nervous energy coursing through Tyler could have lit the entire city. Her hands had been shaking, and there had been sweat starting to pool at the base of her back. Then the doors opened, and Tyler got the first glimpse of the rest of her life, and the entirety of the world fell away. With every step that Brooke took toward her, the nerves seemed to disappear, and a sense of calm consumed her.

There were tears in Brooke's dad's eyes as he walked his daughter toward Tyler. When they finally reached the end, he hugged Tyler and kissed Brooke. He released Brooke's hand and sat next to an empty seat, reserved for his wife.

Brooke stepped up next to Tyler and mouthed "*I love you*" before the judge started speaking. Tyler had never felt so sure of anything. Their lives prior to their meeting didn't matter. The only thing that mattered was that they would be together forever. Tyler didn't need a piece of paper to solidify that, but it was tangible proof to the rest of the world that they were unbreakable.

When it was time for Tyler to say her vows, she took Brooke's hands to stop herself from kissing her when Brooke smiled up at her. "Brooke, you aren't just a person I met and fell in love with. You are something that happened to me. You changed everything. You not only gave me a greater sense of purpose, you gave me a home. You've taught me what it means to be intimate. Before you, I had no idea what intimacy really meant. You showed me that true intimacy is trust. Trust that you can lay everything before another person, all your mistakes, your dreams, your failures, and your aspirations. You trust that person to hold those secrets in their heart and protect them like they were their own. Before you, I couldn't imagine life outside of work. Now, when I look toward the next fifty years, the one constant is you. I can't promise you that I'll never hurt your feelings, that I'll be perfect, or that I'll always do the right thing. I *can* promise you that you will always come before me, that I'll apologize when I've made a mistake, and that I'll always treat you with the respect and loyalty that you deserve. I don't need to promise to love you forever because my love for you is a fundamental part of who I am. I wouldn't be me without you." Tyler placed the ring on Brooke's trembling finger.

Brooke looked at her with so much love in her eyes that Tyler felt it swell in her own body.

"Tyler, I've never told you this, but I knew I loved you from the first time I kissed you. I had never experienced a connection with someone the way I had with you. No one has ever looked at me the way you do every single day. I didn't realize until you that I'd never really been seen before. You're the bravest, most loyal, must decent person I've ever had the pleasure of knowing. There isn't a version of my future that I don't see you in, and I promise there never will be. You're my now, my forever, and whatever comes after that. There is only you, there will only ever be you." Brooke placed the ring on Tyler's finger.

Tyler heard the judge announcing the completion of the ceremony, but she couldn't make out the words entirely. She didn't know if she'd waited for him to tell her to kiss Brooke, she just couldn't stop herself. The cheers and clapping from their friends and family was the only way she registered the ceremony was over. Caden was slapping her back and hugging Brooke. It was so perfect it felt almost surreal.

When they turned to walk back down the aisle, Tyler caught a glimpse of Janice ducking into another part of the building. She glanced over at Brooke, but she hadn't noticed. She was busy hugging her bridesmaids and her father. Tyler hoped Janice wasn't leaving. She wanted her to stay; she wanted her to be part of their family. She wanted that for Brooke.

The pictures took much longer than Tyler could've dreamed. The photographer seemed to want to catch them in every pose that she could possibly imagine. Normally, it would've bored Tyler to death, but that didn't matter today. It wasn't hard to smile at Brooke, laugh at her jokes, or nuzzle up close to her in a variety of angles. She would gratefully cherish every moment.

It wasn't until they were standing outside the reception hall, waiting for the DJ to announce their entrance as a married couple, that she had a moment alone with Brooke.

Tyler cupped Brooke's face and kissed her slowly. "I love you."

Brooke leaned into her touch. "I love you too."

"It was a beautiful ceremony," Janice said from behind them.

Tyler felt Brooke stiffen under her hands. "You weren't there, Mother."

Janice approached slowly, looking meeker than Tyler had ever seen her.

"I wasn't in the front row like I should have been, but I was there." She looked like she was going to reach out to Brooke but changed her mind. "You look beautiful." She looked at Tyler. "You both look beautiful."

Brooke pulled Tyler closer, leaning into her. "What are you doing here?"

Janice looked down at the ground and wrung her hands. "I'm sorry I didn't see it before." She looked at them with tears in her eyes. "I didn't understand how much you loved each other. That's my fault. I never really listened to you, Brooke. I'd like to change that. I spoke with your father at length last night. That's why I've got these terrible bags under my eyes…anyway. We were up all night talking, and he finally got me to understand some things. I realize now that I've been putting my own issues on to you." She straightened her outfit. "My mother hated your father when I met him. He reminded me of how that affected me and my relationship. She refused to see the good in him, and she chastised me for falling in love with him. I'd rail against her ridiculous behavior for hours, because I wanted nothing more than for her to see my love for him. I'm afraid I've done the same to you."

Brooke was hesitant at first but finally reached out and hugged her mother. "Thank you for saying that."

Janice seemed caught off guard by the hug for a moment and then leaned into it. "I want to make things better. This is something I don't understand, but I'm willing to try. I just need you to be patient with me."

Brooke nodded. "That's all I wanted."

Janice let go of Brooke and touched Tyler's arm. "I'm sorry I haven't been more welcoming to you, Tyler. I can see now how much you love my daughter. I'd understand if you two didn't want me in your lives, but I hope that isn't the case."

Tyler hugged her without hesitation. She had no desire to hold a grudge, and this had been what she wanted all along. "Thank you for coming."

Janice took a deep breath and stepped back. "Now, which last name are you two taking? I don't want to mess this up in the future."

"We're keeping our last names. You won't mess anything up," Tyler said.

Janice sighed. "How very modern of you both." She smiled, but Tyler could see a bit of disappointment in her eyes.

Brooke took Tyler's arm. "Actually, I've been thinking about that. We're going to have children eventually. I think it would be easier if we had the same last name."

They'd discussed this at length, and Tyler didn't understand why it was coming up again, now. "Brooke, I told you I wasn't going to give up Monroe. It's the last thing I have from my parents."

Brooke kissed her cheek. "Honey, I don't want you to give up your name. My parents have three boys to carry on the family name. I'd like to be a Monroe, if that's okay with you?"

Tyler kissed her because there were no words to describe her feelings about what Brooke had just said. She knew taking a name wasn't necessary to be a family, and she understood why Brooke had wanted to keep her own. It hadn't mattered. But now, the idea that Brooke wanted to share a last name with her, with the intention of raising children, made Tyler fall even more in love with her.

Janice snickered. "Well, she really must love you. I've never seen her back down from any position."

Brooke smiled at her. "Oh, Mom, I come by it honestly."

"That you do, my dear." Janice kissed Brooke and Tyler again and then disappeared into the reception hall ahead of them.

Tyler kissed their entwined fingers and looked at Brooke. "Have I mentioned how beautiful you look today?"

Brooke smiled. "Once or twice. Have I mentioned how much I love you?"

Tyler heard the DJ announce them and the doors were pulled open. Tyler let Brooke lead them into the room full of their friends and family and toward their forever.

Chapter Thirty-nine

Dylan watched as Tyler twirled Brooke around the dance floor. Even with all the loud music, laughter, and talking guests, they seemed to only see each other. It was almost magical. The ceremony had been beautiful, and the reception was shaping up to be a party that people would be discussing for quite some time. Everyone seemed to be riding the wave of Brooke and Tyler's bliss, just as it should be.

Despite all the love in the air, Dylan still hadn't brought herself to talk to Emma. At first, she'd put it off because Emma seemed busy being a bridesmaid, but she knew that wasn't true. What held her back now was the fact that if Emma turned her down, that would be it. Dylan wasn't sure how to let her go yet, and taking the chance meant precisely that.

Tony leaned over, closer to her ear. "If you aren't going to ask Emma to dance, I'm going to do it."

Dylan hadn't noticed that her leg was rocking up and down until she saw Tony staring at it. "It isn't that easy. She might say no."

He nodded. "True, but there's only a sixteen percent chance of that happening."

Dylan stood, took off her sling, handed it to Tony, and walked toward the front table. She could handle sixteen percent. Hell, she'd beaten much worse odds than that. Emma stopped talking to Jennifer when she noticed her approaching. Emma's face flushed, which was either a very good thing or a very bad thing. It was too late to turn back now, because if she did, she'd regret it forever.

"You look incredible," Dylan said, because it was true and because she needed Emma to know how she still saw her.

Emma blushed. "You look very nice as well."

"Do you want to dance?" Dylan said it much faster than she'd intended, and she was frustrated to be so nervous.

Emma looked over at Jennifer who winked at her before she answered. "I'd like that."

Dylan put her hand around Emma's waist and pulled her closer. She hadn't forgotten the way Emma smelled or the way she felt. She let her mind wander to those memories every chance she had. But the memories didn't do Emma any justice.

"Is your arm okay? I don't want to hurt you," Emma said as she moved closer to her.

A chill went up Dylan's spine at the words spoken against her ear. "It's okay, as long as we're not going running."

Dylan was trying to be funny but immediately regretted it when she felt Emma stiffen against her. "Do you still want to run?"

Dylan pulled her closer so that Emma's ear was against her lips. "No, I don't. I was scared about what not running could mean. So, I stuck to the plan, because I thought it was the right thing. I didn't want to slow down long enough for you to see the real me. I didn't want you to find out the things I've done, and the people I've hurt. I was scared you wouldn't look at me the same. But none of that matters now. I've never felt about anyone the way I do about you."

"What's changed?"

"I never had a reason to slow down before. I've never found anything worth slowing down for before. Until I met you. I never met anyone worth showing my worst parts to." Dylan waited for Emma to pull away, but she didn't. "I've spent every single day since we've been apart wishing I'd done things differently."

Emma wrapped her arms around her a little tighter. "You should've trusted how I felt about you. It's also possible that I was being slightly unreasonable." Emma blushed. "I pushed you away too. Not as directly, but I used my anger to keep you away."

"I should have. I should've told you then what I've known since the first time I touched you. I love you, Emma Quinn. I want you. I don't know if we'll end up here one day." She nodded to Brooke and Tyler. "But I want to try. I want to be the kind of person that you can count on, that you can love."

Emma leaned away from her, her eyes searching Dylan's. "Dylan, you already are. You don't need to change. I love you exactly the way you are."

"You love me?" Dylan knew she heard the words correctly, she just wanted to hear them again.

Emma smiled, her eyes full of love. "Yes, I love you."

Dylan wanted to kiss her. Her whole body was yelling at her to kiss Emma, to claim her. But this final step, this last decision, Emma needed to be the one to make it. Emma leaned in a little closer, and Dylan inhaled the smell of wine from her lips. Emma only lingered there a second longer before she closed the final distance between them. The kiss was slow and sensual. It was filled with a promise of things to come and the connection they shared. It was the best kiss of Dylan's life. She would've gladly stayed there forever, letting Emma's gentle touches to her back and shoulders ignite a spark in Dylan no one ever had before.

It wasn't until she heard Caden right beside her that Dylan finally broke the kiss.

"Well, it's about time you two got your shit together."

Jennifer pushed her back. "Leave them alone. You're impossible."

Dylan leaned her head against Emma's, still laughing at Caden. "I should've come for you sooner. I'm sorry I didn't."

Emma kissed her again. "It doesn't matter now."

A striking couple was walking up behind Emma. Dylan recognized them from the wedding party and was sure they were coming to pull Emma away. She was surprised when the woman said her name instead.

"Dylan Prey?"

Dylan took the outstretched hand. "Yes, hi."

"I'm Nicole Sable, and this is Kyle King. We worked with Tyler while she was at Camp Peary." She pointed to the man next to her. "We hear congratulations are in order. Kyle is still working over at the Farm, but I started at CIAU a few months ago. Everyone is very excited to have you on board."

Dylan could feel Emma's eyes on her, but she tried to focus on Nicole. "Yes, it was made official last week. I start on Monday."

Nicole grinned. "Let's have lunch on Monday?"

Dylan nodded. "I'd like that."

"Great, see you then," Nicole said and pulled Kyle into a slow dance.

Emma pointed to the balcony. "We need to talk."

Dylan followed her, unsure of what the change of expression on her face meant. She thought Emma would be excited to have her here. Well, she'd be excited if things worked out, which Dylan thought they just had. Maybe the idea of having Dylan available and accessible was more commitment than Emma wanted to make.

"What was that about?" Emma asked once they were out on the balcony. But there was no anger in her tone, and she took Dylan's hand.

"I requested a transfer to CIA University. It was approved and I start an instructor gig on Monday." Dylan said the words slowly, unsure how Emma would react.

"I hope you didn't do that for me. I don't need you to be someone different. I don't need you to change. I want you to be exactly who you are. Even if that means I go months without seeing you because you're undercover somewhere," Emma said.

"I didn't transfer for you, I transferred for me. I want to call a place home for longer than an assignment. I want a break from the most vicious men in the world. I want a chance to feel normal. I don't know if I'll do this for two years or twenty, but I want to do it for now. I didn't do this for you, but you made me realize that I wanted something different for my life. You made me realize that I wanted more, that I deserved more." Dylan wasn't sure if she was making sense, but she trusted that Emma would hear her words and believe her.

A smile tugged at the corner of Emma's mouth. "So, you're going to be around for a while?" She ran her hands up Dylan's chest and around her neck, careful to avoid her wound. "I think I could get used to that." She kissed her, smiling as their lips met.

"I was hoping you'd say that." Dylan pulled her closer and deepened the kiss.

Emma ran her hands through Dylan's hair. "I love you."

Dylan looked back into the room. "You want to get back in there?"

Emma blushed and looked away, embarrassed by her thoughts. "I was hoping you'd say you wanted to get out of here."

Dylan took Emma by the hand and pulled her toward the elevator. Brooke spotted them and waved and blew them a kiss as they got into the elevator. Dylan's heart was so full she thought it might burst. The idea of what the future might hold with Emma and what her life could be warmed her soul. She'd never known what it felt like to truly belong anywhere, what it felt like to be home. When she turned and looked at Emma smiling up at her, she knew that's exactly what she found. Home.

EPILOGUE

I hate you both so damn much!" Caden was flat on her back, screaming up into the sky.

"You're without a doubt the most dramatic person I've ever had to deal with." Tyler reached down and pulled Caden to her feet.

"If you weren't staring at Jennifer's chest, you wouldn't have missed that last shot," Dylan said with her hands on her hips. There was sand coating her stomach from the last dig she'd made.

"Shut up, Prey! No one asked you." Caden pulled on her shorts, still trying to right herself from the last play.

Brooke stood behind the service line, volleyball in hand. "Game point. You three are buying dinner when you lose."

Emma held her breath as Brooke tossed the ball in the air. The sound of it smacking her hand made a loud popping sound, and the ball soared over the net. Caden and Dylan both went for it and missed spectacularly. Brooke, Jennifer, and Emma ran to the center of their side of the court and started jumping up and down, yelling and congratulating each other.

"Nice game," Tyler said as she pulled a towel from the bench and started to dry off.

Caden and Dylan were still arguing over who should have gotten to the ball first. Their competitive sides rubbing up against each other was both ridiculous and adorable. Emma would've interfered, but she was enjoying the way Dylan looked covered in sweat and sand too much to intervene.

Jennifer flopped down on the bench next to her. "I don't know how we won that game."

Emma scoffed. "Because Brooke is an absolute beast. She played college volleyball. We're only here to get the ball to her."

Jennifer gulped down her water. "Good point. I'm glad we're on her team."

Emma took the water bottle. "Same." She opened the bag she'd brought with her to extract her shirt when she saw her rosary laying at the bottom of the bag.

It had been a gradual process. A year ago, she would've never gone anywhere without the rosary in her pocket. But over time, it had eventually moved from her purse to her car, and now her gym bag. She no longer needed the security it brought her. She didn't need a reminder that someone had once loved her, had once believed in her. She felt it every single day in the company of these women.

Dylan had approached her new job with the same focus and gusto Emma had seen in her in Russia. She'd completed two quarters in her position and was already talking about a new class she was interested in teaching. It had been eight months since Tyler and Brooke's wedding. Eight months of dating Dylan. Eight months of dinners, movies, laughter, and love. It had been the best time of her entire life, and it showed no signs of changing any time soon. The more time she spent with Dylan, the more she fell in love with her. Dylan had gradually started sharing her secrets with Emma. Stories about the places she had been, the things she'd seen, and the things she'd done. It took time to convince Dylan that she wouldn't turn away from those pieces of her. They made Dylan who she was, and Emma loved her completely.

Dylan sat on the other side of Emma. She leaned over and kissed her cheek. "Hey, beautiful."

Emma kissed her back. "You're sweet, but you three are still buying dinner."

Dylan put her hand over her chest. "You wound me. Do you really think I'd try to get out of it?"

Emma handed Dylan her shirt. "I know you would."

"Where do you guys want to go, anyway?" Caden dumped a bottle of water over her head.

Jennifer stood and pulled her toward the hotel. "I'm not taking you out in public until you shower."

Caden acted offended but followed Jennifer anyway. Emma enjoyed their playful dynamic. It suited them well. They'd just officially moved in together three months before, and they seemed happy as ever. Emma had a distinct feeling that the two of them would be together forever.

Brooke put her bag over her shoulder. "I'm glad we took this vacation. We all needed it."

Tyler wrapped her arm around her waist. "We all deserve a little relaxation now that we know O'Brien and Walker will be behind bars for the rest of their lives."

Carol O'Brien's and Steve Walker's trials hadn't taken long. With the amount of evidence the government had compiled against them, they had no choice but to plead guilty. They were both sentenced to life in prison without the possibility of parole. The death penalty had been taken off the table because of the information they'd provided to the government. They'd spend the remainder of their days in a cell, and the only politics they'd be involved in would relate to the other prisoners. Emma had been relieved they didn't receive the death penalty. She believed a life of isolation with nothing to do but reflect on their decisions was a far worse punishment than death.

So far Nikolai had kept up his end of their agreement. He'd provided the United States with a wealth of information regarding his country's happenings in world affairs. He continued to give the CIA information about competing human trafficking rings, drug running, and nuclear weapon sales. It would make Emma feel better to have him in a dark hole somewhere, but those decisions weren't up to her.

Tyler took Brooke's hand. "We'll call your room in an hour. Then we can decide where to eat."

Emma watched them walk away, and Dylan bumped her. "What are you thinking?"

"I'm just thinking about how happy I am." She put her head on Dylan's shoulder. "I never thought I'd have a life like this. I never imagined being on a two-week vacation in the Bahamas with friends like them. I never thought I'd meet someone like you. I just never imagined I'd be this happy."

Dylan wrapped an arm around her and kissed the top of her head. "Just think, this is only the beginning. We have an entire lifetime to keep making memories like this."

Emma took her hand as they walked back to the hotel. "Promise?"

Dylan kissed her hand. "I promise."

About the Author

Jackie D was born and raised in the San Francisco, East Bay Area of California. She lives with her wife, son, and their numerous furry companions. She earned a bachelor's degree in recreation administration and a dual master's degree in management and public administration. She is a Navy veteran and served in Operation Iraqi Freedom as a flight deck director, onboard the USS *Abraham Lincoln*.

She spends her free time with her wife, friends, family, and their incredibly needy dogs. She enjoys playing golf but is resigned to the fact she would equally enjoy any sport where drinking beer is encouraged during game play. Her first book, *Infiltration*, was a finalist for a Lambda Literary Award, and *Lucy's Chance* won a Goldie in 2018.

Books Available from Bold Strokes Books

Brooklyn Summer by Maggie Cummings. When opposites attract, can a summer of passion and adventure lead to a lifetime of love? (978-1-63555-578-3)

City Kitty and Country Mouse by Alyssa Linn Palmer. Pulled in two different directions, can a city kitty and country mouse fall in love and make it work? (978-1-63555-553-0)

Elimination by Jackie D. When a dangerous homegrown terrorist seeks refuge with the Russian mafia, the team will be put to the ultimate test. (978-1-63555-570-7)

In the Shadow of Darkness by Nicole Stilling. Angeline Vallencourt is a reluctant vampire who must decide what she wants more—obscurity, revenge, or the woman who makes her feel alive. (978-1-63555-624-7)

On Second Thought by C. Spencer. Madisen is falling hard for Rae. Even single life and co-parenting are beginning to click. At least, that is, until her ex-wife begins to have second thoughts. (978-1-63555-415-1)

Out of Practice by Carsen Taite. When attorney Abby Keane discovers the wedding blogger tormenting her client is the woman she had a passionate, anonymous vacation fling with, sparks and subpoenas fly. Legal Affairs: one law firm, three best friends, three chances to fall in love. (978-1-63555-359-8)

Providence by Leigh Hays. With every click of the shutter, photographer Rebekiah Kearns finds it harder and harder to keep Lindsey Blackwell in focus without getting too close. (978-1-63555-620-9)

Taking a Shot at Love by KC Richardson. When academic and athletic worlds collide, will English professor Celeste Bouchard and basketball coach Lisa Tobias ignore their attraction to achieve their professional goals? (978-1-63555-549-3)

Flight to the Horizon by Julie Tizard. Airline captain Kerri Sullivan and flight attendant Janine Case struggle to survive an emergency water landing and overcome dark secrets to give love a chance to fly. (978-1-63555-331-4)

In Helen's Hands by Nanisi Barrett D'Arnuk. As her mistress, Helen pushes Mickey to her sensual limits, delivering the pleasure only a BDSM lifestyle can provide her. (978-1-63555-639-1)

Jamis Bachman, Ghost Hunter by Jen Jensen. In Sage Creek, Utah, a poltergeist stirs to life and past secrets emerge.(978-1-63555-605-6)

Moon Shadow by Suzie Clarke. Add betrayal, season with survival, then serve revenge smokin' hot with a sharp knife. (978-1-63555-584-4)

Spellbound by Jean Copeland and Jackie D. When the supernatural worlds of good and evil face off, love might be what saves them all. (978-1-63555-564-6)

Temptation by Kris Bryant. Can experienced nanny Cassie Miller deny her growing attraction and keep her relationship with her boss professional? Or will they sidestep propriety and give in to temptation? (978-1-63555-508-0)

The Inheritance by Ali Vali. Family ties bring Tucker Delacroix and Willow Vernon together, but they could also tear them, and any chance they have at love, apart. (978-1-63555-303-1)

Thief of the Heart by MJ Williamz. Kit Hanson makes a living seducing rich women in casinos and relieving them of the expensive jewelry most won't even miss. But her streak ends when she meets beautiful FBI agent Savannah Brown. (978-1-63555-572-1)

Date Night by Raven Sky. Quinn and Riley are celebrating their one-year anniversary. Such an important milestone is bound to result in some extraordinary sexual adventures, but precisely how extraordinary is up to you, dear reader. (978-1-63555-655-1)

Face Off by PJ Trebelhorn. Hockey player Savannah Wells rarely spends more than a night with any one woman, but when photographer Madison Scott buys the house next door, she's forced to rethink what she expects out of life. (978-1-63555-480-9)

Hot Ice by Aurora Rey, Elle Spencer, Erin Zak. Can falling in love melt the hearts of the iciest ice queens? Join Aurora Rey, Elle Spencer, and Erin Zak to find out! (978-1-63555-513-4)

Line of Duty by VK Powell. Dr. Dylan Carlyle's professional and personal life is turned upside down when a tragic event at Fairview Station pits her against ambitious, handsome police officer Finley Masters. (978-1-63555-486-1)

London Undone by Nan Higgins. London Craft reinvents her life after reading a childhood letter to her future self and in doing so finds the love she truly wants. (978-1-63555-562-2)

Lunar Eclipse by Gun Brooke. Moon De Cruz lives alone on an uninhabited planet after being shipwrecked in space. Her life changes forever when Captain Beaux Lestarion's arrival threatens the planet and Moon's freedom. (978-1-63555-460-1)

One Small Step by Michelle Binfield. Iris and Cam discover the meaning of taking chances and following your heart, even if it means getting hurt. (978-1-63555-596-7)

Shadows of a Dream by Nicole Disney. Rainn has the talent to take her rock band all the way, but falling in love is a powerful distraction, and her new girlfriend's meth addiction might just take them both down. (978-1-63555-598-1)

Someone to Love by Jenny Frame. When Davina Trent is given an unexpected family, can she let nanny Wendy Darling teach her to open her heart to the children and to Wendy? (978-1-63555-468-7)

Tinsel by Kris Bryant. Did a sweet kitten show up to help Jessica Raymond and Taylor Mitchell find each other? Or is the holiday spirit to blame for their special connection? (978-1-63555-641-4)

Uncharted by Robyn Nyx. As Rayne Marcellus and Chase Stinsen track the legendary Golden Trinity, they must learn to put their differences aside and depend on one another to survive. (978-1-63555-325-3)

Where We Are by Annie McDonald. Can two women discover a way to walk on the same path together and discover the gift of staying in one spot, in time, in space, and in love? (978-1-63555-581-3)

A Moment in Time by Lisa Moreau. A longstanding family feud separates two women who unexpectedly fall in love at an antique clock shop in a small Louisiana town. (978-1-63555-419-9)

Aspen in Moonlight by Kelly Wacker. When art historian Melissa Warren meets Sula Johansen, director of a local bear conservancy, she discovers that love can come in unexpected and unusual forms. (978-1-63555-470-0)

Back to September by Melissa Brayden. Small bookshop owner Hannah Shepard and famous romance novelist Parker Bristow maneuver the landscape of their two very different worlds to find out if love can win out in the end. (978-1-63555-576-9)

Changing Course by Brey Willows. When the woman of your dreams falls from the sky, you'd better be ready to catch her. (978-1-63555-335-2)

Cost of Honor by Radclyffe. First Daughter Blair Powell and Homeland Security Director Cameron Roberts face adversity when their enemies stop at nothing to prevent President Andrew Powell's reelection. (978-1-63555-582-0)

Fearless by Tina Michele. Determined to overcome her debilitating fear through exposure therapy, Laura Carter all but fails before she's even begun until dolphin trainer Jillian Marshall dedicates herself to helping Laura defeat the nightmares of her past. (978-1-63555-495-3)

Not Dead Enough by J.M. Redmann. A woman who may or may not be dead drags Micky Knight into a messy con game. (978-1-63555-543-1)

Not Since You by Fiona Riley. When Charlotte boards her honeymoon cruise single and comes face-to-face with Lexi, the high school love she left behind, she questions every decision she has ever made. (978-1-63555-474-8)

Not Your Average Love Spell by Barbara Ann Wright. Four women struggle with who to love and who to hate while fighting to rid a kingdom of an evil invading force. (978-1-63555-327-7)

Tennessee Whiskey by Donna K. Ford. Dane Foster wants to put her life on pause and ask for a redo, a chance for something that matters. Emma Reynolds is that chance. (978-1-63555-556-1)

30 Dates in 30 Days by Elle Spencer. A busy lawyer tries to find love the fast way—thirty dates in thirty days. (978-1-63555-498-4)

Finding Sky by Cass Sellars. Skylar Addison's search for a career intersects with her new boss's search for butterflies, but Skylar can't forgive Jess's intrusion into her life. (978-1-63555-521-9)

Hammers, Strings, and Beautiful Things by Morgan Lee Miller. While on tour with the biggest pop star in the world, rising musician Blair Bennett falls in love for the first time while coping with loss and depression. (978-1-63555-538-7)

Heart of a Killer by Yolanda Wallace. Contract killer Santana Masters's only interest is her next assignment—until a chance meeting with a beautiful stranger tempts her to change her ways. (978-1-63555-547-9)

Leading the Witness by Carsen Taite. When defense attorney Catherine Landauer reluctantly becomes the key witness in prosecutor Starr Rio's latest criminal trial, their hearts, careers, and lives may be at risk. (978-1-63555-512-7)

No Experience Required by Kimberly Cooper Griffin. Izzy Treadway has resigned herself to a life without romance because of her bipolar illness but wonders what she's gotten herself into when she agrees to write a book about love. (978-1-63555-561-5)

One Walk in Winter by Georgia Beers. Olivia Santini and Hayley Boyd Markham might be rivals at work, but they discover that lonely hearts often find company in the most unexpected of places. (978-1-63555-541-7)

The Inn at Netherfield Green by Aurora Rey. Advertising executive Lauren Montgomery and gin distiller Camden Crawley don't agree on anything except saving the Rose & Crown, the old English pub that's brought them together. (978-1-63555-445-8)

Top of Her Game by M. Ullrich. When it comes to life on the field and matters of the heart, losing isn't an option for pro athletes Kenzie Shaw and Sutton Flores. (978-1-63555-500-4)

Vanished by Eden Darry. A storm is coming, and Ellery and Loveday must find the chosen one or humanity won't survive it. (978-1-63555-437-3)